# PRAISE FOR BRYAN SMITH AND *HOUSE OF BLOOD*!

"Smith promises unimaginable brutality, bile-inducing fear, and unfathomable despair; and then delivers monumentally!"

—Horror Web

"Bryan Smith is a force to be reckoned with!"
—Douglas Clegg, author of *The Attraction*

"A feast of good old-fashioned horror. Don't pass this one up!"
—Brian Keene, author of *Ghoul*

"In the vein of Bentley Little and Edward Lee...sometimes scary, sometimes amusing, *House of Blood* is a quick, enjoyable read suitable for all fans of horror and dark fantasy."
—Michael Laimo, author of *Dead Souls*

"Bryan Smith has a knack for taking the standard horror tale and turning it inside out to show you the dripping viscera at its core."
—Randy Chandler, author of *Bad Juju*

# UNDER HER CONTROL

Craig felt the metallic solidity of the guardrail against the backs of his legs. He considered vaulting over the guardrail, but something kept him riveted to the spot. There was an alien presence in his head. He let out a whimper as he felt its intrusion into his psyche.

Craig whimpered again and his voice emerged as a pitiful whine: "P-please…"

There was another *thunk* from within the car, caused this time by someone pulling the passenger side door handle. The door creaked slowly open, and a woman's long, elegant, stockinged leg appeared. Her exquisitely shaped calf tapered down to a thin ankle and a foot encased in a black stiletto heel.

Then the woman began to rise out of the car and walk toward Craig. The rest of her body delivered on the sensual promise of that first glimpse. The short black skirt and the tight silk blouse further enhanced the impression.

The thing that ruined the picture for Craig was her head.

Her extra one.

"Lady," Craig said, beginning to feel dizzy. "You've got two heads."

One of the heads, the pretty one, laughed.

And that perfect body moved still closer.

Craig attempted to turn away from the insane, impossible vision, but he still couldn't move. The two heads—one radiantly beautiful, the other withered and hideous—grinned in a most unsettling manner.

The ugly head licked its cracked lips and hissed like a snake.

Then Craig knew—that was the one inside his head.

Craig couldn't move, but he could still talk. There was no point in playing at diplomacy now. "Swear to God, if I had a knife right now, I'd cut out my own eyes just so I'd never have to look at you again."

The pretty head's sparkling blue eyes widened with delight. "What an excellent idea. Show me…"

Other *Leisure* books by Bryan Smith:

**DEATHBRINGER**
**HOUSE OF BLOOD**

# THE
# FREAKSHOW

# BRYAN SMITH

LEISURE BOOKS  NEW YORK CITY

*This one's for Rachael,*
*for helping me get through this*
*freakshow called life.*

A LEISURE BOOK®

March 2007

Published by

Dorchester Publishing Co., Inc.
200 Madison Avenue
New York, NY 10016

ISBN 0-8439-5827-8

The name "Leisure Books" and the stylized "L" with design are
trademarks of Dorchester Publishing Co., Inc.

Printed in the United States of America.

Visit us on the web at www.dorchesterpub.com.

# ACKNOWLEDGMENTS

As always, much thanks to my family, including my mom and brothers Jeff and Eric. Thanks also to my friends Keith Ashley and Shannon Turbeville. Let's all go have a beer at the Villager Tavern. Shout-outs must also go to all the supercool Hypericon people, including Darryl and Fred and Stephania Grimm, and to Tod Clark, for the cool books and the place to crash. Thanks again to first reader and friend Kent Gowran, and also to David T. Wilbanks and the whole rockin' crew at Shake It And Break It!

Strange signals in the night.

Dead silence.

Then . . .

. . . a burst of white noise.

Followed by a high-pitched squeal, a warbling sound that rises higher and higher before abruptly flattening out, becoming the low drone of a primitive audio device locking on the strongest detectable frequency.

A six-fingered hand reaches for a dial.

It twists the dial ever so slightly.

Silence again.

Then a baritone voice: *"This is Radio Ether, coming at you live to the Meatside for the first time in almost a year. I know the wait seems like an eternity for many of you, each frozen moment like an eon. But rejoice, brothers and sisters, freaks and geeks, gimps and beasts, for the time has come round again and another Assimilation will soon begin.*"

Another brief period of crackling silence.

Then that smooth, rumbling voice resumes after a deep exhalation of breath: "*Right now things are quiet. It's the stillness before the storm. Take solace in knowing that the trap has been set and will soon be sprung. Any moment now . . .*"

A low, throaty chuckle makes the ancient speaker cabinet vibrate.

"*This moment. Listen . . . yes . . . can you hear their screams? Mmm, what beautiful music they make.*" More throaty laughter. "*I wish you could see the shock on their stupid faces as they leap off the bleachers and stampede for the exits. . . .*"

And the announcer falls silent a moment.

The faint sound of terrified screaming issues through the speakers.

"*So gullible. So like sheep. They deserve to die this way, don't you think?*" A satisfied sigh, followed by a groan of pleasure. "*Yes, yes, yes. The Freakshow has come to town and now the freaks have come out to play-ay.*"

The thing with the six-fingered hand nods and grins.

Then it turns off the old radio and ventures out to join in the fun. . . .

# CHAPTER ONE

Mike Garrett held his breath and waited for the sounds of the tall man's echoing footsteps to fade.

*CLIP . . . CLOP.*

*Clip . . . clop.*

The sound triggered a childhood memory of standing on a sidewalk and watching a lone horse walk down the middle of Main Street near the end of the Dandridge High homecoming parade. And that thought triggered a flood of painful memories of his youth in his doomed hometown. A year ago, everyone in Dandridge died when terrorists detonated a dirty bomb, an inexplicable attack on an ordinary, sleepy town essentially in the middle of nowhere. There had been rumors ever since that the dirty bomb story was purely a government fabrication, a handy cover for something else they couldn't explain—and a way to exploit the lingering post-9/11 paranoia that still gripped the heartland. Mike had moved to nearby Pleasant

Hills only months prior to the tragedy, and his dreams since had been haunted by nightmarish visions of walking corpses and leering, radiation-scarred mutants straight out of a 1950s sci-fi Z-movie.

His therapist chalked the recurring nightmares up to "survivor's guilt." Which made a lot of sense, actually, but knowing this on a rational level had little effect on the nightly torture sessions his fragmented sleep had become. None of the drugs prescribed by his psychiatrist had done any damned good, either. He'd felt at the end of his rope for months now, desperate, about to give up any hope of knowing peace again.

But now the true reason for the endless nightmares seemed clear.

Though the ceaseless stream of horrifying images likely had been initiated by the terrible angst he'd experienced in the wake of his hometown's bizarre demise, he was sure their continuation was a kind of precognition. Some primitive part of his mind, a part accessible only in the murky depths of sleep, had sensed that a similar doom was coming to Pleasant Hills. For all he knew, what was happening now was precisely what had *really* happened in Dandridge.

He shuddered and barely managed to rein in a whine as the images flashed through his mind in rapid-fire fashion, jerky, like the jump cuts in a faux-edgy rock video—the grand entrance of the Ringmaster under the big top, music swelling and blaring as the crowded bleachers rock with applause . . . the subsequent arrival of many hideously deformed "freaks" (as they called themselves) . . . those strange, leering clown-things . . . a brief but dazzling display of acrobatics, ending in the decapitation of a "normal" (by comparison) man . . . the shocked silence of the still crowd . . . the freaks rushing into the bleachers, tearing into the spectators, killing and mutilating them in swift, shocking fashion . . . the disembowelment of Chuck Follett, his best friend since grade school, ropes of intestines spilling on the metal bleacher seats as Chuck's eyes flash pained disbelief . . . then that sense of being swept away by the screaming, fleeing crowd . . .

And since then, hiding wherever he could, frantically ducking here and there like a soldier trapped behind enemy lines, cowering and cringing every time he heard another scream . . .

. . . Clip . . . clop . . .

. . . Clip . . . clop . . .

The tall man's footsteps sounded far away now. Mike at last let out a big breath. He palmed a sheen of sweat from his forehead, wiped it on his jeans, and began to emerge from his hiding place. He gripped the edge of the platform above his head with shaking fingers, waited until he had a firmer grip, then began to slowly rise. His head rose above the level of the platform. He looked left, then right, and let out another sigh.

The midway was empty.

The tall man was gone.

Mike made an involuntary sound that was somewhere between a strangled sob and mad laughter. He lifted a partition board, stepped out of the Punch & Judy booth, and moved carefully into the middle of the deserted midway. Each side of the midway was lined with concession and amusement booths. Their garishly painted façades seemed to leer at him like materialized phantoms from his nightmares.

Mike felt an abrupt welling of tears at the corners of his eyes. It was horrible, what had happened. Of course it was. But it was also kind of funny, if only in a purely insane way. Because he was awake now. The world around him, despite its phantasmagorical qualities, was real, tactile. The ground beneath his feet was real ground. Solid. Definitely not something that would turn to quicksand with his next step. His heaving breath, proof of life and bodily function, fogged the fall air.

And yet, even in his wakefulness, he could not escape the country of nightmares. It felt like the universe was taunting him. Perhaps he'd done something unspeakably awful in a former life, and this was God's way of punishing him. He laughed again, and now the tears spilled forth, etching trails of glittering wetness down his cheeks.

He clenched his fists, digging the fingernails he'd forgotten to trim for too long into the soft flesh of his palms, digging until the flesh yielded beneath the pressure. Blood welled in the grooves. More proof of life. The self-inflicted pain he felt now reminded him of how tenuous life was at the moment. He had to get a grip. Had to stop tittering like a fucking madman. Because if he kept it up, the sound would surely draw the tall man back in this direction.

And he did not want that.

Oh, no.

He had to get out of here. *Now.*

Obviously. What wasn't so obvious was the most efficient way of doing that. The grounds of the Flaherty Brothers Traveling Carnivale and Freakshow were laid out as if there had been some dark design behind the haphazard, sprawling placement of the midways and the tents housing the various grotesque attractions, a design calculated to confuse and disorient. Oh, hell, no "as if" about it. Given what he'd seen and experienced so far, the sinister intent was obvious.

The taint of evil was all around him. Not just in the amusement booths and tents, but in the very air he was breathing. The air was cold. Too cold by far for late September in Tennessee. The grounds of the carnival had its own atmosphere, an alien intrusion that displaced the Tennessee warmth so completely Mike could almost believe he'd been transported to some other entirely different (and terrible) realm the moment he'd stepped through the entrance after buying his ticket. Come to think of it, that didn't seem out of the question. Not at fucking all.

*. . . Clip . . . clop . . .*

Mike swallowed a rising scream.

*He's coming back!*

*Clip-clop.*

The sound was coming from the right. Mike glanced in that direction and thought he saw a hint of long shadow at the far end of the midway. In another moment or two, the ghastly ringmaster of this hellish parody of a real carnival would come around a corner and see him. Mike knew he'd be as good as dead if the tall man saw him. Or worse. Worse was a definite possibility here. He'd seen the awful proof of that up close, hadn't he?

He had two choices. He could either duck back behind the Punch & Judy booth, or he could sprint into the deeper darkness to the left. He imagined hiding again behind the rickety booth while waiting for the tall man to clomp slowly by, with only the deranged-looking faces of the abandoned hand puppets for company. He shivered again at the memory of the puppets' strangely angular and fleshy faces, their eyes gleaming so fiercely in the moonlight, hinting at sentience and life. It should have been an absurd notion, but for Mike the line between the absurd and reality had blurred to near meaninglessness.

*CLIP-CLOP.*

So close.

Cold sweat streamed down Mike's face as he began backing away from the growing shadow, and away from the Punch & Judy booth. He saw the tall man's cartoonish top hat appear over the top of the tent at the far end of the midway and willed his feet to move faster. He stumbled, but somehow managed to maintain his balance. He knew the sensible thing would be to turn around and really put on a burst of speed, but a whispering voice of paranoia made him believe the tall man would be on him in a heartbeat if he turned his back on him.

His heel dipped into a small hole in the ground and he pitched backward. His arms pinwheeled wildly, but this time he'd been put too badly off balance. He hit the ground and let out a cry. A fresh burst of nerve-frying terror followed immediately on the heels of the involuntary squeal.

A sound emanated from the far end of the midway.

An insane, echoing laugh.

Another involuntary cry slipped through his terror-constricted vocal cords. The cry was followed by the helplessly repeated words "Oh god ohgodohgod" as he scooted backward.

Now another voice spoke in the darkness. A breathy whisper that nonetheless filled the night. This is what the tall man said: *"Sweet, sweet, lovely meat, how I love to eat human meat!"*

The insane laughter came again, louder this time,

filling all the dark corners of the midway. The sound rang in Mike's ears like a relentless tolling of some hellish bell. The sound that came from his own mouth now was more of a whimper than a cry. He sounded like a whipped and terrified dog.

Like something defeated.

Something within him rebelled at the thought, a last hidden reservoir of strength and courage he hadn't suspected he possessed. His body went still. He took a steadying breath and got to his feet. He stared for a moment at the now clearly visible form of the tall man at the far end of the midway.

The lean outline of the ringmaster's body looked from this distance like something sketched quickly with a pencil. He stood more than twenty feet tall, and at first Mike had thought he walked on stilts. But that couldn't be the case. His legs were too obviously flexible, and there was none of the stiffness Mike associated with a stilt-walker. That the tall ringmaster was no ordinary man had been clear almost from the beginning, and now Mike was nearly certain he wasn't even human. What sort of creature he might be, Mike couldn't fathom. The ringmaster, along with all the other bizarre beings and ghastly events he'd witnessed over the last several hours, was something beyond his admittedly feeble store of knowledge of things supernatural.

*CLIP-CLOP.*

*CLIP-CLOP.*

The tall man (or *thing*, his cracking mind insisted) strode rapidly down the midway, closing the gap between them at an alarming rate. But now he was running rather than walking; a weirdly gangly, loose-limbed jog. *CLIPCLOPCLIPCLOPCLIPCLOP*. There was a hallucinatory quality to what he was seeing, like something glimpsed in the flashing midst of an acid trip. Mike at last spun on his heels and began to run.

His legs churned beneath him as he bore down with a focus of will and energy exceeding anything in his experience. Though Mike was reasonably fit, he wasn't an athlete, nor did he run regularly. But now he moved with a speed approaching that of an experienced track runner, slicing through the cold night air with the relentless momentum of a locomotive screaming down gleaming railway tracks.

The tall man (*Thingthingthing!*) laughed again.

And again came that breathy, insinuating voice that felt like a graveyard whisper against his ear: *"You run like the wind, human meat, but I blow like a hurricane."*

Mike squealed in panic, freaked out by the tall man's ominous words. He had no clue what they might mean, but it had to be something really fucking bad. Then he heard something he at first thought was the hugely amplified sound of a vacuum cleaner. In the next millisecond he realized it was instead a mammoth intake of breath. There was a pause and Mike cringed, bracing for the exhalation. A rumbling wind, the ringmaster's expelled breath, rolled down the midway, buffeting the booths and shaking free several loose pieces of wood that went sailing into the sky, vanishing for a moment in the blackness, then tumbling down to be swirled about by the rushing air.

A single shattered wood plank sailed over Mike's head, whirling about dangerously like a rogue helicopter blade. The plank struck the ground ahead of him and went skittering down the midway. He felt heat tickle the exposed flesh at the back of his neck, the first warmth of the ringmaster's onrushing breath. An instant later that wind shoved him forward, lifted him off his feet, and slung him down the midway as if he were no more substantial than a discarded candy wrapper.

With his arms outstretched and his legs trailing behind him, he felt for one delirious moment like Superman. But then the cushion of flowing air dashed him against a booth and pain exploded inside him, seeming to reach every jangling nerve-ending in his body in one horrendous moment of blinding white light. Then he bounced off the booth and struck the ground next to a tent with a thud.

He rolled onto his back with a groan. His body was battered and perhaps even broken in places, but the perfect terror overwhelmed the pain. He pushed himself to a sitting position and looked up, expecting to see the ringmaster towering over him. But the tall man was farther away now, and Mike marveled for a helpless moment at the power of a creature able to send a two hundred pound man sailing through the air with a single exhaled breath. How could he hope to get away from such a thing?

The obvious answer seemed to be that there *was* no hope.

On the other hand, there was much more distance between the two of them than before. And the tall man was no longer running—he'd resumed that freaky loping, swaying walk. He was whistling now, a cheerful tune meant to unnerve, no doubt. The tall man was drawing the chase out, toying with his prey, savoring his terror. This realization triggered an emotion that gripped Mike almost as powerfully as the terror he felt.

Hate.

There'd not been time for hate before. There wasn't

really time for it now. But here it was anyway. He
wanted to kill the tall man. Wanted him to suffer before dying in the most agonizing manner possible.
That Mike had no clue how he might do that didn't
matter. He wanted it nearly as much as he wanted to
escape.

The tall man kept coming as Mike sat there stewing
in his anger.

*CLIP-CLOP.*

*CLIP-CLOP.*

Another exhalation of echoing laughter resounded
in the midway. The sound brought Mike spinning back
to reality. He blinked hard and shook his head, forcing
himself to focus on what was really important. Yes, he
wanted to kill the tall man, but this wasn't feasible
given the current circumstances. The tall man was still
a good ways away, so Mike had one more chance to get
away. Maybe his last chance. He braced his hands
against the cold ground and started to push himself up.

He let out a startled yelp as a cold—and very
strong—hand seized his wrist and yanked him back to
the ground. He twisted around and his eyes bugged
out at the sight of a large hand extending from beneath
the flap of the tent. The flap lifted slightly and thick,
muscular fingers began to pull him toward the small
opening. Mike attempted to brace his feet on the
ground and struggle against his attacker, but he was
being pulled forward with too much force. He flopped
forward onto his stomach and his head began to slide
beneath the flap. He detected only darkness within at
first, then very vague forms. He opened his mouth to
scream, but another hand—smaller and softer than the
hand gripping his wrist—clapped over his mouth and

muffled the sound. In another moment he was all the way inside the tent.

A physical weight fell astride him, someone strad-dling him like a mechanical bull at a shit-kicker bar. This, he was certain, was the same person whose hand was over his mouth. A woman. The other person, a man, the one who'd pulled him into the tent, wrenched his hand up behind his back and laid some-thing cold and hard against his throat. Mike gulped when he realized what it was—the exquisitely sharp edge of a very large knife.

Then the man's voice was whispering in his ear: "Stop struggling and be quiet if you want to live. You want to live, don't you?"

Mike swallowed hard and gave the question a mo-ment of intense thought.

Then he nodded, his mouth moving against the woman's soft palm.

The man's whispered voice came again: "Then not another word from you, not another single breath, un-til I say so. Now hold on . . . here he comes. . . ."

Mike listened.

And heard.

*CLIP-CLOP.*

*CLIP-CLOP.*

*CLIP-CLOP.*

# CHAPTER TWO

Craig's nonstop fiddling with the radio dial was getting on Heather Campbell's already edgy nerves. He kept twisting the little silver knob in a vain attempt to get the ancient radio to lock on a single clear frequency. And every time he finally did find a signal that wasn't too badly marred by static, he decided he didn't like what he was hearing and started spinning the dial through the frequencies again. Just now he'd done it again, after less than a minute of listening to an old Smiths song on 96X.

Heather sighed. "You know, I actually liked that one, Craig."

"So you should've said something." Craig's gaze remained trained on the dial as he continued turning it and watching the little orange bar move right-to-left. "What do you think I am, a fuckin' psychic?"

"You could've asked."

Craig snorted. "Yeah, and you could've bought a car

manufactured after the fuckin' Stone Age, but you didn't. Shit, listen to this Barry White-soundin' motherfucker. What the fuck is Radio Ether, anyway?" He winced and cursed as a fresh burst of loud static obscured the disc jockey's rumbling voice. "And you could at least have bought a new fuckin' radio."

Heather bit her lip to stifle the irate reply she ached to unleash. But getting into yet another petty fight with her boyfriend was the last thing she needed right now. She hadn't even wanted him to come along. She had a potentially serious situation to deal with, but you wouldn't know it from Craig's oblivious behavior, which was so typical for him. It was infuriating. He was young, sure, but not so young that he should be so utterly incapable of wrapping his brain around the idea that bad things could (and did) happen every day in this rotten world. When she'd expressed to him concern about not being able to reach anyone in Pleasant Hills (not even any of the emergency services), his response had been typical apathy—a slight shrug while his attention remained fixed on the video game he'd been playing.

Only when she told him she was going to Pleasant Hills to check on her ailing mother in person did he grant her something approximating undivided attention. "Not without me, you're not," he'd said.

She'd tried to tell him to stay home and relax, but trying to tell Craig what to do was a bit like a mountain climber attempting to argue with an avalanche. It drove her insane, the way he needed to be wherever she was. He was so clingy you'd think maybe he actually loved her, but Heather knew the truth. He just didn't like to be alone. Ever.

*What a pain . . .*

She knew she should just break up with him and eventually move on to a healthier relationship. She couldn't fathom the idea of spending her whole life with Craig. It was a horrifying thing to even contemplate. There were, however, a couple of reasons she'd been putting off breaking up with him. For one thing, he was easily the sexiest guy she'd ever dated. GQ cover material. And the sex was amazing, the best she'd ever had by a long shot.

But the bigger reason was fear. He scared her sometimes. Any time she felt compelled to tell him they were through, she would remember the time he told her how he'd chop her up into a "bunch of little pieces" if he ever caught her cheating on him. An assertion lended extra credence by his enthuisasm for the true crime shows on A&E. He'd watch them and snicker over the mistakes made by murderers, frequently saying disturbing things like, "That's not how *I* would do it." A person with that mentality wasn't someone you wanted to upset unless there was absolutely no other choice. Breaking up wasn't quite the same thing as cheating, but she was afraid he might find the experience equally traumatizing.

Craig squealed with delight as the radio locked on a signal as clear as anything processed through a digital dial. The song playing was some generic classic hard rock tune with a thumping beat. So of course Craig turned the volume up to near ear-splitting levels and began manically banging his head like some mullet-haired refugee from the 1980s.

Heather gritted her teeth and clenched her hands tightly around the steering wheel. She didn't know whether to giggle at Craig's ridiculous—though quite sincere—impression of the guys from Wayne's World, or scream from sheer frustration and anger. She made herself think again of her mom and her plight, tried to imagine all the awful things that could go wrong. Mom had lived alone ever since she'd moved out almost seven years ago, but her health had begun to decline within the last year and Heather had gotten into the habit of coming out to Pleasant Hills to check on her just about every other day. Which pissed Craig off, but this was the one way in which she'd refused to yield to his overbearing nature. She would do whatever was necessary to look after her mother and be sure she was okay.

Mom was so frail now, so prone to falling and breaking brittle bones (as had happened twice in the last six months). At some point she hoped to move her into her place in Brighton, but she'd been putting if off because she knew Craig would blow a gasket at the prospect of having to share space with, as he so charmingly put it, "that old hag."

*Face it,* she told herself. *Someday soon you're gonna have to find a bit of backbone and kick this creep out so you can do right by your mother.*

Her hands relaxed on the steering wheel as she let out a long breath.

*Someday,* she reaffirmed to herself with a slight nod. *Hell, maybe even tomorrow. But for now avoid getting into a war with the raving lunatic sitting next to you. Do what you have to do and get through this.*

Craig regularly accused her of overlooking her mother's faults, but that was another thing he was very wrong about. Her feelings about her mother were more complicated than her psycho boyfriend realized. Alice Campbell had given birth to Heather at the age of forty-three, which many now would still consider too old to be having a child. But twenty-six years ago it was considered by most in small-town Tennessee to be an obscenely ancient age for bringing a new life into the world. There'd been times over the years when she'd agreed with the sentiment. It'd been a weird thing to have a mom nearing retirement age just as she was graduating from high school.

The thumping rock beat abruptly stopped. Craig's hand was still on the volume knob. He was staring at her with a discomforting intensity. Her brow furrowed. "What?"

He rolled his eyes. "You looked like you were spacin' out there. What the hell's wrong with you?"

Heather stared blankly at him for a moment. Oh, there were so many things she could say here, a huge arsenal of long-held-in-reserve scathing indictments she'd love to bombard him with, but she somehow found the strength to hold all the venom in one more time.

She sighed and her gaze went back to the road. "Nothing." She cleared her throat and said, "I'm just worried about Mom is all."

Craig snorted disdainfully and shook his head. "Jesus Christ. It makes me sick how much she takes advantage of you. She's not a fuckin' invalid." He laughed. "You ask me, you oughtta hate her guts forever for sticking you with a silly name like Heather."

Heather bit her lip again. "There's nothing wrong with my name."

Craig grunted. "Right." He sneered at her. "I hear your fucking name, and I swear all I can think of is that fuckin' Christian Slater movie. I hate that fuckin' movie."

Heather didn't say anything to that. Craig's reasoning for things rarely made any sense, and when he was being this illogical and mean-spirited there was little point in arguing with him. You couldn't win.

So all she said was, "I liked that movie."

Craig laughed again. "You would. You have no taste."

This from a guy whose favorite movie of all time was *Showgirls*.

He shook his head and chuckled, sounding like a grownup amused by something uttered by a child. "Fuckin' *Heathers*. Fuckin' *Rosencrantz and Guildenstern*. I can't stand the fuckin' shit you like. Everything arty-farty or edgy." He said this with an implied sneer in his voice. "And that tedious fuckin' shit you read, like David Foster Wallace, like you're some kinda fuckin' intellectual. You're so goddamned pretentious. Newsflash, Heather—nobody buys your smart-girl pose. You're a fuckin' college dropout, just like me."

The incessant cursing was another thing about Craig that irriated her. She was no prude. She could unleash an impressive torrent of f-bombs when she felt like it. But Craig's love of profanity was unlike anything she had experienced. His everyday speech made the coarsest hip-hop recording sound tame by comparison. Thinking about it made Heather suddenly tired as she realized again that just about every aspect of her boyfriend's personality was offensive. And his utter disdain for her interests didn't make her love him any better.

*Love.*

What a joke that was—romantic love was not part of their über-dysfunctional relationship, and it'd been a long time since either of them had pretended otherwise. It was all about that sweet ass, baby.

Pathetic.

She sighed and kept her eyes on the road.

He smacked her shoulder. Hard. "What's that fuckin' sigh for?"

*Don't get into it. Don't push him. Let it go. Think about Mom.*

"Nothing."

His fist slammed into her shoulder again. "Bullshit, nothing. You stop being such a fuckin' cunt and tell me what's on your goddamned mind, bitch."

She glared at him. "Don't call me that."

A smirk twitched at the corners of his handsome mouth. "I'll call you whatever I want . . . bitch."

The Chevelle screeched to a jerking, fishtailing halt at the edge of the road as Heather stomped the brake pedal to the floor. Craig squealed and pitched forward, smacking his head against the windshield before falling back into his seat. His wide-eyed expression of fear made her feel at once satisfied and ashamed. Craig's emotions were less complicated.

His eyes narrowed to thin, livid slits, and his face twisted with rage, making him look almost ugly. "You cunt. *You fucking cunt!*" The pitch of his voice dropped abruptly and he smiled—an expression with a hint of evil and a promise of pain. "You're gonna pay for that."

He reached for her purse, but Heather's reflexes were a nanosecond faster. Her hand dove into the open Prada bag and came out with the .38 given to her by a previous boyfriend. She pressed the barrel of the gun to the bridge of his nose. Heather was shocked she felt as calm as she did. There was some anxiety below the cool surface of course, but she felt remarkably composed and her voice emerged with an authoritative edge.

"Get out. Now."

Craig's eyes went wide again and his mouth dropped open in gaping disbelief. But he recovered quickly, the familiar smirk returning as he balled his hands into fists. "I ain't goin' anywhere. You just try and make me."

Heather began to smile. "Okay."

Craig frowned. "What did you say?"

She cocked the .38's hammer and her smile broadened. There was the smallest hint of temporary insanity quivering behind the expression. Her heart was racing now, pounding against her chest wall like some manic tom-tom, and the extra adrenaline coursing through her veins made her feel bolder than usual.

"Get out of my car," she said, calmly as before. "Or I'll kill you."

Doubt flickered in Craig's eyes for the first time. But, like anyone whose bad behavior has gone unchallenged for so long, some part of him flatly refused to accept the conviction that should have been so obvious in her tone and expression.

He sneered. "You know better, bitch. Go through with this and maybe I'll start telling people about that thing we did once upon a time." He chuckled darkly. "You remember, don't you? The last time you pointed that thing in someone's face? Now I fuckin' *know* you don't want anyone to hear about that. Especially not your sweet little old mother. So put the fuckin' gun away."

Heather went cold inside. The thing he was talking about was a thing they'd agreed to never discuss again. She'd spent most of her time since the "incident" (as she thought of it when she was forced to) desperately trying to pretend it had never happened. And she pushed it out of her mind now, forcing it back down deep and hidden where it belonged. But the rage she felt now wouldn't go away. He'd gone too fucking far. Consequences be damned. She didn't want the fucker in her car even one more moment. Her hand shot across his lap, yanked the door handle and pushed the door open so hard the handle broke off in her hand. Aided now by Craig's typical refusal to wear a safety belt, she mustered all her strength and shoved him through the open door. He yelped and cursed as he tumbled to the gravel-covered road shoulder and rolled away from the car. Heather leaned over some more and gripped the top of the door, pulling it shut with an emphatic thunk.

Craig was just getting to his feet as Heather got herself situated behind the seat again. *"I'm gonna kill you, Heather! You fuckin' hear me!?"*

Heather heard his footsteps on the gravel as he staggered toward the car. She put the Chevelle in gear and slammed the gas pedal to the floor. The old car shot away from the road's shoulder and left Craig behind. When she at last glanced in the rearview mirror, she couldn't even see him in all that darkness. She allowed herself the momentary fantasy that she'd seen the last of him. But reality came roaring back a moment later, bringing the anxiety that had been lurking beneath her bravado screaming to the surface. The muscles in her arms began to shake and she had to grip the steering wheel hard to keep from swerving off the road.

*He lives with you, idiot*, the voice of anxiety reminded her. *He'll go back to your place. He has a key, remember? And he'll steal or destroy everything you own. Oh, there's gonna be some serious hell to pay for sure.*

But Heather made the voice hush.

She made her mind empty of thought for a long moment. She listened to the whirring of the tires on highway asphalt, the only audible sound other than her breathing now.

She let out a sigh and began to smile again.

A green road sign came up on the right. It read: PLEASANT HILLS, 7 MILES.

Craig watched the Chevelle's taillights recede until they were almost imperceptible pinpoints of light. Then the lights winked out and he was at last fully aware of being alone and stranded on the highway. As he began to walk toward Pleasant Hills, he consoled himself with fantasies of revenge. He smiled as he imagined the bug-eyed look of terror there'd be on the cunt's face when he took that popgun from her and stuck it in her own face. And maybe stuck it a few other places.

The fantasy went further.

He imagined her shaking, pleading for her life.

He saw himself laughing and pulling the trigger, saw a beautiful explosion of red jump out from the back of her head, just like in the movies.

He smiled again. "Yeah, baby. Daddy's gonna put you in your fuckin' place once and for all."

# CHAPTER THREE

The dwarf clown pranced by the open bedroom door again, skipping over the carpeted hallway floor like a little girl in pigtails on a playground. He was singing a merry song in what sounded like German. Alice Campbell's knowledge of the language was minimal, but the chorus featured the word "fräulein" prominently. She heard the *flap-flap* of the clown's oversized shoes as he (she assumed it was a he) came to an abrupt stop at the end of the hallway, spun on his heels, and came prancing by her door again.

The clown waved as he went by.

Alice Campbell figured she was losing her mind. What else could account for what she was seeing? This had to be a serious sign of senile dementia settling in. Probably the condition had been creeping in for many months, perhaps even years, but only now had become serious enough to manifest in the form of hallucinations.

The little clown looked more like some horror show nightmare than a jolly circus performer. He was freakishly round through the middle. Not fat, but *round,* as if someone had shoved a big beachball down his throat and into his stomach. And every time she glimpsed his face she became more and more certain the red, white, and black clown paint obscuring his true features wasn't really paint. There wasn't that shiny, pebbled look she associated with face paint. The colors looked fainter, bleached into the flesh, as if they were the natural colors of the clown's face. Which was absurd, but she believed it. His hideously bloated red lips looked like plump sausages, and when they stretched across his face in a mad grin, they revealed teeth too long and too sharp to be normal human teeth.

So this was a hallucination. Or a nightmare.

Well . . . there was one other small possibility. Small, because it was an insane and impossible idea she knew she shouldn't grant any real credence. Alice's common sense urged her to dismiss the bizarre notion. But all day she'd felt something calling to her. At first she'd attributed the feeling to the weird way her mind sometimes seized upon random thoughts or ideas, obsessing on them until they acquired a weight they didn't deserve. But this was different. She was certain the calling came from outside, not from her own mind. There'd been a sense of an almost physical *pulling.*

The feeling intensified in the afternoon during a phone conversation with Ruth Irving, her one acquaintance in Pleasant Hills she could almost think of as a friend. Ruth told her about a carnival that had rolled into town the day before and was setting up in Bentley Park. The moment Ruth spoke the carnival's name . . .

*"The Flaherty Brothers Traveling Carnivale and*

*Freakshow. Doesn't that sound awful? It sounds so . . . nineteenth century. I didn't think there were actual freakshows around anymore. But I guess morbid curiosity has gotten the better of me. Frank and I will be there when it opens tonight."*

. . . she instantly associated that sense of calling with the carnival.

Her practical, rational side battled the feeling the rest of the day, but it never went away. She couldn't stop thinking about it, so much so that she entertained the thought of calling her daughter and asking her to take her to the carnival. What on earth a decrepit old thing like Alice Campbell would do at a loud, bustling thing like a carnival, she didn't know. But the compulsion was real, and it was intense. The only thing that kept her from doing it was the thought of making trouble for Heather and that terrible man she was living with now.

So she took a dose of sleeping pills and went to bed when it was still daylight outside. When she came out of her deep slumber, the feeling of being called was gone. She experienced a very brief moment of deep relief—and then the clown's strange Germanic singing began to ring through the hallway, startling and terrifying her so much she was surprised it didn't send her heart a lethal jolt.

That was fifteen minutes ago.

She'd initially believed she was still asleep, still lodged in the midst of a very strange dream. But after watching the clown prance by her doorway a time or two, she let go of that idea and began to accept the notion that her mind was breaking down.

The theory wasn't beyond the realm of possibility. She knew she wasn't as sharp as she'd once been. So some of the signs were definitely there. She was old beyond her years. Her lifestyle in her earlier years hadn't been a particularly healthy one. All that drinking and screwing around with all the wrong men. She'd abused her body in any number of ways. The physical decay had been going on for years. It only made sense that her mind would eventually be subject to a similar decline. It was a horrible thing to accept, but it was better than believing some kind of singing monster clown was dancing in her hallway.

Still, Alice Campbell hadn't gotten this far into her hard life without a strong core of pragmatism to see her through the rough patches. It'd served her well when she was younger and had worked two jobs to properly provide for her little girl. There'd been no one else to help the two of them through those lean years. She'd worked her arthritic fingers to the bone, sacrificing the freedom and comfort that might have been hers if she'd chosen to live out the rest of her days childless. She did it all for the child, the sole shining light in her life, and she'd done it gladly, without hesitation, even on the many occasions when she'd felt too hungover or tired to go into work.

So Alice the pragmatist rolled to her side and opened the nightstand drawer. She removed the pistol—a gleaming snub-nosed .38 she oiled and cleaned regularly—and rolled onto her back again.

She aimed the pistol at the open doorway and waited for the clown-thing to come by again. Hallucination or not, she meant to pop a few rounds at it. She was a pretty good shot. So one way or another her problem was about to be solved. Either the bullets would pass harmlessly through the specter and crash into the wall beyond, or an intruder in her home would get his brains blown out. She suspected the former was the most likely scenario, but she was at peace with the idea of killing the clown if he turned out to be real. If he was real, he was a stranger in her home, an invader, and obviously quite dangerous and deeply disturbed.

So she was ready to do what needed doing, just as she'd always been.

Several long moments elapsed. Long enough for the fear to set in again. Her hands began to shake, and she felt the salty sting of perspiration in her mouth as little beads of sweat rolled off her lip into the corners of her mouth. She eventually became aware of the absence of sound from the hallway. She realized the *flap-flap* of the clown's big shoes had ceased sometime very shortly after she removed the gun from the nightstand. Perhaps he'd peeked in and seen what she was doing, then had ducked back out of sight before she was able to aim the gun at the doorway. The thought of him hiding calmed her. It meant he was afraid. Maybe the clown really was some inhuman nightmare thing, but evidently he feared what Alice's weapon might do to him.

Thinking this emboldened Alice, brought a brittle smile to the dry corners of her quivering mouth. He was probably still out there, cowering just out of sight. And hopefully pissing those silly bright red pants of his. The image this thought conjured nearly made her laugh.

But her sudden good cheer deserted her in the next instant.

She saw a single clown eye peeking around the doorjamb. She'd missed some peculiar aspects of the thing's eyes until now, perhaps because they'd merely comprised one odd detail floating amidst a larger panorama of astounding oddness. But being made to focus on just this one piece of the strange creature's anatomy, the sheer *wrongness* of what she was seeing caused her breath to catch in her throat. There was no iris, no pupil. Just a big black orb beneath a brow arched so high it formed an upside-down V. The eye itself glittered in the light from the hallway, a twinkling light that seemed to cast palpable malevolence into the bedroom.

Alice swallowed hard and remembered to breathe. She shifted her aim now, training the gun's sight on the clown's eye. "I'm giving you just one chance, fella. You can make tracks outta my house or I'm gonna paint that wall behind you redder than those goofy fucking pants of yours. I'm counting to three. If I were you, I'd be outta here long before three."

Alice cleared her throat and began the countdown. "One . . ."

The clown's entire head moved into view now—it grinned at her around the doorjamb, then waddled sideways and filled the doorway.

It stepped through the doorway.

Alice's hands began to shake again, so she shifted her aim to the thing's ample midsection—no way she could miss a shot there. "Two. You got a death wish, boy?"

The clown's grin broadened, exposing more too-sharp teeth.

Teeth like knives.

It shuffled forward

Alice gritted her teeth. "Oh, fuck it."

She squeezed the .38's trigger. Then again. And again. Despite her can't-miss certainty, the first round sailed harmlessly to the left of the still-advancing clown. The clown threw its head back and its belly heaved in a soundless laugh. The second and third rounds punctured its big belly dead-center. There was a popping sound that made Alice think of a punctured birthday balloon. The wide-eyed look of mock shock on the clown's face might have seemed comical under other circumstances. Say, in a scene from a scary movie or TV show. Then Alice screamed as the clown's body blew apart and shot toward the ceiling. Blood rained down on the mattress as the deflated body spun about, caught in the whirring blades of the ceiling fan. More blood spattered Alice's face and nightgown. The salty tang of it in her mouth convinced her once and for all that this was neither dream nor hallucination.

The clown's face—the one part of its body still intact—hung over the end of one of the blades, leering at her. Its mouth moved, the knifelike teeth making a gnashing sound as it began to chew on the wooden blade.

Alice screamed again and reached for the phone on her nightstand. She'd already punched in the emergency number before she realized there was no dial tone. Which made no sense. All her bills were up-to-date. Heather saw to it all every month. She clicked the phone off and on several times. It was definitely dead. She threw the thing aside with a curse and glanced again at the ceiling fan.

The clown's mouth was full of wood shards. It spit them out, and one grazed the side of Alice's head. It saw her watching and grinned again. Then it fell away from the ruined blade and landed on the foot of her mattress. Alice cringed and pressed her back against the headboard. Except for its head, the clown's body did indeed look just like a burst balloon. A balloon apparently comprised of some impossible synthesis of expandable plastic and living tissue.

*This isn't real,* a desperate inner voice told her. *You*

*know that. A thing like this creature simply isn't possible in the real world. You were right the first time. You're losing your mind.*

The clown's head began to move toward her, using its long, gleaming teeth to grip the bedspread and pull itself forward. Alice let out a whimper. She remembered the gun in her hand and gripped it carefully again with both hands, aiming the sight directly at the thing's bulbous red nose.

She squeezed the trigger.

The gun roared.

The bullet punched dead-center through the clown's face. Its nose blew apart, making Alice think of a tick hideously swollen with blood. The clown's head— along with the streaming flaps of its ruined body— skidded back across the bed and tumbled to the floor.

Alice let out a gasp. The gun suddenly seemed to weigh about a million pounds in her trembling hands. But she tightened her grip on it anyway, refusing to relinquish the only protection available to her. She heard a snuffling noise and knew the clown's head was trying to climb up the hanging bedspread.

Alice moaned. "Die, goddamn you!"

*You couldn't kill it. You could definitely wound the abominable thing, but you couldn't extinguish it.*

Alice swung her legs over the side of the bed, reached for her cane and got shakily to her feet. Her hand curled tightly around the cane's handle, holding on to it as desperately as a woman clinging to the edge of a very high ledge with her fingers. She knew she was as good as dead if her grip slipped and she fell to the floor. The walker would have allowed her more speed and mobility, but she wouldn't have been able to hold on to the gun. So she thumped ahead with the cane, using what remained of her upper body strength to vault forward. She moved more quickly than she would have thought possible, perhaps aided by a terror-induced surge of adrenaline.

She gave the foot of the bed a wide berth, but allowed herself a quick backward glance as she hurried toward the open door. The clown's head had nearly reached the edge of the mattress. It seemed to sense her scrutiny. The head tilted backward and those huge black orbs stared at her.

The clown's teeth let go of the bedspread and fell again to the floor.

It began to crawl toward her.

Alice screamed and vaulted through the open doorway. Her heart thumped rapidly in her chest. Maybe too rapidly. She felt dizzy as she propelled herself down the hallway. White light began to crowd the edges of her vision.

A shadow fell across the end of the hallway.

Someone else was here. Probably another monster from that freakshow.

Alice opened her mouth to scream again, but in that moment she lost her grip on the cane and fell to the carpeted floor. She rolled onto her back and brought the gun around in time to aim it at the second intruder.

She pulled the trigger.

And saw the look of horror etched across her daughter's lovely face as the .38's hammer came down.

# CHAPTER FOUR

*CLIP-CLOP.*

*Clip-clop.*

*. . . clip-clop . . .*

Mike listened as the tall man's footsteps grew steadily fainter. He only began to relax when the sound of his own thudding heart eclipsed that sound. Another long, tense moment passed, then the pressure of the blade against his throat eased. The knife was still pressed to his flesh, but it was no longer on the verge of slicing him open. The woman's soft hand slid away from his mouth. He drew in a startled breath as he sensed something coming at him in the darkness—then he felt the woman's lips touch his.

She spoke then, the soft lips moving sensuously against his mouth, the words so quiet they were nearly inaudible. "What Daniel told you still goes. Not a word from you until we say you can talk." She paused, her lips lingering against his. She sighed through his slightly parted lips and spoke again. "I'm pretty sure you're not one of them, but we have to be sure. We have to do the test anyway."

*Test?*

Just a single word, one enigmatic syllable, but it nonetheless sent a shudder of dread through him. What the hell could that possibly mean? His back stiffened and he reflexively tried to twist out of the man's grip. But the man—Daniel—wrenched his arm harder up behind his back and reapplied the pressure of the blade to his throat. His breath caught in his throat and he went very still.

The woman moved away from Mike, scooting backward into the darkness. She stopped and seemed to search for something. He heard a scratch of something in the darkness and then saw a spark of light. A small flame sputtering at the tip of a match. He saw the match dip slightly as it was applied to something else. A moment later, a brighter—though still very soft— light lit the room. The light came from an antique lantern.

The woman met his gaze and smiled.

She was pretty, short and slim, with a choppy pageboy haircut that fell across her face. There was something pixie-like about her. And she was younger than he'd thought, very early twenties at most. He was pretty sure she wasn't one of the circus people. Beauty aside, she looked too normal. She wore blue jeans and a form-fitting black baby doll T-shirt with a glittery AC/DC logo emblazoned across the front.

She edged closer again and set the lantern on the ground next to him. "I'm sorry about this. I really am. You seem like an okay guy. I have a sense about you. But we can't take any chances."

Daniel grunted. "Got that right."

She pried the knife from Daniel's fingers. Daniel clamped that hand around Mike's neck, holding him in place as the girl lifted his shirt and pressed the tip of the knife against his belly button. Mike sucked in a breath, his mind instinctively compelling his flesh to retreat from the touch of the blade.

But the knife pressed forward again.

Mike sputtered. "Wh-what are . . . you . . . doing?"

The girl's gaze was intent, never leaving the blade as she spoke quietly to him. "The test."

"What test?"

The tip of the blade began to pierce his flesh. He felt a sharp, lancing pain as blood welled up from the small wound. The blade pushed in some more, and the blood began to flow. Mike had to fight to keep his whole body from quaking. He was scared, maybe even more frightened than he'd been while running from the tall man, but he had to compartmentalize that fear, had to make himself be absolutely still. The blade moved forward another quarter of an inch. Mike gritted his teeth and his face twisted with the effort of concentration.

Then the girl lifted her gaze and looked him in the eye again.

She sighed. "He's not one of them."

Daniel muttered a curse. "You don't know that. Only the clowns blow up like that. He could be one of those other things. They seem to have all the right inside stuff, organs and everything, just like we do."

Mike wasn't sure what Daniel meant by "other things," though he had a suspicion or two. But his curiosity on that count was overridden by the man's comment about "inside stuff." How would they know that without disemboweling the "things" in question?

The girl sighed and shook her head. "No. He's not one of them."

"How the hell can you know that?"

She made a show of displaying the knife's blade, holding it closer to the lantern. Mike felt bile rise in his throat at the sight of his own blood staining the wedge of silver. "Look at his blood. Bright red." She eyed Mike up and down again before again turning back to Daniel. "You killed enough of them tonight to know their blood doesn't look like ours."

The test abruptly made more sense to Mike. He pressed his shirt aganst the small wound to stanch the welling of blood. He shuddered, recalling his narrow escape from the wholesale slaughter that transpired under the big top. He hadn't killed any of the freaks himself, but he'd seen them wounded. And the girl was right. They didn't bleed like humans. Nor did they all bleed the same. Some leaked a dark, viscous substance from their wounds, while from the wounds of others flowed a strange Day-Glo green fluid that looked more like toxic waste than blood.

The memory diminished his anger somewhat, but there was nonetheless an edge in his voice as he said. "I'm not one of the freaks. You know that now. So let me fucking go, okay?"

Daniel relinquished his grip on Mike's wrist. "I hope you know what you're doing here, Jinx. I hope you're not about to get us fucking killed."

Mike rubbed his aching wrist and frowned. He flexed his fingers and cringed at the sudden jolt of pain that shot down his arm. Daniel had damn near twisted it off. He considered making a snide comment to the effect, but dismissed the notion as probably a monumentally bad idea.

Instead he said, "If either of you die tonight, it won't be because of me, I promise you that."

Daniel grunted. "Right. Well, maybe you're not one of the bad guys after all, but your stupidity could still land us in a world of shit, asshole."

Mike opened his mouth to reply, but a sound from outside the tent silenced him. The sound came again, a noise like the grinding of ancient, rusted metal gears turning. It made him cringe and set his teeth on edge. His gaze flicked to Jinx, who raised a forefinger to her lips in a shushing gesture, then blew out the lantern. The grinding sound came yet again, but this time it changed, gave way to a loud, echoing stutter—*BAMBAMBAMBAM*—that sounded like something powerful, and dangerous, banging against the inside of a metal barrel or chamber.

The sound grew louder still, becoming deafening. There was nothing else in the world now, just that huge, consciousness-obliterating noise. Mike flinched when he felt something touch his hand, then relaxed only slightly as the smaller, softer hand slipped into his and gripped him hard.

*Jinx*, he thought.

He hoped.

She tugged at him, urging him to follow her deeper into the tent. He didn't trust her to take him anywhere safe, but the alternative—remaining where he was, so near the source of that horrible grinding, banging noise—was far more unacceptable. He let her pull him to his feet and began to follow her deeper into the darkness.

Mike heard something else behind him now, something barely audible over the banging. It was Daniel. He was screaming at them. Of course. He'd sensed their movement, would know they were moving away from him. The poor bastard was probably terrified at the notion of being left alone. He'd feel the same in his spot. Mike wondered why the girl had latched on to him and not Daniel. He'd assumed they were boyfriend and girlfriend, but he doubted that now. Jinx wouldn't ditch her boyfriend in favor of someone she'd just met in the middle of a situation as righteously fucked-up as this one.

But there'd be time to think about that later. Maybe.

He felt a strong hand on his shoulder and loosed a shriek he didn't hear. The hand clamped harder on his shoulder and began to spin him around. He couldn't see anything in the darkness, but it could only be Daniel, come to batter him for taking off with the girl who'd been his companion against the darkness until just moments ago. Mike felt Jinx's soft hand slip away from him. He clenched his hands into fists and raised his forearms in front of his face, hoping to at least deflect the blow he was sure was coming.

The grinding, banging sound abruptly stopped. Mike could again hear the sound of his own breathing, as well as a ringing in his ears and the rapid thrum of his terror-juiced heart.

Daniel's voice came to him in the darkness, close enough that Mike could feel the heat of his breath. "Oh, what the fuck now!?"

And now Jinx spoke, her voice quiet but insistent. "Hush!"

Then there was almost perfect stillness and silence. Mike swallowed a hard, bitter lump in his throat. He

experienced a moment of flickering, desperate hope—
*Maybe it's gone*—before a new sound penetrated the
stillness, destroying the absurd notion of hope.

This new sound was very different from the batter-
ing of before, quieter and more subtle, but when Mike
realized what he was hearing the terror gripped him
again, perhaps even more strongly than before. It was
a ripping sound, a sound of . . . fabric being torn apart.

A rumbling, inhuman exclamation resonated outside the tent.

Mike gulped.

And Jinx said, "Oh, hell."

Then all at once they could see again. The top of the
tent had been snatched away, letting in pale moonlight
and a gush of hot, smoky air. Mike blinked hard and
looked up through the opening. The sight of the thing
leering down at him caused his legs to wobble. The
only reason he didn't collapse was because Jinx was at
his side again, clasping hands with him.

Daniel looked up through the opening and said,
"What the fuck is that?"

Mike didn't have an answer. The thing staring down
at them was some kind of giant, mechanical, vaguely
arachnid monstrosity. It had a metallic body that resembled a bizarre synthesis of the turrett of a World
War II tank and an Apollo lunar module. Near the top
of it was a single pulsing, glowing orb, a nightmare vision of Cyclopean madness. It belched hot steam from
several dark exhaust portals. Six jointed metal legs descended from the bottom of the thing's body. It was a
machine, but it was more than that. Mike didn't know
how he knew that, but he did. It was somehow alive,
and it was every bit as malevolent and deadly as the
stilt-legged ringmaster.

Its legs flexed, lowering the thing's body closer to the tent opening. This caused a brief renewal of the horrific grinding sound. The body tilted toward the three defenseless humans and long metal cables with attached pincers snaked through the tent opening.

Jinx took off in the opposite direction, dragging Mike along with her. He stumbled over leaden feet and crashed to the ground. He heard the girl curse and expected her to take off without him. But she knelt next to him and grabbed his hand again, urging him back to his feet. Mike managed to get up and began to stagger after the girl, but he couldn't help a last backward glance—and what he saw then nearly made his heart stop.

Daniel was just standing there, paralyzed by fear and disbelief. There wasn't the slightest trace of bravado left in the man. He gaped up at the spider monster and never moved as one of the cable-tentacles arced toward him. There was a snicking sound and the gleaming pincers flashed in the moonlight. The blades snipped through Daniel's neck and his head tumbled off his shoulders. Bright, arterial blood jetted against the blades before the headless body tumbled to the ground.

Jinx let out a strangled yelp and Mike guessed she'd seen it, too.

She tugged harder at his hand and then they were finally running flat-out, weaving their way through an array of folding chairs and then past a stage. Something odd was on the stage, a multicolored pile of jumbled clothes. Clown clothes. There was also quite a bit of blood. Mike nearly stumbled again as he realized the pile of clothes appeared to be . . . breathing.

As they flew past the stage Mike glimpsed a small

opening at the rear of the tent. Jinx was already moving rapidly toward it. She seemed to know precisely where she was going. He thought of the test she'd performed on him and recalled the things she'd said to Daniel immediately thereafter. And he thought of the lump of breathing clown clothes and had a sudden insight.

She (or maybe Daniel) had killed the thing on the stage. Or had at least disabled it.

*Stick a knife in them and they pop,* he thought. *Like a fucking balloon.*

Weird. But no weirder than the spider machine. Or the ringmaster himself.

And that was the mother of all understatements.

They reached the rear opening, raced through it— and came to an abrupt halt.

Jinx said, "Shit."

A big man who looked like a seventeenth-century pirate grinned at them, displaying a mouth full of bleeding gums and rotting teeth. He was tall, well over six feet, and had to weigh at least three hundred pounds. He wore a ratty shirt that might once have been white, and a black leather vest over it. A black eye patch covered his right eye. In his right hand he held a long gleaming sword with a curved blade and an ornate handle and hilt. The only thing missing to complete the cliché was a squawking parrot perched on his shoulder.

Captain Blackbeard wasn't alone.

Arrayed around him was a motley collection of deformed freaks and slavering, leering clowns with bulbous bellies and black-as-night eyes.

The pirate chuckled. "Jinx, it's good to see you again, dearie." The pirate's good eye fixated on Mike. "And you've delivered fresh meat. How thoughtful."

He laughed again and the demonic clowns began to advance. Mike felt lightheaded. He sagged into Jinx's arms and she guided him gently to the ground. His vision swimming slightly, he looked up and saw a distorted clown face peering down at him. And it was finally all too much.

He closed his eyes and the world went away for a while.

# CHAPTER FIVE

Craig Carpenter's faith in the kindness of strangers had never been strong to begin with, but the last flickering wisp of it blinked out of existence as he watched car number five, a puke-green Datsun dinosaur from the 70s, rattle by him. The driver, some scrawny kid with acne, never so much as glanced in Craig's direction. It was like the little geek hadn't even seen him. The fucker. Craig was standing at the edge of the road with his right thumb extended in a classic hitchhiker pose. Short of standing in the middle of the goddamned highway, he didn't know what else he could do to attract the attention of these heartless assholes.

He'd walked more than a mile along the side of the road since getting kicked out of Heather's shitmobile. That left just under six miles to the outskirts of Pleasant Hills. He was in good shape and could cover that distance easily enough. The problem was time. It was most definitely of the essence. His bitch was probably at her mother's house by now. If something had happened to the stupid old hag, Heather would take her to the nearest emergency room. Craig needed to get to Heather before she wound up in a situation where she was surrounded by medical staff and security people. The only thing working in his favor at the moment was the total failure of all telephone services in Pleasant Hills. No 911 meant Heather would have to get the woman loaded into her Chevelle before heading to the hospital. And Alice Campbell was so frail and slow that doing so would take time.

Maybe long enough for Craig to hitch a ride and get to the Campbell home in time to butcher them both. He grinned.

*Two dead twats for the price of one.*

But the grin slipped again.

Traffic was light on this road tonight, and no one seemed the least bit inclined to pick up a hitchhiker. He did have one last means of attracting attention available to him, one he'd been reluctant to resort to. But he knew he had no choice at this point. If the next car that came along didn't stop for him, Heather and Alice Campbell would soon be en route to the emergency room. Of course, that would only delay the inevitable for Heather. Craig meant to kill her no matter what. But he was into instant gratification. He wanted the bitch dead *tonight*.

So Craig breathed a sigh of resignation and stripped off his white T-shirt. He turned away from Pleasant Hills and stepped again to the edge of the road, displaying a lean, heavily muscled physique. He plastered a fake smile across his face and prayed for some lonely homosexual or desperate fat broad to be behind the wheel of the next car. Appealing to the prurient side of people had obvious potential downfalls, but Craig was prepared to deal with them. Hell, he was already committed to killing some people tonight. Adding one more victim to the list would make no difference to him.

The road leading into Pleasant Hills was a curving strip of black intermittently punctuated by the glow of streetlamps. Craig peered intently into that darkness, hoping to see a pair of headlights appear. While he waited, he tried to imagine what he might say to anyone who actually stopped. He would have to explain the absence of a broken-down car anywhere in the vicinity. People were more likely to stop for you if they thought you were a stranded motorist instead of some drifter. He decided the only thing that might work would be a highly fictionalized version of the truth. Make it sound like Heather was a total cunt with a case of perpetual PMS, and that she'd kicked him out in a fit of unreasoning fury, her anger sparked by his reluctance to badmouth her mother.

He chuckled.

*Yeah, that might work.*

Craig had a degree of charm that usually won people over in the first few minutes, an ability he intended to crank to the max when the time came. Most times, people quickly figured out he was a bastard of the first order, but this time it wouldn't matter. He would only have to be ingratiating long enough to get inside some sucker's car.

Then the fun could begin.

The wait dragged on some more. Deep down, Craig guessed he wasn't surprised it'd come to this. He and the bitch had never had any real feelings for each other beyond the carnal ones. This was typical of his relationships with women and everyone else. Craig didn't have any real friends, not the kind you saw on bullshit TV shows where some buddies bared their souls over a couple bottles of light fuckin' beer. What a bunch of pussy-ass horseshit. Real life wasn't like that. The way Craig figured it, everybody had a lot of wild, freaky-ass ideas running through their heads, things they knew would get them locked up or stashed away in a looney bin if they ever told anyone about them.

The politicians and the flag-waving Bubbas in their fuckin' pickup trucks liked to call the good ol' US of A the "land of the free," but Craig Carpenter knew that was some seriously bogus bullshit. "Land of the repressed" was more accurate by a long motherfuckin' shot, and it was all that repression that was to blame for so much of what had gone wrong in the country in recent decades.

You didn't have to be a genius to get hip to that. All you had to do was flip on fuckin' A&E practically any time of the goddamn day or night and check out one of those true crime shows. America was a big, seething, boiling-over cauldron of repression, and one way the cauldron let off steam was through endlessly fascinating, sex-motivated serial killing.

He'd frequently given some thought to going down that path himself, but the thing that'd always held him back was thinking of himself lumped in with all those sad-sack douchebags on the true-crime shows. They were all so pathetic. Their mommas or their daddies had abused them. Other kids teased them in school and beat their weak asses up for lunch money. Boo-fuckin'-hoo. And boy howdy, but they were pure ugly, as if every night of their miserable childhoods some spiteful gremlin had wailed on them with a goddamned ugly stick from lights-out till sunrise. They all had that greasy unkempt look and those thick-framed glasses with the Coke-bottle lenses.

He snickered again. Fuckin' losers, the lot of 'em.

Craig Carpenter was no loser.

His reasons for finally going over to the dark side weren't as pitiful as the reasons of the geeks on the true-crime shows. Hell, his reasons were practically *righteous*. Putting Heather in her place would be akin to striking a blow against the evils of feminism. Thinking back on his relationship with that gun-toting psychoslut, it was clear he'd failed from the beginning. A chick like that, with ideas of independence and self-respect, he should've shown her what was what from the outset. Should've laid the hurt down on her bigtime. Then she'd be the subservient, mewling wench of his dreams, no doubt.

A flash of bitter memory taunted him now, that image of the shining gun barrel emerging from the purse, the way she'd pointed the thing so unflinchingly straight at the middle of his face. Just as she'd done a year earlier, when they'd done that crazy thing together. Only this time there'd been no wild, gleeful charge to be derived from watching her wield the weapon. Just an instant of utter, primal terror. He'd even wet himself a little. That fire in her eyes, twin blazing reflections of righteous inner fury, had, for just a moment, made him believe she was going to kill him.

His face flushed red from anger and shame. His right arm fell to his side and his hands curled into tight fists. His jaw trembled and pain flared behind his eyes. He was on the verge of screaming. He needed to vent the rage boiling within him, and soon.

He drew in a deep breath and slowly exhaled it, forcing himself to calm down.

A car was coming.

Craig rehearsed his opening rap some more as the headlights grew larger and the shape of the car began to define itself against the darkness. It was a big old boat of a car, long and sleek and dark. It looked vaguely predatory, and its engine emitted a steady, powerful thrum. It swooped around a bend in the road, and the light from a streetlamp glinted off its tinted windshield. It was a Lincoln Towncar, a model that probably rolled off the assembly during the Nixon administration.

Craig thought it looked like a big black shark.

The thought made him gulp and suddenly hope that this particular car would flash by as quickly as the others had. But the Lincoln began to slow as it neared him. Craig felt his balls shrivel to the size of marbles, and a burst of sudden fear propelled him backward, away from the edge of the road and close to the guardrail and the line of trees beyond. The car rolled to a stop. A solid thunk resonated from somewhere within the car. It took Craig a moment to realize this was the sound of the ancient gearshift being ratcheted into the Park position.

He felt the metallic solidity of the guardrail against the backs of his legs. He considered turning and vaulting over the guardrail to take his chances with a plunge into the dense, dark woods, but something kept him riveted to the spot. There was an alien presence in his head. He let out a whimper as he felt its first intrusion into his psyche. He recoiled, grimacing as he tried in vain to force it out with his will. There was no sound, but he sensed something akin to a malevolent chuckle, a psychic impression of amusement from the invader.

Craig whimpered again and his voice emerged as a pitiful whine: "P-please . . ."

There was another thunk from within the car, caused this time by someone pulling the passenger side door handle. The door creaked slowly open, and Craig was able to see just the slightest hint of movement from within. Then he saw something so familiar, a thing he'd seen approximately a gazillion times in movies, that for a moment he was certain he had to be dreaming it.

The door swung open a little wider, and a woman's long, elegant, stockinged leg appeared. The woman's exquisitely shaped calf tapered down to a well-turned ankle and a foot encased in a black stiletto heel.

Craig couldn't help it. He laughed. "I get it. This is a dream. I'm James Bond, and you're Pussy Galore."

Then the woman began to rise out of the car. She stepped past the door and began to walk toward Craig. The rest of her body delivered on the sensual promise of that first glimpse. She had an hourglass figure so perfect it looked like something from a Vargas painting, an exaggerated man's idea of the feminine ideal. The short black skirt and the tight silk blouse further enhanced the impression.

The thing that ruined the picture for Craig was her head.

Her extra one.

"Lady," Craig said, beginning to feel dizzy. "You've got two heads."

One of the heads, the pretty one, laughed.

And that perfect body moved still closer.

Craig attempted to turn away from the insane, impossible vision, but he still couldn't move. The two heads—one radiantly beautiful, the other withered and hideous—grinned in a most unsettling manner.

The ugly head licked its cracked lips and hissed like a snake.

Then Craig knew—that was the one inside his head.

He felt that silent chuckle again.

Craig couldn't move, but he could still talk. He was clearly fucked, so there was no point playing at diplomacy now. "Swear to God, if I had a knife right now, I'd cut out my own eyes just so I'd never have to look at you again, Broomhilda."

The pretty head's sparkling blue eyes widened in delight. Then she uttered a disconcerting giggle and said, "What an excellent idea, Craig."

Craig shivered. Despite the horrendous implication in her words (and despite the fact that this . . . monstrosity knew his name), her voice sent a shiver of extraordinary pleasure rippling through his body. That voice was the essence of sex, the living distillation of every silver screen seductress in history.

The woman dipped her hand into a tiny black purse and produced something small and silver that glinted in the streetlight. She flicked the object with a practiced snap of her hand and a blade snapped cleanly out.

Craig whimpered as the blade was pressed into his hand.

His bladder let go and he felt a hot wetness soak his underwear.

The ugly head cackled.

And the pretty head smiled again and said, "Show me."

# CHAPTER SIX

Col. Luke Braddock popped the top on yet another can of lukewarm Budweiser, grimacing as an eruption of white foam rushed through the opening and spilled over his fingers. He set the can on the control panel and wiped his wet fingers on the hair of the girl kneeling at his feet. She grunted at his touch and attempted to slurp the remaining droplets of beer from his flesh, but Braddock pushed her away and leaned over the command center.

The device was a quadrangle design. The main control panel vaguely resembled a very large ergonomic keyboard, with an array of multicolored buttons, flashing lights, and toggles. It was a strange bit of technology, lacking the precise angles of machines designed by man. The three other quarter panels were also studded with buttons, but the lights there didn't blink and the instruments were nonfunctioning. The control panel's rounded sides and edges and pebbled surface gave it an organic look, like something that had evolved into being rather than something designed and assembled by intelligent beings. This impression was further enhanced by the way the panel would sometimes respond to Braddock's touch, the malleable material shifting slightly as the machine emitted a sound like a muffled groan. As it did now. Once upon a time he would've been frightened and disgusted by the living techology, but after more than twenty years in service with the Freakshow he was beyond jaded.

Rising from the space between the quarter panels was a thick, black column composed of a tarry substance that occasionally twitched. It dribbled droplets of dark goo into a metal gutter that surrounded the base of the column. Pressed into the column at irregular angles were numerous black-and-white television screens. The screens varied in size and picture quality, some displaying images so indistinct they seemed to be relaying a signal from some spirit dimension. One screen with a clear picture relayed scenes from a place Braddock was pretty sure really was some otherworldly realm. The Nothing, maybe, where the freaks came from. The images were disturbing, even for a soul as hardened as Braddock's, and he tried to avoid looking at that particular screen whenever possible.

The screen nearest Braddock—at the base of the column and facing him—was the largest. Braddock gripped a toggle that felt vaguely like molded plastic (except that it adhered to his hand a little too tenaciously whenever he forgot to sheath his right hand in the black leather glove he wore now) and flicked it to the left a few times, switching between views of empty tents and the deserted midway. He saw a flicker of something on the midway and paused there, waiting to see if another poor hick was still lurking in the shadows, thinking he might yet avoid capture. Then the flash of movement came again, and the ringmaster came into view, entering the picture from the lower lefthand corner of the screen and briefly filling the screen before proceeding to a point where he was more or less fully visible.

He stopped and turned slowly around. His gaze seemed to lock on Braddock's and he grinned, displaying rows of glistening razor-sharp teeth. Then he appeared to laugh and turned away, moving out of range again.

Braddock shuddered. Twenty years with the Freakshow and that son of a bitch still gave him the creeps. Braddock's job, ostensibly, was to provide constant monitoring of the Freakshow grounds in the aftermath of an Assimilation, to relay to the ringmaster and his equally creepy cohorts reports of sightings of human survivors. His first night on the job he spotted a young girl who somehow nearly achieved the impossible. She'd managed to reach the Freakshow's outer perimeter and was scaling the high fence. Upon spotting her, Braddock's hand drifted toward a speaker button, but he hesitated. The girl reached the top of the fence and began to swing her legs over the top.

Then there was a flash of gray as something resembling a pterodactyl swooped out of the sky and plucked the girl off the fence. And the ringmaster's leering face loomed up out of nowhere, his maniacal grin widening to fill the screen.

The ringmaster didn't say a word. He didn't have to. The creature's thoughts arrived fully formed in Braddock's head. This was a warning. And Braddock had known he wouldn't get another warning. Another failure to perform his new duties would result in a very miserable death.

And so Braddock committed a kind of suicide of the spirit, willfully shutting down the part of himself that felt concern and empathy for his fellow human beings. At first it wasn't easy. He experienced little flickers of regret. But as the months—and then years—rolled by, even these last vestiges of conscience withered and died. He barely remembered now what it had been like to give a shit about other people.

Braddock felt something nudge him and looked down to see the girl lying at his feet again, her pink tongue lapping at his boot. She sensed his scrutiny and her gaze flicked upward. She smiled and started to rise, her lithe, naked body sliding up his leg like a snake. He pushed the seat back a bit from the control panel, giving her some room. He turned back to the main screen as the girl's teeth worked at unzipping his jeans. Once this task was accomplished, she giggled mindlessly and got to work on him.

The girl's tongue did something that sent a shudder through him and he glanced down at her again. She smiled around his erection and did that thing with her tongue again. He let out a little gasp and leaned back in the chair. When it was over—and it didn't take much longer—he pushed her away and forced his attention back to the main screen.

Braddock gripped the toggle again and flicked through every available angle of the Freakshow grounds. There was no sign of any activity at all. Any humans who'd eluded capture at the beginning of the night's festivities had been rounded up. And all the freaks had gone to wherever it was they went when this first phase of their jobs was done. Still, he'd have to keep watch a while longer. Some more Freakshow operatives still had yet to return from the town, where they were working to collect those few townsfolk who'd somehow managed to resist the Call.

He popped open another beer and settled back in his chair, keeping his eyes on the screen, intermittently toggling to other views out of boredom. He hoped the other freaks would be back soon. The sooner the job was totally done, the sooner he could make full use of his slave's delectable body, then settle in for some much needed sleep.

The girl eyed his beer and said, "I sure am thirsty."

Braddock grunted. "You can have some water later."

"Some beer sure would be nice."

Braddock looked at her. She was smiling, batting her eyes at him like some innocent and playful schoolgirl. Only he'd used and degraded her in nearly every way imaginable, so she could hardly be called innocent anymore. He was pretty certain her IQ fell well short of triple digits. He rarely thought of her as actually being human, and he had to really concentrate to recall her name. He thought it was probably Sharon. Or Cheryl. Or some goddamn thing like that. She was just a thing, a possession, a toy to play with when he needed to keep his mind off the grim reality of his existence. And she wasn't the first. He'd gone through a couple dozen or so over the years. Whenever one of them began to get a little too old or haggard, some of the freaks would come to spirit her off to who-knew-where, and shortly thereafter a replacement would arrive. They always looked the same. Tall and slim with long blonde hair and big tits. That was one thing he could say in their favor—the freaks knew what he liked.

"Listen, Sharon—"

The girl rolled her eyes. "It's Sheila."

"Whatever, Sharon." He sighed. "Look, I've explained this before. The beer's for me. It's one of the few perks of the job. So sorry, but you can't fucking have any."

The girl pushed out her lower lip and batted her eyes a tad more rapidly. "But . . . but . . ." She sniffled and her eyes grew shiny with tears. "My life sucks. Please have mercy on me. I know you're not a bad guy, way deep down inside. A little beer would just be . . . nice. Please?"

Braddock scowled at her. "I thought I taught you better, Cheryl. I get all the beer and goodies. You get shit. Don't make me have to kick your ass all over this goddamn pod just to get that idea firmly planted in your goddamn head again."

The girl's head drooped and she stared silently at the floor. Braddock watched a single tear slide down her cheek and disappear into a corner of her mouth. He looked at those plump, pouty lips of hers and thought for a moment of how nice they felt wrapped around his dick.

"Aw, hell." He sighed again. "Here, take it."

The girl looked up at him, her eyes glistening with fresh tears. But she smiled and took the proffered can from his outstretched hand. "Thank you."

Braddock opened another beer for himself and studied the main monitor in silence for a while. The girl sat cross-legged on the floor, her gaze distant, detached, and she sipped occasionally from the beer, nursing it, knowing this rare display of generosity on her master's part wasn't likely to be repeated any time soon. They were silent for a long stretch of minutes, the only sounds in the pod that of Radio Ether (which currently was playing some annoying techno song) and the occasional mechanical click or whirr that emanated from the command center.

Then the girl said, "Can I ask you a question?"

Braddock's gaze stayed on the monitor. "You sure are mouthy tonight."

The girl waited a moment before saying, "Well . . . can I?"

Braddock frowned. Usually the only things she said were sex related, dirty talk to turn him on. He had to admit, she was damned good at that. And why not? Life as Col. Luke Braddock's flesh-and-blood sex toy wasn't any girl's dream come true, but it was a damned sight better than anything else the freaks would have done with her and she knew it. He'd broken this one in the same as the others, by defiling her in the most vile ways possible from the beginning, and by forcing her to focus on an existence centered entirely around serving his basest needs. This girl was new—having only been in his service for a few weeks—but until tonight she'd shown no indication of being any different from her predecessors. He couldn't remember the last time one of his toys had attempted to engage him in non-sexual conversation. Years ago, at least.

He knew he should ignore her, let his silence put her in her place. And he knew he should be focusing on his job, but he couldn't help himself. Life as pod commander had become pretty goddamned boring after twenty years. He allowed his gaze to drift from the monitor again. He studied her face for a time, peering into her eyes, trying to decide whether he'd misjudged this one. Maybe she wasn't as dumb as she seemed. Maybe the drooling moron thing was just an act.

He sighed. "Okay. Ask me a question, Sheila."

Sheila didn't smile at his use of her correct name, the first time he'd ever addressed her by it. She sipped some more beer, then chewed her lower lip a moment. He could see that she was thinking, trying to decide whether this was a smart thing she was doing, or if she was making a mistake.

Yeah, definitely not as dumb as he'd thought.

The girl sighed and said, "Is it true you can't leave the command center? That you'll die if you ever try to leave the pod?"

Braddock gaped at her for several moments, momentarily stunned and unable to respond. He blinked at the beer in his hand, then brought it to his mouth and chugged it down. He let out a big breath and looked at the girl again, his eyes still wide with disbelief. "Where did you hear that?"

She shrugged. One corner of her mouth twitched. Her gaze met his briefly, then dipped back to the floor. "In the cages. It was just before they brought me here. I heard that one dude, the one who looks like a pirate, talking with some other freak. They thought I was unconscious, and I was at first. I was dreaming about horses, a beautiful dream of riding a stallion down a storm-swept beach, and as I rode their voices came to me like whispers on the wind. I woke up and realized the voices were still talking. I almost screamed. Probably would've if I hadn't opened my eyes and seen them talking outside my cage. The pirate guy turned to look at me and I closed my eyes, pretending to still be asleep."

Braddock frowned. "Why did you do that?"

Her expression this time was absolutely devoid of artifice, and Braddock realized he was seeing the real Sheila for the first time. The hidden intelligence shone as clearly as the midday sun in a cloudless sky.

A corner of her mouth twitched, a reluctant half-smile. "Because knowledge is power. And you can gain a lot of knowledge by letting people think things that aren't true." Her smile broadened slightly. "For instance, I know some things about you. Things you'd never expect me to know."

Braddock chuckled. "Yeah, sure."

"You talk in your sleep." She laughed a little at his shocked expression. "It's true. You say all sorts of interesting things. Things about your mama, things about the army, and you beg people whose names I don't recognize for forgiveness." She leaned forward a bit, peering at Braddock so intently it made him shift nervously in his chair. "Who is Lisa, Colonel? What did you do to her? It must have been something pretty bad, because—"

Braddock surged out of the chair, his mind devoid of thought, all of the world at once enveloped in a red sheen of pulsing fury. The back of his hand snapped across the girl's face, eliciting a startled screech of terror as she tumbled sideways. Braddock gripped a handful of her blond hair and jerked her roughly to her feet. He wound loops of the hair around a tightly clenched fist, stretching the skin of her scalp nearly to the tearing point. She cried and whimpered, pleading for mercy, the insolence of a moment ago dissolving like flesh dipped in acid.

"I ought to snap your neck, bitch." Braddock's voice was a rasp, emerging through teeth clenched and grinding. "You think you're so fucking clever. Thought you spotted a weakness you could exploit, hearing me say my dead wife's name in my sleep. But there's one thing you forgot. It's hard to work a scheme like that when you're dead."

His free hand seized her neck and began to squeeze. She managed to wheeze a single word: "Wait . . ."

Braddock would never be sure why he paused in that moment. He'd never hesitated to eliminate threats before. And this girl was a threat, of that there could be no doubt. But an impulse stayed his hand. He stood there staring at her wide, terrified eyes for a moment, knowing he should finish the job.

Instead, he relaxed the pressure on her throat and said, "Choose your next words carefully, cunt. They may be the last you ever speak."

She inhaled and exhaled several deep breaths before managing to speak. "They talked about you when they thought I was asleep. They said the pod will explode if you ever try to leave it."

Braddock stared at her a long time, weighing how to respond, his face impassive—then he laughed and let go of her throat. "Is that so?"

The girl shuffled backward a bit, putting a few protective feet between herself and the brute who held her life in his hands. "Yeah."

Braddock laughed again, but the display was superficial, the humor never reaching his cold, dark eyes. "People say all kinds of things. Sometimes what people say is the honest to God truth, but mostly people lie, especially around here, and especially if it serves a purpose. Let me pose a question to you, Sheila. Did it ever occur to you that they knew you were awake, that maybe you were being fed a bit of subtle misinformation?"

"Yes."

That took Braddock by surprise. He arched an eyebrow and said, "Oh?"

She nodded. "Yeah. I'm not stupid."

Braddock chuckled, but his eyes remained as cold as ever. "Oh, I know that, sweet thing. But you're real good at playing stupid. You had me fooled. You ever get yourself out of this mess, you might want to consider moving to Hollywood, taking up a career in acting. So, genius, what's your gut instinct here? Were they telling the truth? Will the pod go ka-boom if I ever step out that door?"

Sheila weighed her response; she studied Braddock for several moments, peering into his pitiless eyes longer than any human had had the guts to do in a very long time. She sighed. "Yeah. I think they were telling the truth."

Braddock smiled. "Interesting. That's a helluva thing to do, isn't it? Ensuring a servant's loyalty by installing him in a booby-trapped surveillance device-slash-killing machine." He chuckled again and shook his head. "Why, it's downright diabolical."

The girl didn't react to his sarcasm. "So, it is true?"

Braddock said, "Sort of."

The girl frowned. She started to speak again, but Braddock's fist, lightning-quick, crashed into her jaw and turned out the lights.

# CHAPTER SEVEN

In that fleeting instant before the hammer of her mother's .38 came down, Heather Campbell had enough time to realize her life was at an end. The feeling she had in that moment wasn't the blind terror one might suspect, but rather a simple desire that it not hurt too much.

The terror hit the very next instant, when the hammer clicked down on an empty chamber. She saw her mother's arthritic trigger finger instintively flex again, turning the cylinder to the next chamber. She kicked the gun out of Alice Campbell's frail hand before the hammer could fall again. The .38 skittered across the hardwood floor, coming to rest just outside the open bedroom door at the end of the hallway.

Heather's heart nearly broke at the sight of her mother's anguish, the realization that she'd attempted to shoot her only child fully hitting her. "Mom, it's okay. I'm fine. What's going—"

Alice Campbell's pitiful wail of terror filled the hall-way, making Heather cringe. It was like standing next to a blaring air raid siren. Seeing her mother so dis-traught, so nearly insensible with fear, made Heather just as frightened. She looked past her mother's crum-pled form, searching the hallway for signs of someone or something else. It occurred to her now that her mother seemed to have been fleeing from something. But the hallway was empty. Probably the bedroom was, too. Heather relaxed a little, realizing that what-ever her poor mother had been running from was likely only in her mind.

Heather sighed and knelt next to her, taking one of her withered, knobby hands—the very one that had aimed the gun at her, in fact—and patted it reassur-ingly. "Mom, please, it's okay, really. I'm here now, and I'll take care of you, I promise."

The terror leeched from Alice's face, turning her flesh ghostly pale, and her eyes went wide, beseeching Heather. She gripped Heather's hand tightly and pulled her closer. "You listen to me. I know it looks like I'm losing my mind, but I promise you I am *not*." She spoke with urgency and conviction, a resoluteness that stirred anew the sense of unease Heather had felt a moment ago. "There's something in the bedroom. Something bad. I shot it. I hurt it. But I don't think it's dead. It can still hurt us, and we have to get out of here right fucking *now!*"

Heather frowned. "But Mom—"

"Don't you dare argue with me, not now." Alice's grip tightened around Heather's hand as she hauled herself to a sitting position. She cast her gaze from side to side, her movements frantic, her eyes moving wildly in their sockets, searching for something with a desperation that unnerved Heather. "Where's my cane?" The terror took hold of her again, distorting her voice, each word brittle and teetering on the edge of a sob. "How am I supposed to get out of here without my cane?"

Heather spied a glint of metal on the floor behind her mother and said, "Mom, I see it. Relax. I'll get it for you."

She pried her hand loose from her mother's iron grip, stood, and moved past her. She reached for the cane, which had rolled to a stop against the white wainscotting that ran along the bottom of the hallway walls. And that was when she heard the sound from the bedroom. She froze, her fingertips brushing lightly over the plastic grip of the cane's handle.

She turned her head slowly toward the end of the hallway, brushing back the strands of long blond hair that fell across her face. The sound came again, and this time she heard it for what it clearly was—a wheeze, the sound of someone struggling to draw breath, someone who was maybe dying in there.

"Mom? Who's in the bedroom?" She swallowed hard and her chest felt tight, as if a huge, cold hand had clenched tightly around her heart. "Did you really shoot someone in there?"

Heather stood erect again and took a hesitant step in the direction of the bedroom. "Hello? Is anyone in there?"

"No, no, *no* . . ." Alice Campbell's voice emerged low and scared now, on the edge of becoming a mewl. "Don't go in there . . . please. . . ."

A new emotion, panic, swelled beneath the rising tide of Heather's fear. She heard the labored breathing more clearly now as she moved closer to the bedroom.

There was a desperate quality to the sound, as if the wounded person couldn't get enough air. A collapsed lung, maybe? Heather glanced over her shoulder at her mother, who was on her hands and knees now and facing her daughter, her features a twisted mask of pain and terror. "No . . . Heather . . . please . . . don't. . . ."

Heather felt a sudden lump in her throat, an involuntary sob accompanied by an abrupt welling of tears in her eyes. She didn't know if she could handle this, if what she suspected was true. She'd dealt with a number of difficult things in her life

*The gun in her hands . . . the man's brown face trembling with fear . . . his eyes wide and pleading . . . Craig yelling something at the man, making him flinch and shriek. . . .*

*(STOP!)*

But this was beyond anything in her experience. She wanted very much to hand this nightmare over to someone better equipped to deal with it. A cop, an EMT, hell, anybody at all.

Heather took a deep breath and closed her eyes. She adjusted her grip on the cane, unconsciously wielding it like a baseball bat. Or like a weapon, a caveman's club. She wished she hadn't left her own gun in the car, but there wasn't time to retrieve it right now. There was no telling what awaited her in the bedroom, but whatever it was had to be dealt with very soon. She would allow herself another moment to calm down, then she would do what needed to be done. That burden belonged to her, and she would accept it—she had no choice.

In the same moment she expelled the big breath, her mother screamed.

Heather's heart lurched and her eyes snapped open.

She initially believed her mother was screaming at shadows and phantoms, some figment of a clearly deteriorating mind. The hallway appeared to still be empty. Then a wet hissing sound drew her gaze to the floor.

And Heather loosed a scream of her own.

She gaped at the grinning, impossible thing on the floor, unable for several moments to accept what she was seeing, even as it drew closer and flexed its distended jaw in her direction, displaying what looked like several dozen jagged, gleaming teeth. Teeth that looked like rusty dagger blades.

It was just a head—with a ragged, bloody stump of a neck below. It was pulling itself forward by extending several apparently retractable (and flexible) teeth, then sinking them just far enough into the hardwood floor to gain traction and slide several inches closer to where Heather was standing.

Heather experienced a moment of light-headedness, during which it seemed very possible that she might either faint or lose her mind. The latter possibility even seemed tempting for a flashing moment. After all, who in their right mind would want to go on existing in a world in which being menaced by the severed head of a pink-haired clown monster was even possible?

Then the points of the clown's extended teeth thunked into the floor just a few feet from where she stood and the world snapped back into focus. She blinked at the thing as it retracted its glistening teeth yet again. The thing seemed to sense her more focused scrutiny, its eyes rolling upward to meet hers, the corners of its painted mouth curving upward in a grin that mocked her disbelieving terror.

The grin galvanized Heather. She gritted her teeth,

shifted her body into a position like a golfer's and brought the cane around in a vicious arc. The cane's handle struck the clown's face dead-center and sent it tumbling back down the hallway like some ghoul's idea of a bowling ball. The head struck the linen closet door at the end of the hallway, then rebounded a few feet back in Heather's direction.

The thing immediately resumed its implacable pursuit of Heather and her mother. Heather's mind reeled at the idea. *It's just a fucking head! Those teeth look badass, sure, but we've got legs and feet, we're* mobile, *why the fuck doesn't it just give up?*

Heather glanced briefly at the cane in her hand and felt a moment of frustration. Her mom barely qualified as mobile. If there were any more of these things around—intact ones, especially—escape would prove difficult, if not impossible.

"Mom, we have to get out of here."

She returned to the spot where Alice Campbell remained in a half-sitting position, gripped her under one armpit, and hauled her roughly to her feet, eliciting a sudden cry of pain that stabbed at Heather's heart. She hated to hurt her mother, but this was no time for delicacy. She pressed the cane handle into her mother's hand, forcing the gnarled fingers to curl around it.

Alice looked at her through bloodshot eyes brimming with tears. "I shot it, Heather." She choked out a sob. "I shot the goddamned thing and it blew apart like a fucking helium balloon. How can that be?"

Heather had no clue and said so. "We can talk about this later, if we make it out of here." She half turned, steering her mother toward the living room. "Come on, Mom, you've got to help me out here."

Alice took a lurching step toward the living room,

and another, then her knees buckled and she sobbed again. She would've fallen to the floor without Heather there to keep her upright. "Oh, Heather . . . I don't know if I can do this. . . ." She looked at the front door, which was just visible at the foyer on the opposite side of the living room. "It's so far. . . ."

"Don't think about how far it is, Mom, just keep moving."

They were out of the hallway now and into the living room. Heather kept whispering encouragement to her mother, trying to keep her mind fixed on the goal of reaching the front door, but casting the occasional nervous glance backward. The clown head thing was still coming after them, still moving slower than them, but fast enough to make Heather feel much less than secure.

Several more difficult steps later, though, and they were more than midway to their destination—and the clown head was still about the same distance behind them. Heather felt a spark of hope ignite inside her. If they could just keep this pace up for another minute or so, they'd reach the door and get outside. Heather was pretty sure they would be safe then. The clown head was scary as hell, was probably capable of killing with those teeth at close range, but the ridiculous thing didn't have any arms or legs. A closed door between them and that creature would spell the end of that particular threat.

They were just reaching the foyer when the cane slid out of Alice's sweaty grasp. Alice screamed, and her weight dragged both of them to the floor. Heather tumbled over her mother and reached out blindly, trying in vain to break her fall. The side of her head struck an end table, drawing blood as everything went white for a blinding, painful moment. She wound up flat on her back on the floor, her head swimming again, the way it had in the hallway when first confronted with the clown thing. From a distance, as if through a swirling fog of anesthesia, she heard the thunk of the creature's teeth embedding themselves in the floor yet again. The sound seemed closer than she thought it should have been, and Heather let her head roll to the left.

The clown head was close enough to strike.

It grinned again as its flexible teeth reached for her.

Clarity returned in the space of a heartbeat. A monumental burst of terror pierced her heart, and her lungs involuntarily sucked in air, readying for a scream there'd never be time to unleash. Because it was clearly too late. She must have actually lost consciousness there for a minute, maybe longer. How else to account for the progress the creature had made? In that moment, Heather hated herself. Because not only was she going to die, so was her mother. She'd failed her.

Then, just as the creature's elongated teeth would've penetrated the soft flesh of her belly, something flashed across her field of vision, connected with the thing's chin and sent it rolling under the coffee table. Heather watched it disappear, then wrenched her head back in time to see her mother slump again to the floor, the cane sliding out of her hand yet again, her body deprived of its remaining strength from the desperate—and successful—attempt to save her daughter's life.

Heather sat up and groaned. She touched a hand to her head and felt the sticky blood in her hair. The gash worried her, but the blood wasn't a gusher, so she figured she'd be all right for now. She hoped. She got her feet under her again and stood up. She scanned the living room for something—anything—she might use as a weapon against the clown thing, which even now was emerging from the coffee table and resuming its interrupted pursuit of its prey.

Heather shook her head. "Jesus Christ, it's like the fucking Terminator."

Then a glint of something drew her gaze to the opposite side of the living room. She almost smiled, uttering a single sibilant word: *"Yes."*

She gave the clown head a wide berth as she made her way across the room. Then she seized the poker from its stand next to the fireplace and strode over to a spot behind the head. The thing's attention was on Alice Campbell now. Perhaps it believed Heather had abandoned the older, weaker woman as a liability.

But now, sensing the threat behind it, it ceased its pursuit of Alice. Its flexible teeth turned it around to face Heather. Its black eyes were unreadable, but they widened with some emotion Heather hoped was fear. Then she drove the tip of the iron fireplace poker through one of those eyes, leaning forward and grunting with effort as she worked to drive the instrument through the place where its brain should be. The head's facial muscles twitched and its teeth clacked excitedly for a few moments, then it went still, apparently finally, really dead.

Heather, however, had seen enough tonight to not trust what was apparent.

"Be right back, Mom."

She carried the impaled head outside and wedged it beneath the front left tire of her Chevelle. She got in the car and reached for the keys she'd left dangling in the ignition, half-expecting them not to be there, like in a horror movie. They wouldn't be there, and she'd glance up to see another clown monster—this one whole and capable of tearing her apart—leering down at her through the passenger side window.

But the keys were where she'd left them. She twisted them in the ignition and the engine came to life. She put the car in reverse, tapped the gas pedal, and it rolled backward. The clown's head collapsed with a satisfying crunch. Just for good measure, she shifted gears and rolled over it one more time. Then she parked the car, turned the engine off, and got out to inspect the results of her handiwork.

The clown's head was just a squishy mess, clearly no longer a threat of any kind. She let out a relieved sigh and only then did the terror creep back in, now that she was no longer consumed with saving her own life and defending her mother. But she hadn't been the only one doing the defending, had she? She remembered how her mother had saved her, and she smiled, feeling a surge of pride and love for the woman. But the smile faded as she looked up and down the lonely residential street.

She frowned.

Nighttime in a small town, so you wouldn't expect the area to be bustling with activity, but you'd expect . . . something. Yet there was not the slightest indication of any other human being in the neighborhood. For the first time, her mind was able to return to the insane mystery of the clown monster. It was a thing that shouldn't exist, yet she couldn't deny it. She knew she wasn't crazy. She trusted her own eyes. And where there was one of these things, there would very likely be more. She stared at the silent, dark houses lining both sides of the street and wondered if a similar creature had come to each of those homes. And why not? Why would such a thing, acting alone, single out her helpless mother? It made no sense.

And she thought back to why she'd come in the first place. Her inability to reach anyone in the town who could check on her mom. Every number she'd called either rang endlessly or went to voice mail. Neighbors, friends, the authorities . . . it was as if the entire population had abruptly disappeared.

Or been killed.

The need to be gone from this place shook her out of her reverie and sent her hurrying back to the house. She dashed through the open front door, her mouth opening to again urge her mother to her feet.

But the words never came out.

Alice Campbell was gone.

Heather couldn't breathe for a moment. The world seemed to be closing around her, suffocating her like a dark blanket drawn tightly around her face. Then she heard heavy footsteps coming from the direction of the kitchen and she turned in that direction. Her hands curled into useless fists at her sides, her body shaking with impotent, helpless fury. She'd left the gun in the car again—how could she have been so goddamned stupid?

Then something big stepped through the archway and entered the living room.

It looked like Quasimodo on steroids, a huge, hulking, humpbacked thing. Gripped like a chicken wing in its big, hairy right hand was something Heather at first took to be her mother's cane. But a closer look revealed the pale, thin thing to be a severed arm. The creature sneered, then brought the limb to its mouth and tore off a bite of flesh.

Heather screamed.

The thing swallowed the lump of her mother's flesh and laughed.

And then it came after her.

# CHAPTER EIGHT

The thing staring down at him had a big round head shaped vaguely like a pumpkin, but its gray features were infinitely scarier than any Halloween jack-o'-lantern Mike Garrett had ever seen. Its hairless skull was lined with a network of bulging veins that had a faint pinkish hue. Its eyes were a vibrant, glowing green. Twin air holes occupied the space where a nose would have been on a human face, and its mouth bristled with what looked to be hundreds of needle-like teeth.

Mike thought, *I'm dreaming*.

That had to be it. He did feel light-headed. It was almost a drugged feeling, actually. All sensations seemed to come to him as though from a distance. A low noise he at first thought was coming from another room turned out to be the sound of his own breathing. He felt faint pricklings of pain somewhere in the region of his scalp, but the mental fog enveloping him was so thick the feeling barely registered.

He closed his eyes and even these sensations began to fade.

Then a stray thought interrupted the spiral into deep unconsciousness, causing his eyes to snap open. *Why would I be falling asleep inside a dream?*

A bit of the mental fog dissipated—but he was still feeling everything from a distance. He felt drugged, perhaps by the thing with the gray pumpkin head. Panic flared within him as he wondered what sort of weird chemical was circulating through his veins.

Mike tried to rise, but something was holding him down.

His first thought was he'd been paralyzed, but no, he had sensation in his extremities and could move them very slightly. He fought to stem the tide of his panic in order to analyze the situation rationally. He closed his eyes again and focused only on physical sensation. He curled his hands into fists and tried with all his might to lift them, but couldn't. He felt the same resistance when he tried to lift his feet. Restraints of some sort—*leather?*—bound him to a table.

The drug fog continued to abate as his mind worked, and he soon determined there was another, thicker restraining strap across his forehead. Not only could he not lift his head, he couldn't turn it in either direction.

He opened his eyes and flinched at the sight of the pumpkin-headed thing leaning closer, its bulbous head cocked to one side, its eyes pulsing an even brighter shade of green. The thing's face was alien, but Mike was certain he detected a spark of sadistic delight lurking just beneath the veneer of its curiosity. There was something in its bearing that caused Mike to think of a research scientist studying the effects of some hideously toxic new chemical on a lab rat.

A glint of something bright above the creature drew Mike's attention. It was a huge, shiny, oval thing hanging from a ceiling that looked to be about a hundred feet high. Mike screwed his eyes shut a moment, then opened them again and was able to see a bit more clearly. He was instantly aware of two things—that his initial perception was mistaken (the ceiling *was* high, but only about twenty feet), and that he'd been better off not seeing so clearly.

The thing hanging from the ceiling was a very large mirror. And the image it reflected was of a large room filled with what looked like operating room tables. Many of the tables were empty, but several had nude human beings strapped to them. Their clothes lay in little piles next to the tables. Creatures identical to the pumpkin-headed thing studying Mike hovered near each prone human form. Carts filled with gleaming instruments were parked next to each table. A shudder of revulsion rippled through his body as he began to make out finer details. The skulls of most of the restrained humans had been opened, their brains exposed. Only Mike and an Asian man on a table to his left had thus far been spared the cranial surgery. He and the Asian man were also the only clothed "patients."

Though it made his stomach churn, he continued to study the reflection of horror—and he saw that those with their skulls open were not yet dead. At the head of each table—including the one to which Mike was strapped—was a machine, a black, boxy thing, with an array of wires protruding from the sides. The ends of the wires—electrodes of some sort, Mike supposed—were embedded in the exposed brains. Occasionally, one of the pumpkin heads would touch the black machine, eliciting a variety of reactions from the subjects. The reaction seemed to depend on where they touched the machine, which was weird, because Mike couldn't make out anything that looked like buttons, switches, knobs, or controls of any sort.

But touch the box here, and a man's penis would grow instantly erect. Touch it there, and another person would laugh. Touch it in still another place, and the affected person would sob. The creatures were definitely conducting research of some sort, but to what purpose? He wondered if any of the creatures possessed anything resembling a human conscience, and, if so, if what they were doing disturbed them.

Mike watched in helpless horror as a creature to his right touched the top of his machine and caused the woman strapped to the table in front of him to cease breathing. After several shocked moments of staring at the woman's still form, he opened his mouth to scream at the thing that was playing with her life. It could still bring her back. There was still time. All it had to do was touch the top of the goddamned machine again. But all that emerged from his throat was an unintelligible sound somewhere between a groan and a hiss. His vocal cords felt paralyzed, incapable of uttering even the feeblest protest.

The object of his impotent fury never touched the top of the box again. Instead, the creature wrapped a large, many-fingered hand around the wires embedded in the woman's brain and yanked them out. It then balled the wires up and shoved them into the machine, which seemed to swallow them without a trace. The creature moved to its cart of instruments, extracted something that looked like a large metal spork with a tong attachment. Mike felt bile rise in his throat as he realized the purpose of the instrument, an intuition proven true a moment later when the thing used it to extract the woman's brain from her cranium. It dropped the quivering brain in a white pouch, which it tossed into a bucket half-filled with similar packages.

Mike was so revolted by this casual murder and mutilation he failed at first to note that the creature tending to him was poking around in its own cart of instruments. Then he heard a distressing mechanical whirr and his gaze jerked back to the image of his own helpless form. The terror that came over him then was so strong he thought it might stop his heart. He wished it had. Sudden death would come as a blessing at this point. He did not wish to spend the last moments of his life enduring torture at the hands of one of these evil things. But he didn't die. And his outrage wouldn't help him. In a moment the bonesaw the creature had just turned on would open his skull, and he would have no choice but to bear witness to every miserable moment of his life's sorry end.

The creature turned toward Mike, lowering the whirring blade to a point near the crown of his skull. Mike closed his eyes and gritted his teeth, inwardly sending a flurry of desperate prayers to a God he wasn't sure was there even as he awaited that inevitable first moment of horrible agony.

Then he heard something—a loud *Thunk!*—that caused his eyes to open. His gaze went immediately to the overhead mirror, and he was at first unable to comprehend what he was seeing.

The sound he'd heard was that of a door being flung

open with force sufficient to send it crashing against the inner wall. And through the open door walked Jinx, the cute girl who'd saved him from the ringmaster. He hadn't given her much thought since awakening, assuming she was either dead or in her own place of torture somewhere nearby. He tried, again without success, to work his vocal cords, to urge her to run before it was too late.

But . . . strange thing about that . . .

She didn't seem frightened.

Stranger still, the pumpkin heads didn't seem alarmed by her presence. Nor did they make any move to restrain her as she strode purposefully toward Mike's table. The creature hovering near Mike studied a document she thrust into its hands. Then it nodded. Betraying no discernible emotion, the thing moved away from Mike and focused its attentions on another captive.

Mike's brow creased in confusion. Why did these creatures seem so accepting of Jinx's presence here? She was just like him, a citizen of Pleasant Hills ensnared in the trap set by . . . whatever unfathomable power was behind the Freakshow.

Except . . . now that he thought about it . . . he didn't really know that for sure. He'd just assumed she was from Pleasant Hills, without any explicit confirmation from Jinx. She'd behaved like a person desperately attempting to escape the clutches of the ringmaster and his bizarro cohorts, but perhaps that had been a ruse. Perhaps her intent all along had been to trick him and lure him deeper into the heart of this evil place. Maybe she wasn't really human, was instead some awful thing wearing an alluring costume. It wasn't something he could rule out—he'd witnessed enough seemingly impossible and inexplicable things tonight to know that.

Jinx moved to the head of the table and leaned over him. Her expression was intent, but otherwise unreadable. "I know you're confused, scared, and full of questions, but I'm going to ask you to set all that aside for now."

Mike would've laughed had he been capable of it. Set it all aside. Sure, no problem.

As if he had a choice.

She unbuckled the strap pinning his head to the table, allowing him to move his head side to side. The better view this afforded him of the atrocities surrounding him made him wish she'd just left the damned thing in place. Her face moved from his field of vision and his gaze went back to the overhead mirror, where he watched her extend a foot beneath the table and press on something. He heard a latch give and winced as the table jumped forward a few inches, sprung loose from some sort of mooring device.

Jinx gripped the sides of the table and began to spin it toward the door. Mike felt slightly queasy at the sudden movement, but a little nausea was a small price to pay if it meant putting some distance between himself and the monster doctors . . . pumpkin people . . . whatever the fuck they were.

The table rolled forward, Jinx propelling it at a speed that seemed just a hair shy of reckless. More than once Mike's table nearly clipped the edge of another table or piece of machinery. At one point Mike was treated to a closeup view of another prone victim's empty (but gleaming wet) cranium. His stomach did a slow roll and he felt a fresh touch of nausea at the back of his throat. He wrenched his gaze from the hideous sight and pressed his eyes shut. He held them shut for a time, even as the table bumped through the open door, jerked hard to the left, then began to move even more rapidly down a corridor.

He felt himself edging toward unconsciousness as yet another tickle of bile made him gag. Memories of dead rock stars who'd choked on their vomit ignited a new sense of panic, and his eyes snapped open to blink at a series of dim overhead lights. And now he clung to consciousness as desperately as a shipwreck survivor would cling to a piece of shattered hull.

There was something weird about the corridor—*big fucking surprise*. The walls didn't have the flat, angular planes of buildings made by humans, nor were they constructed of anything like drywall, brick, or concrete. The material used had a molded, organic look, with swirls and ripples everywhere. The ceiling was curved and drooped in places.

The corridor, he began to realize, was also curved, although not as dramatically. He sensed Jinx adjusting their trajectory to account for the curvature every twenty yards or so. It felt as if they were moving in a gigantic circle. Mike raised his head slightly to see if they were actually going toward anything in particular. He could see what appeared to be the end of the long corridor some thirty yards ahead. It gave way to a huge, empty, gray room. A fucking cavern, for God's sake, with a ceiling so high Mike figured you'd need a rocket to reach it.

Jinx kept them barreling along, the table's wheels occasionally bumping against some unseen obstruction. Fighting the strengthening tide of nausea, Mike raised his head again and saw that they were heading straight for the far wall and a large door there. The closer they got, though, the less "door" seemed an apt word for what they were approaching. It was more like a black hole, a large wound in the flesh of some great beast. He tried to discern shapes or movement within that blackness, but saw only impenetrable darkness.

Mike moaned and struggled mightily to make his uncooperative vocal cords work. Every instinct he had urged him to protest. Jinx clearly intended to plunge them right into the heart of that unfathomable blackness, and he had to make her stop. When they were within ten yards of the opening, Mike closed his eyes, clenched his fists, and braced himself for whatever strain of insanity was coming next.

He felt the darkness take them—and then, in a space of time that might have been ten years or one heartbeat, he felt . . . *light*.

His eyes fluttered open and he knew immediately that he had departed one world and entered another. The world he'd left behind was . . . alien . . . and the world he'd reentered was his own. He felt less groggy right away. Still drugged, but more . . . real, more aware of the world around him in a tactile way. Even the air was different. He looked up and saw a night sky speckled with stars, the same stars he remembered staring up at in wonder on camping trips as a boy.

But, unfortunately, they were still at the Freakshow.

Jinx brought the table to a stop outside a dilapidated trailer. She reached under the table and turned a latch to prevent it from moving. Then she quickly undid the rest of the straps and helped Mike sit up on the table.

"Take it easy," she said, keeping a tight grip on his wrist. "You'll feel a little better now, but still a little out of it." She sighed, and Mike heard exhaustion in the sound. Whatever her real story was, he sensed she'd worked hard to get him out of that theater of horrors. He decided then to give her the benefit of the doubt a while longer.

He found he could speak again. "What's . . . going on?" His voice was hoarse, but the words emerged clearly enough. "Who are you?"

"Don't worry about that yet. Let's get you off this table."

Mike shook his head. "I don't know. I feel . . ."

"You'll be fine. It's wearing off. Trust me." She tugged him toward the edge of the table, and he swung his legs slowly over the side. "Now step down. I won't let you fall, I promise."

But Mike stayed where he was a moment longer, taking in the surroundings a bit more. The trailer was just one of many large vehicles. Some, like this trailer, were the sort that would be living quarters for staff. Others were long and windowless, and obviously used for transporting Freakshow equipment. It all looked very normal. Very human. Here and there he could make out the logos of American auto manufacturers. He turned to the left as far as he could and saw the dimmed lights of the midway and the rippling outline of the huge big top tent.

His brow furrowed. "Where did that place go? It was real . . . I know it was real."

Jinx's expression hardened. "Later. How many times do I have to say it? For now can we please just concentrate on getting you inside?"

Mike shook his head. "It was . . . real."

Jinx sighed. "Yes. It was real. There, you happy now? Now, get off this fucking thing or I swear I'll flip it over and drag you inside."

Something in her voice made Mike believe her. He

slowly slid off the table, felt his feet touch the ground, then allowed Jinx to tug him in the direction of the trailer. He saw a dim light glowing through one of its grimy windows. There was a flicker of movement inside—a barely perceptible twitch of shadow—and Mike said, "Wait . . . there's someone in there. . . ."

Jinx, her back to him as she guided him toward the trailer, said, "I know."

Mike dug his heels in the soft earth and said, "We shouldn't go in there."

Jinx stopped and turned to look at him. "And why not?"

Mike licked his lips and looked around nervously. "Because I don't think anyone's watching us now. We could get out of here."

Jinx laughed. "That's where you're wrong, Mike. In the Freakshow, someone's *always* watching you, *especially* when you're sure they're not."

Then she strengthened her grip on his wrist and pulled him toward the trailer. Mike's legs felt shaky as he stumbled along with her. He had no choice but to do as she said. She was stronger than he'd realized, for one thing, and he was still very weak from whatever those pumpkin people had used to drug him.

Jinx hauled him up the short set of retractable stairs, opened the door, and then they were inside the trailer. The interior was sparsely furnished. A single twin bed, with its frame bracketed to the wall, dominated the room.

But what really commanded Mike's attention was the trailer's other occupant.

He swallowed something hard in his throat and realized he was shaking. He tried backing away. At the moment, he cared not one bit about what manner of lurking horror might be waiting to ensnare him out there on the grounds of the Freakshow. All that mattered was getting away from this . . . *abomination*.

The thing slid off the recliner it was sitting in and extended one seven-fingered hand in his direction. Mike stared at the hand in wide-eyed horror. The digits were thicker and longer than human fingers, with hard, knobbed ends that lent them a distressingly phallic look. This hand appeared capable of pushing through the soft flesh of his belly to rip out his intestines. The mental image sickened him, bringing back a vivid picture of Chuck Follett's death. Mike tried to twist out of Jinx's grip, but she continued to hold him fast, barely seeming to strain from the effort.

The thing's expression twisted, forming what might have been a sneer on a human face. "How rude."

Its voice sounded like something emerging from the surgically implanted voice box of a throat cancer survivor. The sound set Mike's teeth on edge and sparked a small ache behind his eyes. He didn't want to hear that voice again. It was nails on a chalkboard times one thousand.

The thing lowered its proffered hand and settled again in the recliner. It crossed its chunky legs and regarded Mike in what might have been a thoughtful or leering way. Again, the thing's strange face was hard to read. The bulbous head was shiny and looked like a piece of blown glass with facial features. The impression was so strong Mike found it highly disconcerting when those features moved with a weirdly liquid kind of elasticity. Its body was short and segmented like that of an insect, with the head, torso, and legs looking as if they could be pulled apart like the pieces of a child's toy.

Mike said, "What the fuck are you?"

The creature made that maybe-laughing sound again. "Why, isn't it obvious?" It sat up straighter and leaned forward. "I'm a . . . freak."

. It made that sound again, and now Mike was certain that it was laughter.

Then it seemed to compose itself and leaned forward still farther. "Do you want to know a secret?"

Mike didn't want anything but to be out of there, but he opted to humor the thing. "Sure."

Its mouth moved. A smile, perhaps. "You have been chosen. You have a glorious destiny to fulfill."

Mike waited a beat. When the creature failed to elaborate, he said, "Say what?"

The creature's gaze shifted to Jinx. "Enlighten our new friend, please. Then . . ."—it laughed again— "then I should like a show."

Mike frowned. "A show?" He looked desperately at Jinx. "What the hell does that mean?"

Jinx wouldn't look at him directly. "It means he wants to watch us fuck."

Mike couldn't have been more taken aback. "Wha . . . ?"

Now Jinx met his gaze, and he saw from the seriousness of her expression that she wasn't joking. "You heard me, and we'll do it. But first I have to tell you some things."

Then she started talking, her voice low and earnest, like that of a saboteur conversing in secret with her cohorts. At first the words didn't register—he was still quite dumbstruck by the notion of having sex with Jinx in the presence of this thing—but soon he latched onto an alarming phrase or two and really began to hear her. When she was finished speaking, he shook his head and said, "My god . . . you can't be serious. . . . How could we possibly . . . ?"

Then Jinx began to undress, and he fell silent again.

# CHAPTER NINE

While it was happening, Craig was simultaneously aware of exquisitely intense sensations of pain and pleasure. The feelings didn't alternate—they coexisted. The pleasure was such that he didn't want the two-headed woman to ever stop doing what she was doing to him. And the pain was so intense it threatened to grind what little remained of his sanity to ash and cast it skittering into the wind.

This thing happening to him was so surreal a part of him refused to accept the reality of it, the part that was left of his rational self. The rest of him was too aware of everything to deny its reality. Between the moans of ecstacy and howls of agony that burbled past his trembling lips, he kept thinking things like, *Oh, man, this is about seventy-seven shades of fucked up right here.*

The woman's soft palm and fingers felt so good wrapped around his engorged penis, and the way she slowly stroked the throbbing shaft was the most exciting thing he'd ever felt. He'd enjoyed fucking Heather, but nothing she'd ever done for him had ever felt anywhere near this good. Which was weird, because, really, it was just a handjob. He suspected the exquisite sensation was largely the result of his mind being manipulated by his captor. But knowing this did nothing to diminish his pleasure. She also seemed to be regulating his ability to reach climax, sustaining him just shy of that threshold for far longer than he ever would have imagined possible.

Which he didn't mind.

It helped offset the disgust he felt at the way the ugly head's withered tongue kept sliding in and out of the bloody socket formerly occupied by his left eye. Worse still were the moments when that crusty mouth suddenly locked firmly around the socket and slurped at the pooled blood and small bits of leftover optic tissue.

Mike tried to keep his one good eye trained on the pretty head, with its flowing blond hair and movie starlet face, but every once in a while he would feel a psychic pressure that forced him to watch what the hag head was doing. Then the hag head would smile and cackle in that awful wheezing way it had.

This went on for what seemed like hours, but was really more like half an hour. Then there was an abrupt relaxing of the control the woman was exerting over him. Her hand gave his penis one final squeeze and he erupted, screaming long and hoarse in one moment of perfect ecstacy. Then, as that sensation crested and quickly faded, the pain washed in, and it was worse now, so bad he wished he could die so it'd be over. He screamed again, this time in unbearable agony, then he screamed some more.

The woman watched him for a while, enjoying his

pain. He wanted to rip her throat out, but she seemed to know his thoughts and only laughed harder. After a time, the pretty head leaned close to his face. And the mouth opened wide, those full, sultry lips stretching themselves so thin Craig thought the flesh would split. But that didn't happen. What did happen was much worse.

Or so Craig initially thought.

She vomited on his face. He gagged and tried to move away from her mouth, but he couldn't. She moved her mouth closer still to the empty eye socket and vomited on him again. He felt the thick, viscous fluid dribble down his face. It had a jellylike texture. There was a lot of the stuff on his face now, and when she started stuffing it into his socket, he thought he might do a bit of vomiting of his own.

But a strange thing happened.

The pain began to fade.

Weird. Whatever this puke jelly was, it seemed to have an anesthetizing effect. He even felt a bit of numbness where it'd dribbled down his cheek and spilled past his lips into his mouth. Now that he wasn't consumed with mind-shredding agony, he was able to ask himself some pertinent questions. Like, what was this creature?

Craig figured he might as well just ask: "What are you?"

The two-headed woman extracted a tissue from a small black handbag and dabbed jelly from the mouth and chin of the pretty head, holding the head at an angle that almost seemed regal. She snapped open a compact mirror, examined herself, then, seemingly satisfied, smiled and put the mirror away. Only now did

Craig note how surprisingly little of the jelly stuff had wound up on the woman's slinky black dress—just a speck here and there that she casually swept away.

The pretty head laughed.

The hag head scowled and hissed. *Fucking bitch.*

The pretty head's eyes widened and her lips pursed, a look of mock surprise. "Oh, Craigy. That's . . . not . . . nice." She made a tsk-tsk sound and waggled an admonishing finger at him. "You want to know what I am?" She giggled. "Well, I'll tell you. But first, a lesson in manners seems in order."

Craig scowled. "What in the name of sweet creeping fuck are you talking about?"

The pretty head's smile faded slightly. "This."

A psychic tendril did a little wiggle inside his brain, causing his body to spasm uncontrollably for several moments. His teeth chattered as his head and arms flopped against the leather upholstery, and his remaining eye jittered wildly in its socket. Then something twitched in his head and the wild spasms abruptly stopped.

Craig was still shaking, but the cause now was abject terror. "Please . . ."

The pretty head smiled again, a beaming, radiant expression so perfect it belonged on the cover of a fashion magazine. "Oh, the magic word. P-L-E-A-S-E. Please." That incongrously girlish giggle trilled from her mouth again. "Now I know I have truly broken you. I had you on the ropes before, to use one of your race's charming sporting metaphors, but, despite the extreme trauma you endured, you retained a remarkably high degree of insolence and bravado. But no more!" And here she clapped her hands in glee. "You are thoroughly cowed. You are ready to beg for your putrid life." She leaned close and clamped a strong hand on his thigh. "Aren't you?"

Craig nodded emphatically and struggled to speak. "Y-y-yes," he said, his lips trembling. "A-a . . . any-thing . . . you say."

"Yes." The woman's hand moved to his face and stroked his cheek. "My pet, you will indeed do any-thing I say. What's more, I feel confident you will find great joy in serving me."

Craig wondered whether the comment was intended to be sarcastic. He supposed it didn't matter, because she was right about at least one thing: he was broken. At least as far as his resistance to her will was con-cerned. So, what the hell, he decided to cling to the hope there was truth in what she was telling him.

He coughed and loudly cleared phlegm from his throat. "So . . . what do you want me to do?"

"*There's* a good boy." She pinched his cheek like a grandmother praising a precocious child. "So eager to please." She giggled again. "It's like this, Craigy. I've seen inside you. I know the whole truth of you. Your essence. Your soul. And what I have seen is dark. Very, very dark indeed. Why, I do believe that if our paths hadn't crossed this evening, you would've gone on to murder quite a significant number of relatively inno-cent human beings."

Craig felt a strange chill slither up the length of his body and nestle in the back of his brain. As he looked into her eyes and noted the knowing smirk at the edges of her mouth, he knew it was true—this woman, this *thing*, knew absolutely everything there was to know about him.

He felt fear, of course, as well as a deep sense of violation. The violation, in some very profound ways, was more unsettling than the fear. It left him feeling exposed. And vulnerable. And Craig didn't like that one bit. He began to fidget like a nervous first grader made to sit at the front of the class. He may even have whimpered a bit. It was hard to tell, the frantic way his thoughts were racing. He needed a place to hide, a dark, secret place where all his inner thoughts could be private again. He wondered if this was anything like the way a woman felt in the aftermath of a rape, and almost—but not quite—felt a tiny flicker of genuine empathy.

"You need to calm down." The woman's voice was hard, devoid of the playfully sadistic tone of before. The hag head hissed and writhed like the head of a cobra. Its crusty tongue slid from between its parched lips and flicked at him. The sliver of putrid flesh was still wet with his blood, and Craig tried—in vain—to suppress the memory of the sickening thing sliding in and out of his eye socket.

Craig managed a jittery chuckle. The sound surprised him. There wasn't a damn thing funny about this situation. No, sir. Just further proof his mind had completely cracked. "Yeah, okay. You're right. I'll just go ahead and calm down." He shrugged expansively and smiled. "Things can't get any worse, right?"

The pretty head's expression was flat, unsmiling. "I have a job for you, Craig. More of a test, actually. A way of proving your mettle. Perform the task I'm about to assign you satisfactorily, and you'll have a place in my world."

Craig had no idea what she was talking about, but it hardly seemed to matter. She would tell him at some point, he assumed. "And if I don't?"

And now, at last, she smiled again. But that playful quality remained absent. This smile was a quietly savage thing, more frightening by far than the hungry, angry snarl of a rabid animal. "Then I will have you tortured over an extended period of time. You'll endure agonies so extreme, and so prolonged, that you'll recall the pain you've experienced tonight with wistul nostalgia."

The pretty head held its chin at a haughty angle, looking down at him, challenging him to disagree.

The thing was, he believed her.

"What do you want me to do?"

The woman pressed a white button set in a recessed panel between the seats, then spoke in a way that indicated to Craig she was talking to someone else—the Towncar's driver, presumably, who was hidden behind a partition of black glass. "Joseph, have we arrived at our destination?"

A tinny but gruff voice responded through a speaker set in the same recessed panel: "Yes, madam. We're outside the preselected target."

"Excellent. We're ready back here, Joseph."

"Very good, madam."

Craig heard a door open, then slam shut, followed in short order by the sound of the rear door to his left opening. He saw a large man in an immaculately tailored chauffeur's uniform standing on the sidewalk. The polished brim of his chauffeur's hat showed a glint of reflected streetlight. The man looked like a bizarre cross between a professional wrestler and a proper English butler. He was massive, with a barrel chest and a neck as thick around as the base of a hundred-year-old oak tree. His hands were equally large and looked capable of squeezing Craig's head off with a single flex of those powerful fingers.

Craig didn't want to get out of the car.

"But you must," the pretty head whispered, her soft lips brushing his earlobe.

Craig sighed. "Yeah. I know."

Taking a deep breath, he slid out of the car, stepped up to the sidewalk, and sidled a few very deliberate steps away from the chauffeur. One corner of the chauffeur's mouth might have moved just the slightest little bit, a there-then-it's-gone smirk indicating a casual, almost bored disdain. The big man sensed Craig's scrutiny and began to turn his head in Craig's direction.

Craig quickly averted his gaze, deciding now was an excellent time to apprise himself of his surroundings. They were on a residential street in some nowhere town. Pleasant Hills, most likely. It had that typical look of bland small-town smarminess he so despised. The houses lining each side of the street were all small, one-level brick structures, all very modest, though each and every tiny patch of green lawn was immaculately, even lovingly, maintained. It was the kind of place that normally made Craig want to either puke or rip his eyes out. Huh. Now that he'd actually been made to cut out one of his own eyes, that observation no longer struck him as funny. Life sure had a way of blindsiding *(hah!)* a guy with a big ol' irony wallop now and then.

The two-headed woman was on the sidewalk with them now. She took Craig by the crook of an elbow and turned him toward the nearest house on that side of the street. This house had an actual white picket fence lining the front of the property. Other than that quaint touch, there was absolutely nothing to distinguish it from any of the other houses.

Craig grunted. "Okay. Nice house. If you're a fuckin' suburban asshole." He glanced at the two-headed woman. "What are we doing here?"

The pretty head smiled. The hag head made a sound suspiciously like a cackle, which did nothing to allay any of Craig's fears. The pretty head said, "The test, Craig. Remember? Inside that house is a living human being. Your task is to cause it to stop living."

Craig frowned and gnawed at his lower lip a moment. He stared at the house a long while, considering. It looked empty. No lights were on, nor could he detect the faint flicker of a television screen through any of the windows. He looked up and down the block and saw that the same was true of every other house on this street. Weird. Sure, he was in Bumfuck, Nowhere, populated entirely with good, church-going, god-fearing people, all of whom likely believed in getting to bed at a decent hour, but—well, it wasn't *that* late. This house—and each of its neighbors—resembled a mausoleum more than a home.

He looked at the two-headed woman. "This place . . . this whole fucking street . . . feels empty. You sure there's anyone here?"

The pretty head smiled faintly. "Quite sure."

Her tone was too confident—bordering on smug—so he believed her. "Okay. So I'm supposed to kill somebody in that house." He arched an eyebrow. "The way you said it . . . you sounded pretty sure there's just one person in there."

"Yes."

The answer was so vague it bordered on not being

an answer. Craig chose not to press her on the subject, but he was starting to feel exasperated. "How exactly am I supposed to do this? I don't have a weapon. Is the person in there asleep, or are they hunkered down in there and watching us through a window?"

The two-headed woman shrugged. "These are things you must discover on your own. I'll grant you two more bits of information, then Joseph and I will retire to the car to await your return. Your quarry is more or less alone in the house. Also, the front door is unlocked, so you needn't concern yourself with breaking and entering." The pretty head's smile brightened a smidgen. "Just entering."

She stepped off the sidewalk and stood next to the Towncar's open rear door. "Oh, and one more thing. Once you've ended your quarry's life, I'll want a trophy."

Craig frowned. "A trophy?"

The woman slipped inside the car. Her last words before Joseph threw the door shut made Craig gulp: "Bring me your quarry's heart."

Joseph shot a final penetrating glance Craig's way, then returned to his place behind the Towncar's steering wheel. The chauffeur sat there with the door open and his left leg out of the car. He looked far more relaxed than a man driving the getaway car for a murderer ought to look.

Craig turned and faced the house again. He remained utterly paralyzed for a few more moments. While he stood there, he pondered some things. Why, for instance, were these strange people so apparently unconcerned about the police? The possibility that the person he was supposed to murder would hear him enter the house and subsequently call 911 terrified him—until he remembered why Heather, *that fucking bitch,* had been so hellbent on coming tonight in the first place. The phone lines weren't working in Pleasant Hills.

Craig smiled.

He began to walk up the length of white sidewalk leading to the front porch of the house. It was strange how good he suddenly felt; a near giddiness reflected in the broad grin stretching across his face. He wondered if maybe it had something to do with some sutble influence of the two-headed woman, a gentle subconscious prodding via the mental pathways that existed between them now, but intuition told him otherwise. No, this was rooted in something more basic, and he realized what it was in a moment of pure epiphany.

He was free. Liberated.

He was finally being allowed to be what he'd always wanted to be.

He was so caught up in the moment, so swept up in a wave of happiness unrivaled at any point in his life, that he wasn't even aware he was laughing softly as he ascended the two steps to the front porch. He crossed the porch with a brisk, confident stride, then gripped the brass door handle and turned it without hesitation.

He pushed the door open and stepped into a deeper darkness.

# CHAPTER TEN

The metal wheel latch squeaked loudly as Braddock turned it to unlock the pod's hatch. The large hatch popped out of its metal frame and Braddock shoved it open the rest of the way. A view of the Freakshow grounds and the wide world beyond taunted him, as alluring to him as the airbrushed image of a centerfold model was to a teenage boy—and just as out of reach.

A cool night breeze rolled in and fell across his face, so refreshing after so many hours cocooned in the stagnating warm air that circulated inside the pod.

He fished a pack of Winstons from his front shirt pocket, tapped out a cig, and rolled it into a corner of his mouth. He lit the smoke and stood inside the hatch frame, which was as far as he could go without detonating the device the freaks had implanted in his brain. The story the girl had overheard only hinted at the real truth. Braddock would indeed die if he ever left the pod. But the pod itself wasn't booby-trapped. At least not in any way Braddock knew about.

The only booby trap he knew of was sitting there in his head, a little nodule the size of a pinhead, waiting like a dormant tumor. Braddock never ceased being aware of its presence, which was the real reason he drank so much. A thing like that, a guy could go crazy thinking about it. Maintaining a steady level of inebriation—never sober, but never too drunk—was the only way he could ever get any sleep. Otherwise he would obsess over it, perhaps even to the point of taking a suicidal swan dive out the pod door. Which was something he occasionally considered anyway, but never very seriously. He didn't much like being trapped here, but things could be worse. The freaks kept him well supplied in life's necessities—booze, pussy, and food. Hell, some guys would probably consider this a dream gig.

*Yeah*, Braddock thought, taking a slow drag off the Winston. *Some guys . . .*

"It doesn't make sense."

The girl's voice startled Braddock. He jumped, and the half-smoked cigarette slipped from his fingers. He saw it fall away from him, its lit end fluttering in the night air. For one wild moment, Braddock seriously thought about leaping after it. The weight of his body shifted subtly forward, and he could feel how easy it would be to just go.

*What the hell are you doing?*

His hands shot out and gripped the edges of the doorframe so fiercely his large knuckles turned white. He drew in a deep breath to steady his nerves, then pushed himself back from the precipice. He tapped another cig from the pack of Winstons and lit it before turning to face the girl.

She stood very close. Too close, as far as Braddock was concerned. If she tried, she could easily push him through the pod's open door. It was what he would do in her position. But then, she didn't know what he knew. He'd wondered why the freaks would want her to know Braddock couldn't leave the pod, but feed her that one deliberate bit of misinformation. Now, though, he began to see a tiny sliver of method in their madness.

They wanted her to know Braddock was a prisoner. Never mind that it was supposed to be a secret. They wanted her to know and so she knew. It was a dangerous piece of knowledge. He didn't socialize with the other humans held captive here, for obvious reasons, but he knew he was regarded as a collaborator. Some probably even believed he was in charge of the whole shebang. The pod, after all, was naturally seen as a position of power. It sat atop a mobile killing machine that had wiped out countless scores of them, so this was a natural assumption. The prisoners probably spent much of their time fantasizing about ways of killing him. This girl, Sheila, had probably given that very notion a great deal of thought.

Which was why they'd allowed her to believe the pod was booby-trapped. They hadn't wanted her to know there was a way of eliminating Braddock without killing herself. This obviously meant they didn't want Braddock dead, at least not for a while yet. For which he was very grateful, fuck you very much, but knowing that did little to reassure him. Why let her know anything, even if it was just a piece of a larger secret? He had a feeling some weird, subtle game was being played by the powers that were, and he didn't like it one bit.

Braddock exhaled smoke in Sheila's direction, smirking as he watched her nose crinkle at the smell. "Damn, but I must be losing my touch. I thought you were down for the count."

Sheila put a hand to her jaw, slowly rubbed the tender place where his fist had connected with it. "It hurts."

Braddock snorted. "Too bad." He wedged the cig into a corner of his mouth and stepped toward her. She flinched slightly, but didn't try to retreat, not even when he gripped her small shoulders in his big hands. "You got taught a lesson, little girl. Too many questions equals pain." He squeezed her shoulders, his fingers digging hard into soft, bare flesh, making her wince. "But I'm guessing maybe the lesson didn't take, because it sounds like you've got some more questions."

The girl sighed. "It doesn't matter what you do to me."

Braddock frowned. "What?" His tone was incredulous. He must have misunderstood her. "Are you serious? I've shown you what I'm capable of. . . ."

The girl shook her head. She maintained eye contact with him the whole time, her gaze as unwavering as that of a marine sniper. "Yes, you have. And I don't care."

Braddock's features twisted in a scowl of disbelief. "Bullshit. I could end this tough broad charade of yours *tout suite*, believe me."

The girl sighed again and this time her gaze did slide away from him. "It just . . . doesn't make sense."

Braddock knew he should just rap her upside the head again. Maybe two or three times. Or more. Whatever the hell it took to shut her up. But he didn't do that. Because now his own curiosity was piqued. "Okay, tell me. What doesn't make sense?"

She looked at him again, and now he did see a bit of apprehension there. "Well . . ." She hesitated, her brow furrowing as she chewed her lower lip. "It's just that . . ." Yeah, she was really nervous now. He could feel the tension in her body. But she wasn't backing off. He could feel that, too, could see it in the way her eyes suddenly came into intense focus. She was just gathering her courage. And then it came: "I just don't get why they would booby-trap the pod. It makes no sense."

Braddock strove to project an outward calm. He puffed smoke around the dwindling cig wedged in the corner of his mouth. "Oh yeah? You mind explaining that?" He chuckled and shifted one hand to her throat. "Because, it's funny, I'm not sure what you're trying to say."

Sheila had to be aware of the threat implicit in the presence of his hand at her throat, but she pressed on anyway. "You're just a man. They can replace you as easily as you or I would change a burned-out lightbulb. But this machine . . . there's just the one."

Braddock felt himself edging toward real panic. "You don't know that."

"I don't know it. But I believe it." And now she smiled. "And so do you. This machine . . . it's . . . it's capable of amazing things. Crazy, horrible things. And it's just . . . weird, like a cross between a U-boat and something extraterrestrial."

Braddock let go of her throat. "The freaks aren't aliens."

"Okay, and that just makes it weirder." Sheila put a hand to her throat and absently massaged a tender spot. "This machine, it feels like it's something left over from a bygone age, like something salvaged from the ruins of Atlantis."

"That's quite an imagination you've got, lady."

Sheila shrugged. "Okay, so maybe it's not from Atlantis. Atlantis was just a myth. But it's something like that. I know it. I *feel* it. Which is why I say this thing has to be more valuable to the freaks than you are. It's just simple logic. If they lose the pod, they can't just order up another one."

Braddock laughed. "There's the flaw in your reasoning right there. Don't look for logic where there isn't any." He flicked the smoked-down cig out the door and instantly flared up another. "This 'artifact' does possess a self-destruct capability. I even know how to enable it. Not that I ever will. I've been with this whacked-out dog and pony show more than twenty years, okay? I've seen a lot of things, and I know some of what they do." He indicated the column of video screens rising from the command center with a nod. "Hell, I've had a front row seat most of those years. Once a year the Freakshow rolls into some backwater nowhere town. Somewhere small enough that the whole population can be sucked in. And you know what happens once that population is contained. It was your town last year, right?"

Sheila's eyes brimmed with moisture as her expression hardened. "Yes. Stewartsville. My family . . . my . . . girlfriend . . . They're all dead."

Braddock grunted. "Girlfriend, eh? Anyway, same

story for me, minus the same-sex lover aspect, all those long-ass years ago. We also know the rest of the world's completely oblivious to these slaughters. Because as far as the rest of the world is concerned, nothing in those towns has changed." He smirked. "Why, right at this very moment, somewhere in Stewartsville a gal who looks just like you and has your name is walking around and doing the normal things a young honey like you would be doing."

"I'd heard . . . stories like that. It's true?"

Braddock exhaled smoke and looked steadily at her through the haze. "Yep."

Sheila frowned. "But . . . why?"

Braddock smiled. "See, now we're reaching the heart of the matter. Why, right? Why any of this?" He shrugged expansively. "Who knows? I'm not sure they even know. It's just a pattern that repeats, year after motherfucking year. And far as I can tell, they were doing it long before I came into the fold. I used to think maybe they were trying to take over the world, one shithole town at a time. But if that's their game, ain't no way you or I'll be around to see it happen."

Sheila shook her head, her frown deepening. "It would take centuries at that rate." She heaved another big sigh. "The whole thing is . . . insane."

Braddock flipped another smoked-down butt through the open door, then reached outside, grasped the wheel lock, and pulled the door shut. He spun the wheel until the latch snapped home again, then moved past Sheila to return to his place at the command center. He gripped the toggle handle and said, "Come here, I want to show you something."

Sheila joined him at the command center, sidling up next to him to lean against the armrest of his chair.

The way she shifted her weight to one leg did things that emphasized her body's lovely curves. She was just tired and lacked a chair of her own to sit in, but the stance was sexy as hell. Braddock's libido stirred. He recalled the stray comment about her "girlfriend" and that further stoked the fires of lust. He could just see that pretty face of hers buried in some hot young thing's snatch. The image sent a shudder of desire pulsing through him. He considered throwing her on the floor and having a good, savage go at her, but damn her, she'd engaged his intellect, too, and it'd been a very long time since that had happened. Until this moment, he hadn't realized how starving some suppressed part of him had been for a substantive conversation with another human being.

He nodded again at the column of screens. "The Freakshow's a façade. You know that already. There's something much weirder than a menagerie of misbegotten genetic unfortunates lurking behind the illusion. And when I say that, I don't mean behind a fucking curtain. Behind our reality, on another plane of existence, that's what I mean."

Sheila smirked. "Bullshit."

"After everything you've seen, everything you've experienced, belief in alternate realities shouldn't be that big a leap." He jogged the toggle to the left a bit, then squeezed the handle and pulled it slightly backward. "See that oblong-shaped screen just below the biggest one? Watch that."

Sheila leaned forward a bit, peering intently at the wavering, indistinct images on the screen. The shift of her body presented a very pleasing view of her ass. He fought an impulse to bite the perfectly round left buttock, finding it as tempting as a piece of fresh fruit.

"What's going on in that room? What are those hideous things?"

Braddock tore his gaze away from the young girl's shapely posterior long enough to see that the image on the screen had come into sharper focus. Then he resumed his study of her ass, able to address what the girl was looking at without seeing it himself. He'd stared at similar images enough times to know precisely what she was seeing. It was the operating theater, the place where the pumpkin heads performed their odd experiments in genetic engineering. "Those things are in that other place I was telling you about, a realm that occupies the same physical space as the Freakshow, but on another level of reality. Another frequency on your radio dial. What you're seeing is as close a glimpse as you or I will ever have of the reality behind the Freakshow."

Sheila crossed her arms beneath her breasts and shuddered, causing her buttocks to jiggle slightly. Braddock couldn't stand it any longer. He put a hand on her ass. She surprised him by leaning into his palm a little.

She glanced down at him and said, "They look like monsters from outer space, like something from a fifties sci-fi movie."

Braddock shook his head. "I told you already. They're not aliens. They're a different species, visitors from another version of this world."

"But how do you know that?"

Braddock grunted. "You learn a lot of things in twenty years, girl. Every so often I'm fed a snippet of real information by people like Captain Ahab."

"You mean the pirate, right?"

Braddock licked his lips. "You are full of fucking

questions. It's annoying. I have half a mind to bend you over my knee and spank you."

Braddock rose from his chair and placed a hand at the flat of her back, pushing Sheila forward. "Brace your hands against the edge of the command center and lift that sweet ass of yours up."

She did as instructed, but glanced back over her shoulder at him. "I should've kicked you out that door when I had the chance."

The comment gave Braddock a moment's pause as he positioned himself behind her. "You thought about it, huh?"

Sheila's face was blank. "Yeah. I did."

"But you didn't."

"No."

Braddock's eyes narrowed. "What stopped you?"

"Because I didn't want to die when the pod exploded."

"Right." Braddock's hands dug into her waist. "I thought you didn't believe the pod was booby-trapped."

"You always believe the things a girl says, Braddock? Really?" There was an archly mocking tone to her voice now. "I hadn't pegged you as being that stupid."

Braddock's hands squeezed harder.

And Sheila licked her upper lip. It was strange. She seemed to be taunting him, almost goading him on. Almost eager for what was about to happen. And it wasn't just acting, the way it normally was with these girls. Seeing that flare of erotic hunger in her eyes made Braddock's pulse race. He entered her roughly and experienced a moment of grim satisfaction at her startled yelp. But then she shifted her weight back and wriggled against him in a way that elicited a sound from him that was part snarl and part moan.

When it was over, Braddock collapsed into his chair, panting hard, his body covered in a sheen of sweat. "Goddamn."

Sheila retrieved two more beers from the icebox and passed one to Braddock, who accepted it gratefully. He nodded at the can in her hand. "I say you could have that?"

She popped the can's top and drank deeply from it. Then she wiped her mouth with the back of a hand and said, "I guess I figure I deserve it."

Braddock chuckled. He was too tired, too spent, to give her any shit over it. "I guess you do, at that." He popped the tab on his own can and sipped some foam. Then he heaved another big breath and slid down farther in his chair. His gaze slid appreciatively up the length of her body before settling on her clear blue eyes. "You're something else, you know that?"

Sheila didn't say anything to that. She took a seat on the floor, crossing her legs beneath her. She looked at the column of organic video screens. Braddock's gaze remained on her, but when she reacted visibly to something on one of the screens, he turned to see.

The ringmaster's eerie visage filled the largest screen.

Braddock sat up straighter in his chair.

An enigmatic smile touched the corners of the tall man's pale, bearded face.

Sheila said, "I think he was watching us fuck."

Braddock's head snapped in her direction. "What? How could—"

She smirked. "Because of the Seeing Orb implanted in my brain."

Braddock's eyes widened with shock. His first impulse was to deny what she was saying, but he felt the truth of it in his gut. His mind reeled at the implications and he began to be really afraid, now that there was a very real possibility that the ringmaster had seen them and had eavesdropped on their conversation. His heart pounded and sweat filled the grooves of his palms. He tried to tell himself he had nothing to worry about. They'd only shared some theories about the Freakshow. There'd been no talk of rebellion or escape.

*Yeah,* he told himself. *I'm cool. Everything's fine. This is just business as usual.*

So, naturally, that was when the nodule in his brain finally detonated.

The top half of Col. Luke Braddock's head exploded, showering the command center console with blood, bits of bone, and pulped brain tissue.

Sheila barely flinched.

She remained in her cross-legged position on the floor awhile longer, staring up at the ringmaster's grinning face as she took her time finishing her beer. Then she crumpled the empty can, tossed it aside, and got to her feet. She tugged Braddock's body from the blood-spattered chair and dragged it across the floor to the pod's hatchlike door. She cranked the wheel lock and popped open the hatch. Braddock's body tumbled through the opening a moment later and landed with a wet splat on the ground below.

Sheila stared at the indistinct blob on the ground and said, "You got played, you stupid man." And she laughed.

Sheila closed the door and grabbed yet another beer from the icebox. Then she returned to the command center, where she allowed her fingers to drift over the keys she'd been able to access while Braddock was fucking her, that glorious opportunity she'd

waited so many maddening days for—days she'd
spent either chained to the wall or servicing the old
man sexually. The killing sequence was still so vivid in
her mind from the weeks she'd spent memorizing it.
She still wondered why the freaks hadn't just eliminated the vile old man themselves. It would have been
so easy for them. But she decided it didn't matter just
now.

She settled into the chair and considered how long
it'd been since anyone other than Braddock had sat
there and smiled. It felt good to sit there. This was a
sturdy thing. And so unexpectedly comfortable. And
still so sticky with Braddock's blood.

She dipped her fingers in a pool of it and put them
in her mouth.

On the screen, the ringmaster's head tilted to the left
a bit.

Sheila dipped her fingers in the blood again. This
time she smeared the stuff on her flesh, tracing a
moist, red trail from her throat to her abdomen.

"What do you think?" she said, addressing the
screen. "Did you pick the right girl for the job?"

The ringmaster laughed and laughed.

And Sheila continued to paint herself with Braddock's blood.

# CHAPTER ELEVEN

The big hunchbacked thing was fast, but Heather was faster. She spun toward the door with all the fluid grace of a prima ballerina, then she bolted through the opening with a speed that would have impressed an Olympian. She flew down the front steps and sprinted toward the Chevelle. Her pursuer thundered after her, its footsteps unnaturally loud in the otherwise silent night.

Heather dove through the Chevelle's still open driver's side door, snagged the .38 from the passenger seat, and backed out of her car in time to raise the weapon and fire it point-blank at the beast's massive chest. The gun's reports rang out in the night as each of the slugs found its target, drilling impressive holes through the center of the thing's torso. The .38's hammer clicked on an empty chamber, and the pistol slid out of her grasp, landing with a clunk on the driveway.

The beast had been staggered by each bullet's impact, but now it was standing fully erect again, its bloated upper lip curled and trembling. Heather's retreat as it advanced on her was a product of reflex, despite the obvious hopelessness of her situation. In a moment it would have her, and there would be nothing she could do to prevent it from ripping her apart. Just as it had ripped apart her poor mother.

Its approach was unhurried now. It seemed to be savoring her terror, anticipating the things it would do to her. Heather stopped moving as it closed to within grabbing distance. On some level, it seemed, she'd accepted the fact of her imminent demise and just wanted this night of worry, grief, and torment to be over.

One huge hand began to reach for her throat. Heather closed her eyes and prayed it wouldn't hurt too much, or for too long. Her throat trembled, the nerves within it almost seeming to know in advance how the creature's cool, crushing embrace would feel. But that never happened.

The night exploded.

Or, at least, that was Heather's initial impression of what was happening. There was a sudden cacophony. A thunderous, repeating noise that obliterated—for a moment—the rest of the world. Then she felt something wet and clingy splatter her face and the front of her blouse.

Then her eyes opened and she saw that much of the creature's grotesquely deformed head had disintegrated. She glanced down at her blouse and realized she'd been doused with the thing's green blood. Another blast resonated in the night, and she saw an exit wound bloom like a scarlet rose just below the creature's shoulder. It was then she realized the explosions were blasts from a pump-action shotgun.

The creature's body stumbled forward, its arms still stretching toward her. Heather thought the thing meant to take her with it into death, but then whatever spark of life still powered its ravaged body abruptly winked out and it fell to the ground. Heather stared at the corpse in shocked disbelief for a moment, her mind unable at first to process this turn of events.

She gradually became aware of a voice calling to her. It seemed far away at first, like a whisper from a dream. There was a sense of urgency in the voice, but she was unable to make sense of the words. They were like a foreign language, strange patterns of sound whirling about her head.

Then one of the patterns coalesced into something she could understand: "Goddammit, are you okay? Can you not fucking hear me?"

Heather blinked. She lifted her gaze from the dead creature and for the first time glimpsed her savior. The man holding the shotgun had the classically chiseled jawline of a movie hero. He was well-built and stood a shade over six feet, had more than a day's worth of stubble, and unruly dark hair that fell to his shoulders. He wore a tattered flannel shirt open over a red T-shirt. The front pocket of the flannel shirt was stuffed full with spare shotgun shells. The shotgun was still pointed vaguely in her direction. Heather's eyes went wide with alarm. Apparently thinking she was frightened of the gun, the man let the barrel tilt toward the ground.

"You don't need to be afraid of me. I'm—"

But Heather wasn't really hearing him again. Now that the immediate threat of the monster was removed, her mind focused with laser intensity on a single notion—getting to her mother. The rational part of her mind realized she was likely dead—a sickening image of that beast gnawing on that limp limb flashed through her mind—but the love she felt for her mother overwhelmed reason. She had to see for herself.

Which was why she suddenly sprinted past her rescuer and plunged back into her childhood home's darkened interior. She stood huffing in the foyer a moment, then gathered her breath and called out, *"Mom!"*

The shotgun-wielding man's booted feet clunked on the hardwood floor behind her. "You shouldn't yell. You'll just draw their attention."

"Fuck you." Heather whirled on the man, her face contorting in a venomous expression. "My mother is in here and I mean to find her. She needs . . . help." Tears erupted from her eyes. "That thing hurt her . . . maybe killed her . . . I . . ."

The man's expression remained mostly stoic, but a flicker of what might have been compassion touched his eyes. "Okay. Let's find her, then. I reckon the damage is already done, what with all the gunfire." He paused to feed some more shells into the shotgun's chamber. "Once we find her, though, we'll want to get out of here in one hell of a hurry."

Some of Heather's rage had retreated, but she remained jittery, a lit fuse sparking toward explosion. "No shit."

She moved away from him and into the living room, where she immediately spied the cast aside limb. She knelt next to it and felt her heart lurch at the sight of a turquoise ring she'd given her mother for her birthday several years earlier.

She stood and saw the man staring down at the arm, his face a pinched mask of revulsion and concern. It was obvious what he was thinking—that her mother was clearly dead and any hope of coming to her aid in time to pull off a miracle was pointless. But it wasn't his loved one in trouble (or dead).

He could leave any time.

Some small part of her was aware she could stand to be a bit more charitable toward this man, considering he'd just saved her life. That was the civilized part of her, but these finer impulses were being overwhelmed by other emotions. There'd be time for apologies later. Or maybe not. Maybe they'd both be dead, slaughtered by more of the bizarre creatures loose in Pleasant Hills. Right now she only had time for one thing.

Heather raced through the living room and then through an archway into the shadow-cloaked kitchen. At first she couldn't see anything. The windows here were smaller than those in the living room, with no streetlamp light to diffuse the darkness. She slapped a palm against the nearest wall, her fingers searching frantically for the switch she knew was there.

Just as her fingers skidded across the switch, she heard a faint moan from the far side of the kitchen, on the opposite side of the black blob she knew to be the dining table. A fresh jolt of adrenaline sizzled through her veins.

"Mom!"

She flipped the switch and the overhead flourescent light flickered on. The sight of the bright swath of blood sprayed across the cupboards and counter jolted her heart again. All this blood *couldn't* have come from her mom's body. There was too much of it. Surely too much for a person to lose and still be alive.

She dashed across the kitchen, sliding for a millisecond on another patch of coagulating blood on the floor tiles. She righted herself and continued around to the far side of the table, where her mother was slumped in a corner on the floor.

Alice Campbell looked even more haggard than usual. In fact, she looked like a corpse. Only the sound of her breathing, which was very faint, indicated she was still alive. Her eyes were glassy, unfocused.

Heather's eyes filled with tears again as she knelt next to her mother. "Mom? Can you hear me?"

Alice Campbell's head turned in the direction of her daughter's voice. "Heather . . ."

Heather sniffled. "Mom, yes, it's me, and I'm going to get you some help."

Even as she said this, the impossibility of what she'd just promised hit her. *She's going to die, and there's nothing you can do about it! Nobody can lose that much blood and live! The shock alone will probably kill her!*

But Heather gritted her teeth and managed to at least temporarily mute the manic voices of doubt. She opened her mouth to say something else, some other empty platitude, but the words were never spoken. She'd noticed something peculiar about her mother's wound.

The stump was red and glistening, but there was no longer any blood flowing from it. In fact, the red substance she'd initially assumed was blood appeared to be something else entirely. The texture was all wrong.

She frowned and leaned in for a closer inspection. "What the hell is that?"

A shadow fell across her, triggering a fresh jolt of fear. But it was just Mr. Shotgun. She'd been so focused on her mother she hadn't heard him enter the kitchen. He was standing just behind her, leaning down slightly to get a better view of Alice Campbell. "What is what?"

Heather touched the tip of an index finger to the gelatin-like substance and immediately felt a mild sting. She jerked her finger back and swiped the substance off on her jeans. "This . . . stuff. My mother's wound is packed with it."

The long-haired man frowned. "Just a guess, but I'd say that thing I just blew away did that to keep her from bleeding out."

Heather shook her head. "But . . . why? Why not just kill her outright?"

The man grimaced. "Uh . . . this is just a guess . . . and kind of a ghoulish one at that . . . but . . . well . . ."

Heather rolled her eyes. "Jesus Christ. We're hip deep in carnage here . . . whatever your name is. We're past putting things delicately, okay?"

"It was saving her for later. The name's Josh, by the way. Josh Browning."

Heather frowned. "For later? Why?"

Josh shrugged. "To eat, I think."

Heather's stomach churned. "Ugh."

"You said we were past being delicate. And I didn't catch your name, by the way."

Heather's attention remained on the glistening stump as she said, "It's Heather." She became aware of a tingling in the tip of her index finger, and she probed it with her thumb. "My fingertip is numb."

"Sure. I reckon whatever that jelly shit is, it acts like an anesthetic."

"We have to get my mom to a hospital."

"Main thing we've got to do now is get out of this house, make tracks to some place else." Josh stepped past her and knelt next to Alice Campbell. He placed the shotgun on the floor and slid his arms under the woman's limp body. "We don't make ourselves scarce pronto, there won't be a chance to get to a hospital."

Heather's eyes widened. "What are you doing?"

"Trying to save your mother's life." Josh stood up with Alice cradled in his arms. He held her easily, as if she were a small child. "You're gonna have to carry the shotgun. I can give you a quick primer on how to use it."

Heather snatched the shotgun off the floor and surged to her feet. She looked Josh square in the eye and said, "I know guns."

Josh smiled slightly. "Yeah, I saw you blastin' at Quasimodo with that .38. You're a crack shot with a pistol. A normal man would've been dead instantly."

"Well, trust me, I'm just as good with a shotgun, or pretty much any other weapon. I had a boyfriend who was big into guns and he taught me to shoot."

"Okay, then." Josh nodded at a door. "I reckon that leads to the backyard. It's a fenced yard, right? You know if she keeps a lock on the gate?"

Heather shook her head. "I'm sure she doesn't."

Josh nodded again, as if affirming something to himself. "Yeah. Get that door open. You go out first."

Heather's brow furrowed. "Why?"

The look on Josh's face was one Heather knew would normally be reserved for addressing idiots. "Because you're the one toting a shotgun. Anything's out there, you're gonna need to blast a path clear for us."

Heather still didn't move.

Josh shifted his grip on her mother. "This is a text-book case of time being of the essence. What's the holdup?"

"Why go out back? Where are we going?"

"Away from here? Of course, we could just hang out here, wait for more weirdos to show up. If that's what you want, cool. Me, I'd rather get moving."

Heather's expression hardened. "Stop talking to me like I'm a fucking moron, okay? I just think we ought to get in my car and burn rubber out of here. So what's the deal with going out back?"

Josh sighed. "I'm sorry if I sound condescending. I mean no offense. I'm rattled, okay? Just like you. And I think taking the car is a mistake because it means being out in the open. We'll attract attention immediately and likely be fucked as fucked can be. We do it my way, we can move cautiously through the neighborhood and eventually be able to hunker down in the woods. I know this neighborhood and the woods real well, and I'm pretty sure I can get us to safety that way."

Heather shook her head. "That'll take forever. My mom doesn't have forever. In the car, we can be out of this shithole town in five goddamned minutes. And, hell, there can't be that many of those things. It's not like we're in a war zone. There's not gonna be snipers on roofs or roaming freaks patrolling the streets in armored tanks."

"Gotta tell ya, Heather, I wouldn't rule any of that out."

Heather took a deep breath. This conversation had quickly become exasperating. Now it was edging toward infuriating. "I would ask you why you'd say something so stupid, but my mom could be drawing her last breaths while we stand here arguing. I'm done with this bullshit."

She backed up a bit and aimed the shotgun at Josh.

Josh's eyes reflected fear in that first instant, but then his features took on an incredulous cast. "Put that down, please. You're as likely to hurt your mom as me if that thing goes off."

Anger stronger and more frightening than anything she'd felt before propelled Heather forward. The barrel of the gun was pressed against Josh's forehead. His eyes gleamed with fear again—and this time it didn't fade quite so quickly.

"Maybe you didn't really hear me before, asshole." She made a deliberate show of curling her finger around the shotgun's trigger. "I know guns. I handle them very well. And this isn't the first time I've put one in someone's goddamned face. If you don't turn around and head back through the house right now, I'm gonna blow your brains out and do what I need to do on my own."

Josh sagged slightly. "Fine." He backed away from her deliberately, turned, and began to move toward the living room. He said over his shoulder, "Just don't blame me when they blow us off the road with their freak tank."

Heather followed him into the living room, keeping the shotgun's barrel trained on the back of his head the whole time. Josh earned a brownie point when they moved through the archway, turning sideways and stepping carefully through in order to avoid banging any part of Alice Campbell against the jamb. The conscientious gesture produced a flicker of guilt in Heather. Now that the initial flash of fury had passed,

Heather couldn't believe she was pointing a gun at the man, threatening him. She could tell he was a decent guy. He didn't deserve this kind of treatment. It was insane. Which made it appropriate in a really twisted way, what with the whole fucking world apparently gone crazy.

They passed through the living room without incident. At the front door, Josh again turned sideways and moved through carefully. Heather experienced another stirring of warm feelings for the guy. She wanted to thank him for being so careful, but she found herself tongue-tied. There was something a bit wrong about expressing gratitude to a person you were holding at gunpoint.

Well, fuck it. She could apologize later.

As Heather walked through the front door, she caught a glimpse of something moving rapidly out of the shadows. She called out a warning, but it was too late. Josh let out a yell as the assailant tackled him at knee level, tumbling him off the porch. Heather saw her mother fly out of Josh's arms and screamed. Alice Campbell landed heavily in the front yard, the impact bringing her back to consciousness with a scream. The sound of her mother's agony was like a knife through Heather's heart.

She leaped off the porch and rushed to where Josh and the attacker were savagely wrestling on the ground. She aimed the shotgun at the thrashing bodies and felt a wave of revulsion as she got her first good look at their new adversary. The naked creature was humanoid. And it was female. That was evident from the lack of external male genitalia—and by the creature's huge flopping breasts. All three of them. The thing had a squat, powerful body covered in hair so thick it could almost be called fur. Its lower body was especially formidable, with massive, flaring hips and thighs as thick as tree trunks. Its head had a conical shape, with a snoutlike mouth that had a definite canine aspect. Its teeth flashed and tried to rip at Josh's flesh. Josh was holding the thing off, but it was clearly requiring every bit of his strength to keep those snapping teeth from plunging into him.

Heather watched helplessly for several very long moments as they rolled back and forth on the ground. She knew she had to act, but she was terrified she would accidentally kill Josh instead of the three-titted wolf lady.

But then the creature finally managed to pin Josh, getting her elephantine legs straddled about his midsection. Josh held her head back with one hand clamped to her throat. He used his other hand to bat away her hands, which sought the soft tissue of his eyes. Josh was fighting valiantly, but he was losing the battle.

Lucky for him.

Heather, grateful to at last have a stationary target, armed at the back of the creature's head and squeezed the shotgun's trigger. The blast punched a big hole through the base of the thing's skull and the exit wound obliterated much of its face. Josh yelped in disgust as a soup of blood and brains fell on his face. Heather rushed forward and kicked the thing off him. She jacked another round into the shotgun's chamber and aimed the barrel at the creature's midsection. Another blast resonated in the night. And then another. More blood burbled out of the area where Heather estimated its heart to be, which hopefully now was shredded.

Josh was still flat on his back, breathing heavily and

wiping blood from his face. Heather kicked him in the hip. "Get up!"

"Ouch!" Josh managed to heave himself to a sitting position. He wiped more blood from his face and stared at her in disbelief. "You can stop kicking me now, okay?"

He got to his feet with a grunt and hobbled over to where Heather's mother lay unmoving on the ground. Groaning, he knelt and scooped her up again, then turned to face Heather. "I think she's okay. Unconscious again, but that's probably for the best." He was still hobbling as he carried his burden toward Heather's car. "I'll lay her out in the backseat, okay?"

Heather nodded. She frowned and bit her lower lip as she observed his stiff gait. "Are you okay, Josh?"

"Banged my knee up a bit when that thing knocked me off the porch, but I'll be all right." He reached the driver's side door and turned to look at Heather. "Can you push the seat up a bit?"

Heather brushed past him, then knelt to press a handle that flipped the seat forward. She stood back up and moved out of Josh's way while he slipped inside the car and gently spread Alice Campbell across the backseat. He then backed out of the car and flipped the seat back up.

When Heather thrust the shotgun into his hands, he fumbled with it at first but then got a solid grip on the stock and barrel. He shook his head. "You're an awfully trusting lady, Heather. I could be a real vindictive asshole, you know, the type who'd turn the gun on you now, maybe even kill you."

"Right." Heather brushed past him and dropped into the driver's seat. She looked up at him. "But you're not. Now get in. You're gonna be riding shot-gun. Literally."

Josh laughed softly. "Christ." But he did as she in-structed. Then he looked at Heather. "What makes you think that?"

Heather started the Chevelle, then backed quickly out into the street. She glanced at Josh as she changed gears. "Think what?"

Josh gulped when the car leaped forward, tires squealing on the asphalt. "Goddamn, I think we're about to make the jump to hyperspace." A look of pained distress crossed his face and the tires squealed loudly again. He sighed. "Anyway . . . what was I say-ing . . . oh, yeah . . . why do you think I'm not an ass-hole?"

Heather grunted. "I never said you weren't an as-sole. You kind of are, you snide fuck. But you're defi-nitely not a *vindictive* asshole. You're a decent man. I know it."

"And how do you know that?"

Heather shrugged. "A combination of intuition and the obvious. The obvious being that only a decent man would've come to my aid in the first place. A man without a conscience wouldn't have risked himself that way."

"Wow." Josh chuckled. "You're right. I'm great. Thanks for reminding me."

Heather rolled her eyes. "You're welcome."

"So what's the plan here?" Josh shifted slightly in his seat, getting more comfortable. "Is there one?"

"There's an interstate junction a couple miles from here. That's where we're going. And once we're on the interstate, we're gonna go hell-for-leather until we reach the nearest neighboring town." She smirked. "That's my plan. Simple, eh?"

Josh pursed his lips, considering it. "Uh huh. Say . . . what speed, precisely, is hell-for-leather?"

"Approximately as fast as this motherfucker will go."

"Ah. I see."

They drove in silence for the next several moments, and Heather had occasion to reflect on her last comment. It'd sounded very much like something Craig would've said. She hadn't thought much about Craig since abandoning him on the interstate. She'd been way too busy trying to stay alive to give him even a moment's consideration. But now that she *was* thinking about him, a creeping dread began to steal over her. Even if she got out of this mess alive, there'd still be Craig to deal with. He would certainly come sniffing around looking for her. To get revenge.

She sighed heavily, drawing Josh's attention. "What's wrong?"

She didn't want to get into a discussion of her other woes just now, so she forced a smile and said, "Nothing. I'm just tired. I want to be beyond this craziness, that's all."

Josh laughed. "That's the right term for it, for sure. Crazy."

They were out of the neighborhood now and zipping down a long loop of a tree-shrouded secondary road. Heather eased off the gas a bit and held the steering wheel a little less loosely to accomodate the seemingly endless curvature of the road. "So what the hell is going on in Pleasant Hills, anyway?" she asked. "What are all those hideous things, and where do they come from?"

Josh grunted. "I don't know what they are, but I'm pretty sure they're from the freakshow."

Heather cocked an eyebrow at him. "What freak-show?"

"The one that rolled into town yesterday." Josh said it as if it should have been obvious.

Heather said, "I don't live in Pleasant Hills. This is the first I've heard of it."

Josh nodded. "Ah, okay. That explains a thing or two." He coughed. "Anyway, this freakshow showed up out of the blue yesterday. It's a big traveling carnival thing. Rides, a midway, sideshow freaks . . . the works. I spent a big chunk of the day at the park yesterday watching them set up. Me and my bud Chico. We got baked and wasted hours snickering over how beat-up all their gear and vehicles looked. I mean, you couldn't imagine a more decrepit operation. Looked like they'd been hauling the same shit around back country roads for fifty years at least."

Despite the gravity of their situation, Heather couldn't help feeling amused by Josh's narration. "You really have a friend named Chico? Who you get stoned with in the park?"

"His real name's Ken. See, there was this TV show in the seventies, and—"

"Yeah, yeah," Heather cut him off. "I've seen the re-runs. And sorry, I can do without the funny story of how your stoner buddy earned his nickname. Tell me why you think the things that tried to kill us tonight are from this freakshow."

Josh's voice adopted a markedly more serious tone than before. "I don't just think it, I *know* it. And you would too if you'd been there. The freakshow looks so

ramshackle it borders on pathetic. So much, you'd
think they wouldn't be able to operate. Who's gonna
pay admission to something so clearly not worth a
fucking dime? But here's the funny thing. Funny curious, not ha-ha." He paused a moment and stared at the
road ahead, marshalling his thoughts. "They drew a
big crowd of onlookers the moment they showed up. A
shitload of people like me and Chico who hung out all
day watching them set up. But it was different for the
others. Maybe because they weren't stoned, I don't
know. There was this strange feeling, as if something
about the place was hypnotizing them. And, you know,
I think maybe something was, because everyone was
so excited. I tuned in randomly to a bunch of different
conversations, and every single one of those dumb-
asses was making plans to show up for the freakshow's
opening tonight."

Heather frowned. "Weird." The road began to
straighten out a bit and she applied more pressure to
the gas pedal. The interstate juncture was less than a
mile ahead of them, around one more slight bend in
the road. "So what happened tonight?"

Josh made a sound somewhere between a sad, dry
laugh and a sigh. "As it was getting dark, a lot—maybe
even most—of Pleasant Hills's citizens gathered at the
park, waiting for the opening of the freakshow. It was
so damned crazy, more like a church congregation
than a loose collection of people waiting to get into a
carnival. I tried talking to some of them, but in most
cases it was like talking to a brick wall. They were all
in some kind of trance. Chico, too. He'd worked that
day and didn't smoke with me."

"You get high in the middle of the day a lot, Josh?"

"Hell yeah, I do. And you know what, I think being baked saved my ass tonight."

Heather smirked. "Oh, really?"

"Yeah, really. This'll sound crazy, but I got the sense that something in the freakshow had called them there, that they were under a spell. The more I hung out there, the later it got, the more it seemed the whole damn town was there. And they were all like that. Everybody but me. Then, just before I bugged out, I began to feel it, too. That sense of calling."

Heather shuddered. "And you managed to resist when no one else did? How?"

"I really think it was something to do with being high. No joke." He regarded her now with an expression as solemn as any she'd seen. "Something about my altered state of consciousness interfered with the calling."

"But you're not high now. And neither am I. Why don't we feel that calling?"

Josh shrugged. "Hell if I know. But it was scary as hell, even for just that one minute when I felt it. I got out of there and got baked again. I just couldn't deal. I knew something freaky was happening, but I never suspected it'd be quite this fucked-up. That calling, whatever it was, ended around the time the freakshow opened its gates. I hate to think what happened to all those people who went in there. Whatever it was, it was Bad with a capital damned B. And these freaks we've fought off tonight . . . I'm pretty sure they were sent out to round up the stragglers like me and your mom."

Heather didn't reply immediately. It sounded loony, of course, but in light of everything she'd seen tonight Josh's theory made a disturbing amount of sense. So

disturbing, in fact, that she was almost too preoccu-
pied considering the bizarre implications to notice the
roadblock.

Josh said sharply, "Oh, shit!"

Heather sucked in a sudden breath as the sight of
the big trucks blocking both the road ahead and the interstate ramps finally registered. She tromped on the
Chevelle's brake pedal and the car fishtailed to a halt
in the middle of the road. Dark figures milled about
outside the trucks. They looked up at the sound of the
squealing tires. There was a moment of frozen recognition from both sides, then some of the figures
jumped into the trucks. Still others came sprinting toward the Chevelle at a speed that should have been impossible for anything on two legs.

Or four legs, in some cases.

Josh rolled down his window and pumped a round
into the shotgun's chamber. "Now would be a good
time to turn around."

Heather cranked the Chevelle's steering wheel hard
to the right, tapped the gas pedal, and steered the car
onto the road's shoulder. She continued turning the
wheel and applying the gas, spinning the car around
until it was pointing back toward town. She glanced at
the rearview mirror at the same moment she was at
last able to apply full pressure to the gas pedal.

Something lithe and powerful-looking took a flying
leap at the Chevelle in that same instant, landing with
a thump as the car rocketed back toward Pleasant
Hills. Josh cursed and began to climb through the
open passenger side window.

A moment later the shotgun discharged and Heather
screamed.

# CHAPTER TWELVE

A tide of mixed emotions flowed through Mike as he watched Jinx undress. She was lovely. Okay, that was an understatement. She was sexy as hell. And when she pulled the AC/DC T-shirt off over her head, exposing her larger than average breasts, he felt a stirring in his groin. Then, as she wriggled out of her skintight jeans, the stirring became something more pronounced. He felt his mouth fill with moisture as she stepped free of the jeans and stood fully nude before him.

His heart was racing and he was having a hard time swallowing. Despite the awful circumstances, he wanted her. He wanted to taste every inch of that ripe, delectable flesh. Her breasts, her belly, her pussy, her thighs, her plump, tempting lips. The need to seize her and thrust himself inside her was as intense as it'd ever been with any girl.

But the need was tempered by the unavoidable presence of the freak in the recliner. Every few seconds Mike's gaze would helplessly slide away from Jinx's succulent body and get another shudder-inducing glimpse of the thing leering at them. Those glimpses were the sole reason he'd yet to shed his own clothes.

The strange, almost translucent flesh around the freak's mouth crinkled. Mike was still having a great deal of difficulty interpreting the thing's expressions. This might have been mirth, or it might have been anger.

Then it spoke: "What are you waiting for, boy?"

There was an impatient edge to its voice. And something else. An unspoken implication that failure to accede to its wishes would result in some very unpleasant consequences for Mike. And still, Mike made no move to get undressed. He remained aroused, but he felt paralyzed, unable to act. His hands were shaking. His legs felt weak. He wobbled slightly and knew he was just moments from toppling over.

The freak made a sound of disdain. "Pathetic."

But Jinx came to his rescue. She stepped toward him, gripped the zipper tab of his jeans and pulled it down. She gave the button a twist and it popped free, then she began to push the jeans down past his hips. She gave him a gentle nudge and he fell backward, landing hard on the cot. Mike watched her kneel before him in wonderment, amazed at how calm she appeared. It was as if she'd done this many times before. The thought made him sad, but he couldn't dismiss it.

Jinx untied his shoes and tugged them off his feet, and after that she peeled off his socks. Then her hands, so soft, slid up his legs, over his thighs and hips, and gripped the bottom edge of his T-shirt. Mike lifted his arms in numb cooperation as she pulled the shirt away from his body and tossed it aside. She pressed herself against him, and he drew in a sharp breath at the delightful sensation of her breasts pushing against his bare skin, the erect nipples sliding across his chest. She pushed him backward until he was flat on his back and she settled atop him, writhing slowly but forcefully against his body. It felt so good he was almost able to forget about the freak.

Which was probably the point. This suspicion was confirmed when she whispered in his ear, "Don't think about him. Just focus on me. Enjoy this and pretend nothing else exists for a while."

Then she sat up and straddled him, guiding his hardness inside her so quickly there was no time to give the matter of the voyeuristic freak any further thought. Jinx took her time riding him, controlling the entire performance and guiding his rhythm. Her body glistened in the weak lamplight. He stared at her in rapturous wonder, thinking he'd never seen anything so exquisite. For a time, he thought their coupling might go on forever, and a part of him would've been more than okay with that.

But then Jinx quickened the pace subtly but deliberately, triggering a building physical reaction within him. He tried to hold it back, but he couldn't. Jinx screamed, feigning a level of ecstasy far higher than what she really felt. All part of the "show" for the freak's benefit, Mike was certain.

One instant Jinx was there with him, the next he was alone on the little bed, panting heavily and listening to the manic thudding of his heart. Then he became aware of another sound, a muffled slapping noise. Mike lifted his head slightly and saw the freak slowly clapping its pudgy hands together in mock applause.

"Bravo," it said, making a little hiccoughing noise Mike assumed was sarcastic laughter. "A brilliant show, indeed."

Mike turned away from the disgusting creature and saw that Jinx was getting dressed. Her jeans and boots were already on. She picked up her T-shirt and in the instant before she pulled it on Mike was allowed one more glorious glimpse of her bare torso.

Then she looked at him, her expression unreadable. "Get dressed, Mike. Now."

Mike heard and felt the imperative in her voice. This was a command, not a suggestion. He was worn-out. All he wanted to do was lie here and let his eyes close, let sleep take him away from the freakshow. But her tone compelled him to rise. He swung his legs over the side of the bed and reached for his clothes.

Once he had his clothes back on, he looked first at Jinx, who wouldn't meet his gaze, then at the freak. "I want out of this place. I think your plan is nutty as hell, but fuck it, I'll go along with it."

The freak chortled. "As if you have any other choice. . . ."

Mike smirked. "Actually, I do. I could go find that ringmaster dude, or that pirate, and let them know what you've got in mind."

Jinx moved so quickly the motion of her body was a barely perceivable flash in the semidarkness. Her hand whipped toward him, an uncoiling flash of white flesh that made him think of a cobra striking a victim. Her open palm struck his cheek with such force that it drove him off the bed to the floor.

Mike gingerly touched his stinging flesh and stared up at Jinx, who looked calmer, more composed, than a person should in these circumstances. "Say anything like that again," she said, her voice so cold it sent a shiver through him, "and I'll kill you myself."

The freak laughed his strange laugh again. "Drama!"

Mike sat up. He scooted away from Jinx, eyeing her warily the whole time. "I never suspected you were such a hardcore bitch. I thought you were cool. I thought . . ."

"It doesn't matter what you thought. I'm using you. Same as Jeremiah here is using me." But then a bit of the hardness leeched out of her demeanor as her expression softened. "If it makes you feel any better, I don't want to hurt you."

Mike touched his cheek again, scowling at her. "Could've fooled me."

She shook her head. "That was nothing. Just a bit of needed discipline." She extended a hand to him, and he reluctantly took it, allowing her to pull him up. She maintained her grip on his hand when he was on his feet again. "You listen to me. I know how much this sucks, okay? It's no fun being used. Being a pawn in someone else's game. I know. I've been there. But don't mistake empathy for vulnerabilty. You'll do what I need you to do. It's our one chance of finally getting free of this place. And I mean to see it through."

Mike fumed inwardly, but all he said was, "Even if it means my life."

Jinx squeezed his hand. "Yes."

Mike twisted free of her grip and backed away from her. "This is so fucked up." He sneered at her. "You weren't really trying to escape when you and Daniel rescued me from the ringmaster. It was a ruse. You were looking for a sucker. Daniel was your first choice, but he got himself killed. I'm your fallback plan. You disgust me, Jinx. You're no better than they are."

"The alternative to our plan is at least as bad as what you face now." She moved to the window, staring out at the dark freakshow grounds. "You may also want to consider that there are a lot of potential fates here far worse than physical death."

The freak said, "I can attest to that."

Though every instinct in him railed against the idea, Mike allowed his gaze to fully settle on the creature for the first time. His simmering anger was building toward a potentially dangerous explosion. "I'd like to know just one thing." He glared at Jinx now and pointed a wavering finger at the freak. "How did you come to be with this thing? Why didn't you wind up with your skull cut open on a table?"

Jinx's pale face flushed. "The deal with that," she said, her voice lower than before, straining at the edge of some sensitive territory she didn't like to visit, "is that some freaks, mostly older ones in positions of power, are allowed to . . . sort of . . . adopt . . . a human. As pets. My life was spared when Jeremiah selected me. You also owe your life to him. Without his pull, we wouldn't have been able to bring you back to this world."

Mike was astounded by what he was hearing—Jinx expressing gratitude to this . . . monster. But he knew he had to put aside the loathing he felt for the freak long enough to get this situation sorted out.

He drew in a deep breath and released it very slowly. "So, let me be clear about this. We're going to hijack that mechanical spider tank-thing, that big metal whatsit, and invade the world behind our world. Where we'll seek out the powers-that-be and annihilate them, thereby bringing an end to the freakshow."

Jinx grunted. "It's slightly more complicated than that, but essentially, yes."

Mike laughed. "Can you explain to me why no one's ever attempted this before?"

The freak (Jeremiah, Mike reminded himself) spoke up now: "I cannot say with certainty that it has never been tried. However, I suspect it has not. There are too many safeguards in place, too many traps to ensnare a saboteur."

Mike laughed again, and said to Jinx, "Yeah? Won't those same safeguards keep us out, too? I have to say, the more I learn about this plot of yours, the stupider it sounds. And him?" He gestured in a derisive way at Jeremiah. "What the hell could his motivation possibly be? Won't the end of the freakshow mean the end of him, too?"

The freak nodded. "It shall."

"And yet you don't strike me as the self-sacrificing, noble type."

Jinx said, "That's because you don't know everything yet."

"Really? Why don't you clue me in?"

Jinx and the freak shared a lingering, meaningful glance. Mike wanted to scream at them, but he managed to rein his fury in a bit longer.

At last, Jinx turned back to him. "Okay. We'll tell you."

Mike smirked. "Great. Happy to hear it."

Jeremiah's bulbous head swiveled in his direction. "Listen carefully. It's almost time."

Mike frowned. "Almost time? Almost time for what?"

Then Jinx started talking again. As Mike listened, a new sense of oppressive forboding began to take hold deep within him.

# CHAPTER THIRTEEN

The interior of the house functioned for Craig as final proof of the old axiom that you can't judge a book by its cover. In this case, the home's pristine suburban exterior was like the happy, colorful cover of a child's storybook. Then, imagine opening that cover and finding out that, whoa, this story is no sunshine and puppydogs parable for impressionable and fragile little minds. Instead it's a hardcore, blood-splattered nightmare from the freakiest, screaming recesses of some psycho motherfucker's fractured psyche. Pure NC-17 territory, baby.

Craig could dig it.

He had smelled the stench of death the moment he'd entered the house. The odor drew him through a dining room and then through an archway into a much larger room, a room Craig suspected the homeowners would have referred to as their living room. But a better name for it now would have been the dying room. Craig grinned at his own cleverness. Dying room. Yeah, that was a good one. So good he wanted to share it with someone, but he was pretty sure none of these dead motherfuckers would find it half as amusing as he did. And, anyway, they were fucking dead, a condition that tended to hurt a person's sense of humor.

Like, for example, this sorry sack of shit over here. The dude was a middle-aged guy with a sensible haircut. A small-town businessman's haircut. His cheeks were puffy and he was tending toward the jowly side just a bit. The small nose and thin, bloodless lips looked out of place in the middle of that pudgy face. You could almost imagine the skinny teenager he might have been long ago. Craig thought it was within the realm of possibility that he'd been a handsome dude in those days. But now he was a real Fatty McDeady. If some monster hadn't ripped open his abdomen and spread his internal organs around the room like party streamers, his saturated fat-filled diet likely would've killed him soon anyway. Hard to feel sorry for a guy like that, really.

The man's wife and teenage daughter were another story altogether. They were dead, so he didn't have confirmation of their relationship to the disemboweled lardbucket, but the truth of it was plain enough. The adult woman had been about the right age to be the dead man's wife, and the daughter's face was too obvious a mix of their features. The two females had been in much better physical condition than the rotund family patriarch, with long, lean but nonetheless shapely figures. The daughter looked particularly ripe, with her hiphugger jeans and perky breasts displayed so pleasingly in a tight purple sweater. Looking at her now, Craig fervently wished her head wasn't turned at so freakish an angle. The way the back of her scalp had been ripped off diminished her attractiveness a little, too. But twist that head back around and she'd still be fuckable. It was something to think about.

In fact, he took a moment to think about it now. His whole world, his very conception of reality, had been turned inside out. Things were different now. So different that things he once found repulsive now possessed a glorious, electric allure. The full implications of his new status in this radically changed world truly hit him for the first time. There was nothing he couldn't do now. There was nothing so twisted, nothing so deviant, that it was out-of-bounds anymore.

Like, for instance, screwing a dead girl.

Craig's mouth went dry and he licked his lips. He felt a swelling at his groin, straining the tight fabric of his jeans. The dead daughter's body was splayed over a plush blue sofa, her legs spread in a way that made her look whorish. Her back was arched, making the purple sweater ride up, revealing a toned and tanned midriff that looked absolutely delectable.

He took a tentative step toward her. He waited a moment, then took another. The reason for his hesitation was the task appointed him by the two-headed bitch. He expected to feel the hag head's psychic tendrils any moment now, urging him back to business, perhaps threatening him with another painful convulsion. But he continued toward the dead girl without receiving even the slightest of warnings. He had to wonder what that meant. A tacit approval of this deliberate descent into depravity, perhaps? Or maybe they just weren't monitoring him for the moment. The more he thought about it the more the latter possibility seemed likely.

They'd set him upon this path with a set of explicit instructions. It would be purely up to him to sink or swim. Craig reached the sofa and stared down at the dead girl, his gaze slowly, admiringly moving over her limp body's exquisite curves. He was now pretty sure he was on his own, his mind his own again, for as long as he was in this house. He didn't doubt the two-headed woman would take control again if he attempted to leave the house without accomplishing the job assigned to him.

The smart thing to do would be to quickly explore the rest of the house and flush out the lurking sole survivor of this massacre. Kill the fucker fast, cut his or her heart out, and get out. But Craig's instincts were guiding him in another direction. He wasn't in seek and destroy mode—at least not yet. He wanted instead to take his time with this, to wallow in the gore and savor the sweet, psychotic joy to be found in an absolute corruption of the soul. Though he couldn't be sure why, he had a strong feeling things would work out the way he needed them to just by doing exactly what he wanted.

His heart was thudding hard in his chest as he knelt over the girl and undid the snap of her jeans. He splayed his fingers over that taut midriff and felt a shudder ripple through his body. She was still warm. Whatever had killed these people must have done its work within just the last half hour. For a fleeting moment, he was disturbed by the notion that the killer was still somewhere nearby, perhaps still in the house.

But Craig dismissed the idea. He felt sure this family's killer was controlled by the two-headed woman and that it had already vacated the premises.

His hand slid up under the girl's sweater, roaming over flesh so smooth and unblemished it was nearly perfect. He squeezed her plump breasts through the cups of her bra. His gaze went to the ruined back of her head, but rather than diminishing his arousal as he'd suspected might happen, the sight only inflamed it. He decided he wouldn't twist her head back around after all.

He slipped his hand out of the sweater and undid the fly of his own jeans to relieve the swelling pressure. Then he began to tug the dead girl's designer jeans down past her hips. Craig whistled at the sight of her smooth, shapely thighs. He ran a hand up one of them. God, her legs were even better than Heather's, which was really saying something. He got the dead girl's shoes off, then tugged the jeans the rest of the way off. He was laughing softly as he spread her legs farther and adjusted her body on the sofa to comfortably accomodate his own.

Then he stood up and began pushing his own jeans down. He chuckled and said, "Too bad you ain't alive for this, baby, because you'd be screaming your lungs out with me inside of you."

He kicked his shoes off and stepped out of his jeans. Then he leaned over the dead girl and began to position himself. That was when the scream came, so piercing and startling it nearly burst his eardrums and gave him a heart attack at the same time.

Something came charging into the living room so fast he didn't have time to react before it attacked him.

He felt something hard crash against the side of his head, and he collapsed atop the dead girl. His face fell against the exposed portion of her scalp, his mouth tasting blood. He was in too much pain to be disgusted. Whatever weapon his attacker had wielded had been something blunt and hard, but not something as potentially lethal as, say, a baseball bat. Also, there'd been a bit less force behind the blow than Craig might have expected. But now whatever it was cracked against his skull a second time, making his head swim and his eyes mist over.

He became aware of a high, reedy voice screaming at him: *"Get your hands off my sister, motherfucker!"*

Craig sensed something descending toward him again and at last had the presence of mind to roll out of its path. He rolled off the couch and thumped to the floor, looking up just in time to see a bespectacled nerd slam a rolling pin against the side of the dead girl's head. The kid shrieked, then began to babble insanely, apparently unhinged at the thought of further damaging his dead sister's body.

Craig laughed. "I got news for you, kid. She didn't feel it."

The nerd looked down at him through eyes that looked huge behind his large lenses. And Craig couldn't help it—he started giggling like a schoolgirl. "My God, I don't believe it—serial killer glasses!"

The kid scowled at him, an expression that conveyed equal parts rage and incredulity. And Craig laughed some more. Here this guy was, a scrawny little nothing in a black Weezer T-shirt, no doubt a wimp in every way, and yet he'd worked up the nerve to defend his dead sister's honor. This, presumbably, while cowering in some corner while his family was slaughtered, probably watching through splayed fingers as they were torn to pieces. And now that he'd at last found it within him to fight back, his adversary was laughing at him and cracking jokes about his glasses. You kinda had to feel a bit sorry for the little wuss.

But not *too* sorry.

Craig's eyes went wide as nerd boy quickly shifted position and brought the rolling pin down in an arc that should have nailed the middle of his face. But Craig's survival instinct kicked in at the absolute last possible moment, and his right leg shot out, his foot delivering a blow to the kid's shin hard enough to sweep his feet out from under him. The kid pitched to the floor, cracking the side of his head against the edge of a coffee table as the rolling pin went spinning across the carpeted floor.

The kid got to his feet again faster than Craig. He was already halfway to the spot where the rolling pin had come to rest—against a bookcase filled with DVDs rather than books—by the time Craig was upright again. Craig didn't bother trying to beat him to the fallen weapon. Now that he was no longer in so vulnerable a position he no longer considered it a serious threat. He struck a nonchalant, relaxed pose—to the point of folding his arms and assuming a bored expression—and waited for the kid to come at him again.

But that didn't happen.

Nerdo, apparently expecting Craig to be right on his back, made a desperate dive for the rolling pin. But his trajectory was off a hair and he collided with the bookcase, rocking it back against the wall. The kid cried out and fell away from the bookcase, just as it tipped forward and rained DVDs all over him. A strap connecting the bookcase to the wall prevented it from toppling all the way over, but the kid nonetheless reacted as if he'd been crushed beneath it anyway, loosing a terrified scream and batting at the flying DVDs like a person swatting at swarming bats in a cave.

Craig laughed some more. Holy shit, this kid was excellent entertainment. In a way, it was gonna be a damned shame to have to kill him. Craig retrieved his jeans and stepped into them while he waited for the kid to stop screaming like a little bitch. By the time the kid realized he hadn't been crushed by a falling bookcase, Craig was fully dressed and ready to start.

He stomped on the kid's head like a workman driving a shovel into hard earth. Then he did it again. The thick eyeglass lenses shattered and the frame slid off his head. The kid went still. But he wasn't dead. He groaned and looked at Craig through eyes that looked defeated and pathetic. A person with a remaining ounce of human conscience would have put the guy out of his misery then and there.

Craig flipped the teenager onto his stomach, elicting a howl of pain. Craig cackled at the sound. Then he lifted one of the boy's legs, got a firm grip on his ankle, and stomped down on the limb with all the strength he could muster. Which was considerable. The kid's shin snapped like a tree branch. The boy screamed again and tried to crawl away. Craig allowed him to move several feet away, just far enough that the poor bastard might have time enough to imagine that there might yet be a way out. He watched with amusement as the boy angled toward the foyer and the front door beyond. What the hell did he think he was gonna do— crawl all the way to the sheriff's office?

Craig finally grabbed the kid by his broken leg and

hauled him back to the living room. The kid's screams were beyond anything Craig had ever heard. Loud, continuous, and full of desperation edging toward insanity. It reminded him of the original version of *The Texas Chainsaw Massacre*, with that wildly screaming bitch running from Leatherface and his family of cannibal crazies.

Craig paused for only a moment in the living room, realizing he would find the tools needed to finish the job in another room. Again, he pulled the boy by his broken leg, eliciting another series of piercing screams. Craig had enjoyed the sound at first, but it was beginning to give him a fucking headache. Once he'd gotten the kid to the kitchen, he stomped on his head again and that shut him up. He laid the teenager's body—still alive, just barely—in the center of the kitchen's tiled floor, then began pulling open drawers and rooting through their contents. The third drawer contained a cutlery tray, and in one of the plastic recesses was a big, thick carving knife, the sort the family's dad would've used to carve a Thanksgiving turkey.

He threw the drawer shut and turned back to face the boy.

He blinked.

The body wasn't where he'd left it. The floor was empty. A sudden panic ignited in Craig's heart. What the fuck? How could that crippled son of a bitch have gotten away without making a shitload of noise? Whatever had happened, Craig had to locate the bastard fast. His ass was on the line. If the kid managed to get outside, that was it, game over. He was shaking now, half-expecting to feel the hag's cold psychic tendrils entering his brain at any moment.

Then he sensed something at his feet and glanced

down. Craig shook his head slowly, an expression of abject amazement on his face. Somehow, the kid had managed to move quickly across the floor on his belly and get behind him. How he could've managed this without making a fucking sound, Craig couldn't imagine. Unless he'd been making enough noise rifling through the drawers to cover the sound of the kid's approach. But no way, he hadn't been making anywhere near that much noise, so what the hell . . . ?

Craig's frown deepened as the kid tried to bite him through his jeans. "Christ, you're one slippery motherfucker. I'll give you that. But you ain't no Rottweiler, boy."

The kid glanced up at him and did the damnedest thing—he grinned. Then he lifted the cuff of Craig's pants leg, exposing a stripe of bare, vulnerable flesh. A hiss issued through his lips and his head snapped forward like a snake's, his teeth sinking into the bare patch of flesh and drilling deep an instant before the pain could register. Then, *oh boy,* there came the pain, and now it was Craig who was screaming like a little bitch. He tried to kick the boy loose, but his jaw was clamped about his ankle. And now the son of a bitch was wrenching his head back and forth, working at his wounded ankle like . . . well, like a fucking Rottweiler.

Craig screamed again and tottered sideways. He fell against the kitchen counter and grabbed desperately at its edge. He just managed to remain upright. The boy pressed the attack, taking advantage of Craig's pain and momentary disorientation. He pushed the pants leg up higher and sank his teeth into the meatiest part of his calf. Craig screamed again and fell backward, landing hard on his back on the floor.

This time pain seemed to lance every nerve ending in his body. He almost blacked out for a moment, then everything snapped back into focus and for just one perfectly crystalline moment he wished he had blacked out. Because now he knew how the boy had been able to sneak up on him.

He'd had help.

A huge spiderlike creature was attached to the kitchen ceiling. Spider*like* because it had many more than the eight legs of a spider. Maybe three times that many. Each furry leg was approximately the width of a coaxial cable. The thing's body was an abomination. Even now, after all he'd seen and done, Craig couldn't think of it any other way. A humanoid head protruded from an amorphous blob. Humanoid, yes, but grotesquely deformed, like something that would have caused the Elephant Man to recoil in disgust. It had a twisted, swollen face that looked like it'd been boiled in acid, and red, pulsing eyes that looked like the eyes of the devil himself.

Not for the first time that night, Craig pissed himself.

Two of the abomination's legs were coiled around the teenager's waist. The fucking thing had lifted the boy off the floor and placed him in position to attack Craig. It dropped the teenager right on top of Craig. Craig screamed as the boy howled with righteous rage and went for his throat. He barely managed to block the attack, wedging the base of a hand under the boy's jaw and pushing his head back. And at last things were working in his favor again, because he'd somehow managed to hang onto the carving knife. He swept it around in a vicious arc and slammed the point of the blade through the boy's right temple. The boy's eyes went wide for a moment, then his body convulsed and fell away from Craig, the knife sliding out of the wound as he rolled to the floor.

Craig lay panting on his back for several moments, his gaze riveted to the spider creature. He swallowed hard and realized his whole body was shaking. Craig felt certain the thing would soon pounce on him and inject him with some kind of spider-monster venom. It was toying with him, enjoying his terror. He supposed this thing had killed the teenager's family, under orders from the two-headed woman. Which pissed him right the hell off. They'd sent him here to do a job—why test him by putting obstacles in his way?

Well . . . that was his answer right there, wasn't it? He was being tested. He got it now. This was a trial-by-fire sort of deal. He began to smile. Then he was laughing. And the spider-thing was laughing, too.

Craig took a deep breath and sat up. He looked at the kid's limp body. The feisty motherfucker was clearly dead. He felt a flashing moment of . . . not pity, as that implied empathy. Respect, that was the word he was looking for. The guy had been a pitiful geek, sure, but he'd fought hard. If the breaks had gone his way, he might well have ripped Craig's throat out.

Craig rolled the body onto its back and used the carving knife to slit the bloodied Weezer shirt down the middle, exposing a scrawny, sunken chest. Then he lifted the knife high over his head and slammed it down, punching the big blade all the way through the wisp of a body. He extracted the blade and brought it down again, then again. His knowledge of human anatomy was very basic. He made a huge mess of the "operation" (as he thought of the process), but eventually managed to excise the organ he'd been sent to fetch.

The heart in hand, he got to his feet and stood in the middle of the kitchen, trying to figure something out. Something had . . . *changed* during his assault on the kid's body. Instinct caused his head to snap up. The spider-thing wasn't there anymore. Craig couldn't say he was sad to see it gone. Nor was he surprised. It had clearly served its purpose. He still felt some anger over the way the thing had been used against him, but even that was fading now, displaced by a much larger sense of relief and accomplishment.

He searched the kitchen for an appropriate container for the bloody organ. A cooler was his first hope, something he could fill with ice to preserve the thing. He opened cabinets and looked through the pantry, finding nothing like what he was looking for. When he opened the cabinet beneath the kitchen sink, he saw an array of kitchen cleaners, insecticide spray cans, a nearly empty box of plastic trash bags, and, nestled behind a stinky mop bucket, a brown burlap bag with a drawstring. He stared at the bag for a moment. Then he grabbed it, stood up, and dropped the heart inside it. What the hell, it wasn't like he needed to keep the thing fresh for an emergency transplant.

He grabbed a beer from the fridge, popped the tab, and drank deeply as he reentered the living room. He paused for a moment at the sofa and stared longingly at the dead girl. Her whorishly spread legs still presented an exquisitely tempting tableau, but he made no move to drop his pants again. Not because he'd suffered any late-arriving pangs of conscience, but because he could feel the hag reaching into his mind again as he thought about it. Some of his facial muscles twitched and he felt an odd strain elsewhere in his body, a razor-wire tension hinting at imminent seizure.

"Okay, okay," Craig muttered and walked out of the house. The twitching ceased as soon as he acceded to his new mistress's wishes. The Towncar was still waiting for him at the curb, the big chauffeur standing at the open rear door. Craig glimpsed the two-headed woman's shapely legs through the opening. He slid into the backseat without acknowledging the chauffeur's scowl and the door thunked shut behind him.

The hag head leered at him in its usual disgusting way, but the pretty head smiled at him. She indicated the burlap bag with a slight inclination of her elegant chin. "I see you brought me your prize. Show it to me."

Craig opened the bag and pulled out the heart, offering it to her. She took it from him and brought it to her red lips, opening her mouth wide to take a bite from it. She chewed slowly, making a sound that conveyed sensual delight. "Mmm, delicious." She pushed the torn organ at him. "Here, have a bite."

Craig frowned. "Um . . . I'm not really hungry."

She pushed the bit of bloody muscle against his mouth. "Eat." The single syllable crackled with an implied threat and would've been enough to make him yield to her command, but she nonetheless added, "Eat, or I'll tear your own heart out and feast on it."

Craig didn't give it another moment's thought.

He ate.

# CHAPTER FOURTEEN

Josh's shot went wild. Of course it did. You'd have to be one hell of a marksman to hit your target while leaning out the window of a vehicle moving at high speed on a bumpy road. Heather nonetheless found herself cursing his inaccuracy. The combination of adrenaline-fueled desperation and fear had rendered her absolutely unforgiving.

"Goddammit, shoot that fucking thing!"

Josh's voice came back muffled by the rush of wind: "I'm trying."

Heather's gaze ticked back and forth from the dark road ahead and the rearview mirror. She knew she should just watch the road. But she was so afraid of the beast clinging to the rear of her car, she couldn't keep her eyes off it for more than a moment. She was sure they'd all be dead if she didn't keep the awful thing in view.

The Chevelle's driver's side tires left the paved part

of the road and skidded for a long, wild moment on the gravel shoulder. Heather screamed and Josh let out a cry as he was nearly pitched from the speeding vehicle. Heather wrenched the wheel hard to the right and brought all tires back onto pavement. Josh cried out again and slapped his free hand on the roof, holding on for dear life. Heather glanced his way and was stunned to see the shotgun still clutched in his flapping left hand. Then her eyes flicked back to the rearview mirror again and she shrieked. The thing wasn't just clinging to the car's rear anymore. It'd somehow gained a secure hold and was climbing onto the trunk.

Heather's whole body shook as her hands closed around the steering wheel in a deathgrip. She screamed again: *"Josh!"*

The answer this time was another blast from the shotgun. The sound simultaneously startled her and sent a thrill of improbable hope coursing through her. Somehow Josh had managed to bring the weapon around to bear again. It discharged once more in the time it took to look again at the rearview mirror. The blast ripped through one of the thing's membranous wings, causing it to shriek in pain. The hope Heather felt swelled for a moment at the sound of it. But the thing failed to let go of the car. In fact, it was advancing again. And now its face was pressed against the rear windshield, its black lips open wide in a mad grin. The creature was lithe, wiry and thin, but powerfully built. It looked like a fusion of man and vampire bat, complete with pointy, furry ears. The thing met her gaze in the rearview mirror. That moment of accidental intimacy nearly caused her to lose control of the car. She glanced at the road just long enough to be sure they weren't about to go sliding into a ditch, then looked again at the creature, her heart nearly stopping as she watched it swing a raised fist at the rear windshield.

The fist punched a hole through the window and safety glass rained down on the still barely conscious Alice Campbell. Heather screamed and screamed as the creature punched a larger section of glass away and reached through the opening for her mother. Josh slid back into the car and aimed the shotgun over the passenger seat. One thing she had to give Josh—he didn't give up or back down in the face of danger. He jacked another shell into the chamber and quickly pulled the trigger. This time the blast took out a segment of the thing's head.

But it wasn't dead.

The thing seized Heather's mother by the throat and started dragging her limp body through the shattered windshield. Josh vaulted through the opening between the seats, jolting Heather and causing the steering wheel to slip briefly from her shaking fingers. The Chevelle looped rapidly from one side of the road to the other and would've gone straight into a ditch had Heather not managed to seize the wheel again at the last possible instant. By the time she had the car under control again, Josh had gotten to the backseat. Heather looked in the rearview and saw the big man jam the barrel of the shotgun against the creature's muscular chest. He pulled the trigger and the thing screeched in pain and flew backward. Josh fired yet again and a larger section of its head disintegrated.

Still, it didn't die, continuing to pull Alice Campbell with it as it slid backward across the trunk. Josh cursed and reached through the shattered windshield to batter the creature with the shotgun's stock, whacking at its arms in a desperate attempt to make it let go of the frail woman. But the creature seemed impervious to assault of any kind, and in another moment it had Alice the rest of the way out of the car. Josh dropped the shotgun and made a last futile lunge at them as they slid off the trunk and tumbled to the road.

Heather jammed the brake pedal to the floor, bringing the Chevelle to a fishtailing, screeching halt. She yanked up the parking brake and propelled herself out of the car. Josh hurried after her as she raced toward a dark spot on the road some twenty yards to the rear of the Chevelle. Josh fed more shells into the shotgun, slammed the breech shut, and said, "That's it. No more ammo after this."

A few more rapid strides toward that dark spot in the road was all it took to reveal the truth—that Heather's worst nightmare had come true. Her knees went weak at the sight of her mother's crumpled, road-scarred form. Alice Campbell was dead. Really and truly dead this time. There wouldn't be another reprieve. No miracle. And now nothing else mattered. Her own death seemed imminent, was barreling down on her even now, but she couldn't care less about her own survival. She'd come so far, fought so hard, and all that effort had come to this ugly conclusion. Her mother's blood and shredded flesh spread across so many yards of blacktop.

Josh dropped a hand on her shoulder. "Heather, we should go."

She shrugged the hand off. "I'm not leaving my mother here."

She continued forward, her knees growing weaker with each step. She became light-headed as the mess of her mother's corpse became clearer. The last of her strength gave out and she dropped to her knees a few feet away from her mother. Sudden tears blurred her vision and a sob from somewhere deep inside tore out of her, then spiraled away into an anguished wail. She tried to speak, but her words were unintelligible, even to her own ears. She didn't even know what she was trying to say, just some primal cry of regret and pain.

When her vision cleared, something drew her attention to the body of the thing that had caused this. The creature was several yards to the left of Alice's corpse. The road had done its brutal work with it, as well. Its freakish body was just as broken as Alice's, its flesh and blood smeared across the road in equal measures. Heather found no consolation in this, but when she saw one of its long, taloned fingers twitch slightly, something awoke inside her. Something as undeniable as her grief, an emotion and need so strong it momentarily overwhelmed her pain. Searing rage brought her to her feet. And thirst for revenge caused her to rip the shotgun from a startled Josh.

She jammed the barrel into the pulpy remains of the creature's head and squeezed the trigger. The recoil nearly knocked her off her feet. She pumped another round into the chamber and braced herself better, adopting something approximating a proper shooter's stance. She pulled the trigger and continued the obliteration of the creature's head. There was precious little left of it now, only a piece of its jaw and a blood-obscured portion of the right side of its face. Another shot took care of the remaining bits.

The creature's body was now still. Heather stared at its ruined form numbly. She felt empty, hollowed out. For one dazed moment, she felt less than human, just a flesh and blood *thing* bereft of any emotion. She thought it might be good to spend whatever remained of her life this way. It would be good to never feel anything again. But then the numbness dispersed and she could feel things again.

The haze enveloping her mind vanished and the world came back into stark relief. Her ears were ringing, a lingering effect of both the shotgun blasts and the endless screams that had peeled out of her in those last desperate moments before her mother was plucked from the car. Her throat felt raw, her vocal cords ravaged. Drying tears commingled with snot on her glistening face.

She heard the faint but rising buzz of engines coming their way. In a few moments a contingent of freaks from the roadblock would be upon them. Their headstart—flimsy from the beginning—was on the verge of amounting to nothing. Heather felt a reflexive jolt of fear, but then she wondered why she should care. There was precious little left in the world she cared about anymore. Part of her wanted to make a stand right there. They would take her down, of that there could be no doubt. But if she could even kill just one or two of the godforsaken things, it might be worth it.

But then Josh did something that snapped her out of the defeatist train of thought. He scooped Alice Campbell's body off the road and started walking toward the Chevelle. Heather followed him, the shotgun pointing vaguely in his direction. "What the fuck are you doing with my mom?"

Josh didn't acknowledge her question (or the hint of implied threat in her tone), just nodded at the Chevelle. "Get that trunk popped."

Heather's face contorted with sudden rage. "I asked you—"

Josh whirled on her, surprising her with his own display of anger. His eyes were wide and gleaming and his jaw a quivering line of tension. "Shut up. Just shut the fuck up. There ain't time for this shit. We're not leaving your mother on the road to be run over by those fuckers. Now get the goddamn trunk open and let's make tracks outta here before it's too late."

His demeanor now was so unlike anything she would've expected of him that it (at least temporarily) burned away her own rage, spurring her to action. She hurried past him, tossed the shotgun into the Chevelle's backseat, and slid into the car through the open driver's side door. She pulled the trunk latch and yanked the door shut, then looked in the rearview mirror. The trunk lid stood open, blocking her view. Then Josh slammed the trunk shut and for a moment she saw his silhouette standing like a lonely phantom in the middle of the road. Somewhere behind him, a tiny pinpoint of light appeared. Then another. Their pursuers were closing the gap in a hurry. They had a few seconds remaining, and Heather could feel the tension building within her again as each one burned away. She was about to scream at Josh to hurry up, but it wasn't necessary—he was already sliding into the shotgun seat and pulling the door closed.

Heather didn't waste another second. She put the car in gear and stomped the gas pedal to the floorboard before the door was fully shut. Tires squealed on asphalt and the Chevelle shot forward, streaking down the winding road as Heather kept the pedal all the way down, the red speedometer needle climbing past fifty miles-per-hour. Then past sixty. Then seventy. The posted speed limit was forty, and sixty was probably the top end of the safe range. And still the red needle climbed, closing in on eighty miles per hour. Heather only eased off some as she whipped the Chevelle around a particularly hairy curve, but then she floored it again.

Josh spoke up then, sounding remarkably composed for someone in his position: "You'll want to take the first turn you see. Wickman Road. It's coming up any second now."

Heather scowled at him. "Yeah? You mind telling me why?"

"Just do it." He sat up straighter and pointed to her left. "There it is."

Heather looked that way and she saw the narrow road appear. The hell with it, they were probably screwed no matter which way they went. She eased off the accelerator some and cranked the wheel hard to the left. The car spun into the turn and its whiplashing motion caused Josh to fall against her. A heartbeat later she cranked the wheel just as hard to the right, sending him the other way. Then she jammed the pedal to the floor yet again and the Chevelle zipped down Wickman Road. This side street wasn't nearly as well lit as the road they'd left, and the tall trees that lined each side of the narrow passage were cloaked in shadow. At first, the encroaching darkness spooked her, but the feeling abated somewhat as she realized it would slow down her pursuers.

She glanced in the rearview mirror and felt an immediate easing of tension when she spied no pursuing headlights. It didn't mean they weren't still after her, but it did mean they'd gained an advantage again. She suspected their pursuers would split up, some taking the turn at Wickman while others continued along the main road back into Pleasant Hills. Then she frowned, realizing her assumption was based on the way rational human minds made decisions. The things coming after them weren't human, so they couldn't be counted on to act in anything resembling a logical fashion. It was a distinction that could mean nothing at all, or could well mean the difference between life and death.

She smacked the steering wheel out of frustration. "What do we do now? Please tell me going this way was part of some clever strategy for getting us out of here that you devised on the fly."

Josh shrugged. "It wasn't, really."

Heather grunted and shook her head. "Well, that's fucking great. Why are we going this way, then?"

"Why? Lack of any better alternative, that's all." He laughed softly, a sound devoid of humor. "I wish I had a better answer for you."

Heather grimaced. "So do I."

She looked again in the rearview mirror. The road behind them was still empty, wrapped in a cloak of impenetrable darkness. Josh noticed what she was doing and twisted around in his seat to get a look for himself. After a long moment, he turned back around and settled in his seat again.

"I think you can slow down. They're not back there, Heather."

Heather was still scared shitless, and a stubborn part of her did not want to trust what Josh was saying. She chewed her lower lip and allowed herself another, longer glance at the mirror. The darkness remained unbroken, so complete she immediately thought of it as a living entity, a huge, unstoppable thing bearing relentlessly down on them. But this, at least, she recognized as nothing more than paranoia.

She let out a big breath and allowed the gas pedal to lift another inch or so from the floorboard. She looked at Josh and said, "Why did they break off the chase?"

Josh shrugged. "Couldn't say for sure, but I have an idea."

"So share it."

"I think all they cared about was herding us back toward town." Josh looked out the window on his side, his gaze fixated either on the line of dark trees flashing by or on nothing at all. "They don't care if we're alive, at least for now. They just don't want anyone getting in or out."

Heather snorted. "Your theory has one big fucking flaw, Josh. If what you say were true, there would've been no reason for that bat-thing to kill my mother." She struggled to keep a quaver out of her voice. "But it did, Josh. It fucking killed my mom." By now her hands were shaking and it was impossible to sound like someone who had her shit together.

Josh didn't say anything for a while, allowing the silence to lengthen as Heather struggled to regain control. The wave of emotion rolled back as quickly as it had come rushing in, and she breathed a steady sigh Josh interpreted as a subtle signal to continue. "I can't explain that in a way you'll find comforting. I'm sorry. I think that thing seized an opportunity. It didn't really matter whether it killed any of us or not, but as long as it had the chance . . ." He sighed. "It would've killed us all, given the chance."

Heather derived a small measure of solace in the strength this man projected. "Yeah, I guess you're right." She looked at the dark road ahead. "So where do we go from here? Do you know another way out of town from here?"

"Actually . . . ," Josh cleared his throat and seemed to brace himself for an argument, "I think you should pull over."

"Say what?"

Josh didn't waver. "I'm serious. Pull over."

"Why?"

"Just do it, okay? Humor me."

Heather grunted and shook her head, but she let the gas pedal up and applied pressure to the brake. She guided the Chevelle off the road and parked on the shoulder. She moved the gearshift to Park and looked at Josh. "There, we've pulled over. Now what?"

Josh retrieved the shotgun from the backseat. "Now we get out."

Heather stared at Josh a moment longer before glancing at the rearview mirror. She half-expected to see headlights appearing behind them, dashing Josh's theory. For now, though, the road behind them remained deserted. So maybe he'd been right about that. But even if they weren't being followed anymore, abandoning the car wasn't something she was eager to do, especially with her mom's corpse stowed in the trunk.

Heather shook her head. "No."

"Look, there's not gonna be an unguarded road out of here. You know that. I told you before, back at your mother's house, that I thought I could get us out of here on foot. Well, now it's the only real choice we've got. If you'll just think about it a minute, you'll see I'm right."

Heather did think about it. She hated to admit it, but he was almost certainly right about the odds of finding an unblocked road out of Pleasant Hills. Still . . .

She studied the line of dark trees visible through the driver's side window and shuddered. Had she thought the forest creepy as it was rushing by? Well, that was a laugh. Now the tall trees seemed more like an ideal hiding place for things that would be most comfortable lurking in shadows. She could too easily imagine something freakish skittering out of the woods to snatch them from the fragile safety of the car.

She looked at Josh. "You have a point. I'll give you that. But do you honestly expect me to believe you can lead us out of town through the forest? It's dark as hell out here, and it'll be twice as dark in the thick of the woods. We'd get lost in no time. More importantly, we'd be vulnerable. Who knows what's waiting out there for us?"

Josh breathed slowly through his nose. He was losing patience with her. "I know my way around these woods, girl. I grew up in this fucking town."

Heather grunted. "Yeah? So did I. And unless you can convince me you're some kinda Grizzly Adams master woodsman motherfucker, I'm not getting out of this car. I'll crash my way through the next roadblock if I have to."

Josh examined the shotgun, checking the chamber. Heather assumed he was stalling for time, stewing over what she'd said as he worked out some counter argument. But then he looked at her and smiled. "There's one shell left in this thing."

Heather smirked. "Great. So we'll have one shot at any monsters or bad guys we run into in the forest primeval. Might as well leave the goddamned thing behind."

But Josh was already shaking his head before she'd

finished speaking. "Nah. One shell's all I fucking need at this point."

Heather frowned. Her heart was suddenly beating very fast. Something in his tone was deeply disturbing. She spoke her next words quietly, struggling to keep her voice steady: "What do you mean?"

He pointed the barrel of the shotgun at her head. "Heather . . ."

Heather's heart raced faster. "Josh . . . why are you aiming that thing at me? What—"

He shoved the barrel against her head and it scraped her temple, drawing a thin trickle of blood from the cut. "Duck!"

Some primal part of Heather's psyche reacted immediately to the explosive urgency contained in that single word. She slipped past the looming shotgun barrel and flattened herself across his lap. An instant later the shotgun boomed, a concussive wave of sound that battered her already abused eardrums. The driver's side window exploded, raining safety glass on the ground. Somehow she was able to dimly perceive another sound—a heavy thump.

It was the sound of something outside the car hitting the ground.

Heather remained where she was a moment longer. She clutched at Josh, her fingers digging into his leg so hard it had to be painful. She heard him toss the empty shotgun into the backseat. Then he just sat there, saying nothing and making no attempt to dislodge her. A few more shaky moments elapsed, then she drew in a deep breath and forced herself to a sitting position.

She regarded Josh with a dazed expression. "I

thought you were going to kill me. Or . . . or worse. I thought . . ." She trailed off and shook her head slowly. "I don't know what I thought."

Josh ran a hand through his hair, sweeping long locks back from his forehead. "I know what you were thinking. And I'm sorry." He touched her face with the back of his hand, a gentle caress. "I'm sorry I scared you, Heather. But I think you'll see I couldn't help it."

Heather managed not to flinch at his touch, which was shocking given how terrified of him she'd been mere moments ago. He abruptly broke off the contact and got out of the car. She watched him circle the Chevelle's front end, then come to a stop near the driver's side door.

His gaze was downcast, and Heather figured it was high time she discovered why Josh had seen fit to scare the shit out of her. She pushed the door open carefully, wincing as several bits of safety glass slid away from the bottom edge of the frame. Then she stepped out of the car and got her first look at what Josh had killed.

She gasped. "Oh my God."

Josh shook his head. "You dumb son of a bitch."

The dead kid couldn't be any more than eighteen years old. His hollow cheeks bore the evidence of a recent acne outbreak. The front of his white T-shirt was stained a deep crimson, and his glassy eyes stared up at the night sky. The eyes haunted Heather, the way they seemed to be looking at something beyond this world. Her own eyes misted with tears. The kid wasn't a monster or a freak. He'd been a human being, just like them, with a life full of potential ahead of him. A dangerous rage built within her, and she might have lashed out at Josh had her gaze not finally alighted on the 9mm pistol still clutched in one of the kid's out-stretched hands.

She swallowed her anger and looked at Josh. "Now would be a good time to tell me what happened here. Why did this kid have to die?"

Josh said nothing at first. He knelt next to the dead kid and pried the pistol from the lifeless fingers. He then popped the magazine out, examined it, and slapped it back in. "Magazine's full." He aimed the gun at a tree, squinting an eye as he lined up a shot through the sight. But instead of actually firing the weapon, he made a noise meant to mimic gunfire. "Bang."

Heather rolled her eyes. "Explain to me why this happened, Josh."

Josh stood up. He flipped the gun's safety to the on position and tucked the weapon in the waistband of his jeans. The way the hanging shirttail obscured the firearm made him look like some television show's idea of an edgy undercover cop. "I saw the boy come out of the woods." He nodded toward the line of trees, and Heather directed a nervous, fleeting glance in that direction. "Saw the gun right away, too. Didn't say anything because I didn't want to tip him off."

Heather shook her head. "Say what? Somebody was coming at us with a gun and you said nothing because—"

"If I'd said anything, you might have looked his way. At that point I didn't know if I'd have to kill the boy, but I did know that if it became necessary, I'd only have one shot at him. So I let him get close."

Heather shuddered, picturing the scene in her head—the boy approaching the car, his gun drawn, the nickel plating glinting faintly in the moonlight, drawing close to where she sat behind the wheel, facing Josh and oblivious to the predator outside. "So . . . there must be more to this. How did you know he was a threat and not just some scared kid who'd come out here to hide when the freaks came to town?"

Josh shrugged. "You want an easy answer, Heather. I wish I had one, but I don't. The kid raised his weapon and aimed it at your head."

Heather flinched at the revelation. "Oh."

Josh nodded. "Yeah. Now, maybe he wasn't a threat. Maybe he was just scared. Could've been he wasn't sure about us, thinking maybe we were from the freak-show." And now Josh sighed again, a sound mixed with equal measures of regret and resignation. "Or maybe he was a psycho son of a bitch. Maybe he meant to kill us both and take your car. Probably not, but I couldn't know that. All I did know was this dude was pointing a gun at your head. So I shot the fucker. I hope you can see I didn't have a choice."

Heather said nothing. Josh was right. But knowing that did little to ease the sick feeling that knotted her guts every time she looked at the dead kid's face. And of course that made her think of her mother's twisted and road-scarred corpse, stashed away now in the Chevelle's trunk like a bag of trash.

But that was when she heard it.

The whimpering.

She took a shaky step toward the tree line, straining her ears, wondering if her senses were betraying her. She glanced at Josh. "Did you . . ."

Then she heard it again, more clearly this time, and followed by a shuddering sob. Heather was moving before she even realized it, crossing the ditch beyond the road's shoulder en route to the dark tree line. She heard Josh calling after her, alarm in his voice, but she kept running toward the woods. Fear reared up inside her as she reached the edge of the woods. She was crazy to be doing this, she knew that, rushing into who knew what kind of danger. But neither the fear nor the uncertainty did anything to stop her.

She heard Josh scrambling to catch up as she stepped through the line of trees and into the woods. The whimpering came again and she was able to get a lock on its general direction almost immediately. It was definitely a human sound and female. She turned to her left and beat her way through the brush. "Hello! I can hear you out there. We're coming to help you!"

Josh stumbled through the woods behind her, cursing as he blindly crashed through low-hanging tree limbs and brush. He called her name and urged her to stop, implored her to stop making so much noise before she attracted the attention of the creatures. Which was ironic, given that he was generating a great deal more noise.

Then she passed through another tangle of brush and stepped between two large trees into a small clearing. When she saw what was tied to a tree at the opposite end of the clearing, she came to an immediate stop and slapped a hand over her mouth.

Josh emerged into the clearing a moment later, drew up beside her and just stood there for a long moment, as stunned by the sight as she was. Then he groaned and said, "Oh, Christ."

The girl was naked and dirty. She had long, dark hair that fell over her breasts. Her body was bruised and scratched all over, and here and there were thin red lines that looked like . . . whip marks. A strip of duct tape covered her mouth. On the ground nearby was the body of another girl, approximately the same age. She was dead, her torso separated from the lower half of her body. Near the ravaged corpse lay a blood-spattered chain saw. There were other tools, other implements of torture.

Heather at last snapped out of her shock and crossed the clearing in several long strides. She pulled the duct tape from the girl's mouth and made mindless cooing, soothing noises.

Then the girl's eyes went wide and she said, "You have to get out of here. H-he's coming back."

Heather attempted a small reassuring smile. "No, you're wrong, sweetie. The guy who did this to you, he's not coming back. My friend killed him."

The girl frowned a moment, then gave her head an emphatic shake. "No, he didn't. You have to leave. He's coming back."

Heather started to say something, but another voice cut her off: "The bitch is right."

Heather gasped and turned to her right, where a tall, heavily muscled naked man had emerged from a place of hiding into the clearing. Josh pointed the 9mm at the big man and ordered him to freeze.

The man just smiled.

Then he crossed the clearing with a speed that belied his size, closing in on Josh in barely more than an eyeblink. He crashed into Josh and drove him to the forest floor. The 9mm discharged, the bullet zipping harmlessly straight up into the night sky. Then the big man had his hands around Josh's throat and began squeezing the life out of him. Josh couldn't aim the pistol, because his attacker had his arms pinned to the ground.

The girl whispered in Heather's ear as the two of

them watched Josh losing the fight for his life, "You can't save him. Or me. Run."

Heather wanted to run. More than fucking anything. She had no hope of winning against this monster-sized man. Making a dash back to the car was her only hope of survival.

She took a step, was on the verge of really running . . .

Then she hesitated, her gaze sweeping the clearing.

She listened to Josh's dying gurgle and made a decision.

# CHAPTER FIFTEEN

Sheila started getting bored about an hour after taking control of the pod. She'd just finished taking the lurching machine on patrol around the freakshow's perimeter, enjoying the opportunity to familiarize herself with the command center's odd instrumentation. The machine's controls were very intuitive and soon she'd worked out how to maneuver the thing in just about every direction. Unfortunately, however, there'd been no opportunity to test the pod's killing capabilities. Braddock seemed to have eliminated any remaining human stragglers prior to that glorious moment when his head exploded, raining gore all over the command center console.

Even looking at the monitors embedded in the fleshy, trunklike column that rose to the pod's ceiling stopped being fun pretty quickly. The flickering screens displayed a few scenes of things outsiders might label "atrocity," but it was nothing Sheila hadn't seen up close before. Just as boredom was settling in, a high-pitched tone from the command center signaled an incoming message. Moments later a message appeared on the largest screen. She read the words, smiled, and went to the hatch. She cranked the wheel lock and shoved the squealing metal door open. Suspended in the air via crane was a cage. Inside the cage were two young humans. One male, one female. Both were nude. The crane operator maneuvered the cage closer to the open pod door, jostling its clearly terrified occupants. When the cage was properly aligned with the door, an electronic buzz sounded and the front of the cage swung open.

Sheila waved a metal rod that resembled a police baton at the shivering new arrivals. "Step inside and be quick about it." She chuckled softly and licked her lips. "Seriously, you don't want to piss me off. Get in here."

The captives exchanged a last nervous glance, then the young man stepped out of the cage and into the pod. Sheila touched the tip of the metal rod to the small of his back, pressed a switch, and delivered an electric jolt that sent him tumbling to the floor. The girl shrieked and paused at the edge of the cage.

Sheila's smile faded. "You're scared. Which is understandable. You'd be stupid not to be scared. But if you're not out of that cage by the time I count to three, you're gonna die. And trust me, it won't be an easy death, girly."

The girl shivered as she took one tentative step out of the cage. "But . . . you're gonna k-kill me a-anyway . . ."

Sheila arched an eyebrow. "Oh? And just how do you know that?" She licked her lips again and eyed the girl up and down. "You're very pretty. Who knows? Maybe I won't kill you if you . . . please me." Her smile had a vaguely conspiratorial quality to it. "Hell, I think I like you already. Now get in here and help me torture this stupid boy."

Some of the nervousness went out of the girl then, her body assuming a less guarded posture as she stepped fully into the pod. She even smiled. Stupid thing. The girl's gaze flicked briefly to the prone form of the young man. Then she looked into Sheila's eyes and her smile broadened. "I never liked him anyway."

Sheila smirked. "We're going to have fun, I think, you and I." She nodded at the open hatch. The cage had disappeared, the crane returning to some other part of the freakshow grounds. Close that door."

The girl nodded. "Okay."

She turned away from Sheila and reached through the opening to grasp the wheel lock. She pulled the door shut, then spun the lock until the latch snapped home. Then she turned to face Sheila with an expectant smile. Sheila relished the way that slightly smug smile gave way to a look of wild terror as the tip of the shock rod came at her. A jolt from the instrument drove her back against the closed hatch before she fell in a twitching heap to the ground.

Sheila savored the small betrayal a moment longer, then turned her attention to the young man, who had recovered somewhat, rolling onto his back and groaning like a person in the grip of a debilitating illness. She pointed the rod in his direction and smiled again when she saw his eyes focus on it. "You stay right there, boy. You make the slightest move, you'll regret it. Understand?"

He managed a shaky nod. "Y-yes."

"Good."

Sheila went to the girl and stood over the bitch as she slowly recovered. When the girl's body stopped shaking, she placed her right foot on the girl's throat and pressed lightly down, enjoying the way her eyes suddenly bugged out. She showed the girl the rod again, waving the tip of it around her trembling face. "I bet I know what you're thinking. Aside from how scared you are, I mean." She touched the tip of the rod to the girl's nose, but didn't press the switch. "You're thinking if I knew how awful it felt to get zapped with this thing I would never use it on anyone else." She moved the tip of the rod along the girl's trembling, delicate jawline, then placed it firmly against her lips, applying pressure until the lips parted and allowed the rod to enter her mouth. "But that's flawed thinking. You see, I know just how it feels. The man who had this job before me used it on me numerous times. The agony that jolt induces is just out of this world." She giggled. "As you've learned. But, for me, what was even scarier was the loss of control of my own body, the way the electricity made me flop around like a fish out of water. There were times I was afraid I'd never stop convulsing."

She pushed the rod deeper into the girl's mouth. She also applied more pressure to her throat. The girl's pale face began to flush red. Sheila giggled again. "You should see yourself. You look like you're sucking a giant robot dick. I wonder how much worse it'd be for you if I were to press the zapper button now, with the shock rod inside you like that." She pursed her lips, made a contemplative sound. "I guess there's only one way to find out. . . ."

Her index finger glided over the switch and the girl cringed, whimpering again, sounding to Sheila like a wounded animal caught in a trap. "But I think I'll give you a break. Just a little one. I'm not quite ready to get so hardcore with you." She smiled as she withdrew the rod from the girl's mouth.

The girl let out a sob. "Th-thank you."

Sheila removed her foot from the girl's throat and positioned herself so that she was standing directly over her head. "I wasn't lying before. You really are very pretty. Your face, in particular, is just lovely. I think I'll sit on it for a while. I'll just trust that you know what you need to do to make me happy."

The girl started to say something, but Sheila shut her up by doing what she'd threatened to do. It took a moment, but the girl soon responded in the proper way, and Sheila settled in for a very pleasant fifteen minute ride. When she decided she'd had enough of the girl's oral ministrations, she abruptly stood up and smiled down at her glistening face. "My. You've done that before, haven't you?"

The girl managed a shaky smile. "Yes. . . ."

"I'll tell you the truth. I meant to kill both of you after putting you through a few hours of hell. But, baby, you're giving me some real second thoughts."

The girl licked moisture from her lips. "I'll do anything you want."

Sheila laughed. "Of course you will. Your boyfriend's another matter entirely. Him I'm going to kill. Do you have a problem with that?"

The girl shook her head. "No, ma'am. He's not my

boyfriend. I don't care what happens to him. I'll even help you hurt him."

Sheila frowned, studying the girl's face a moment. "Say . . . you look kind of familiar. You're not a cage slave, are you?"

"I started out in the cages, but I was adopted by a freak named Jeremiah a few years ago."

Sheila nodded, as if the words only affirmed what she'd known all along. "Yeah, I figured it was something like that. Jeremiah must've decided to dump you, huh? So the tall man sent you here to be my plaything, I suppose. Tough break for you. What's your name?"

"Jinx."

Sheila grunted. "How odd. That's not your given name, is it?"

Jinx placed a hand on Sheila's leg and began to gently caress it. "I'm afraid it is. My mom didn't mean to get pregnant and didn't really want me to be born. Only reason she didn't have an abortion was she figured out she could get on welfare by having me. She said she named me Jinx because the man who knocked her up was always bad luck."

"That's about enough of your life story. I'm the star of this show, bitch, and don't you ever forget it. When I want a bunch of goddamned little details, I'll fucking well let you know. Okay?"

Jinx cringed. "Yes. I'm sorry. . . ."

Sheila smirked. "You sure as shit are. Like I said, I'm the star. You want a bio? Of course you do. I'm the fucking star." She laughed. "I bet you think I must have some sob story like yours. Product of an abusive environment or some such weepy shit, right? Well, you're dead wrong, bitch. I was a rich girl. A daddy's girl. My parents loved me and spoiled me. I had a handsome boyfriend. I even had a secret girlfriend. She was very pretty—prettier than you. I was the most popular girl in town. Everybody either wanted to be me or fuck me. I had the perfect life until that stupid night I went to the freakshow a couple years ago. Makes you wonder, doesn't it?"

Jinx's brow furrowed. "Um . . . I'm sorry. . . . Wonder about what?"

Sheila chuckled and tapped the side of Jinx's head with the shock rod. "About how I got to be the sadistic cunt I am today. Aren't you curious about that? I would be, in your position."

Jinx frowned. "It's not any of my business." She saw the dark look that crossed Sheila's face then and hastened to add, "Unless you want it to be."

Sheila sneered. "I want, bitch. I fucking well want."

Jinx stroked Sheila's leg again. "So tell me."

Sheila smiled. "Oh, I will. The truth is, I've always enjoyed hurting things. Always. From the time I was a little girl, I got off on causing pain. It was the one secret about me I kept from everyone, even my secret girlfriend, who knew more about me than anyone else did. It started off with bugs and animals. They were easy. I could hurt them all I wanted. Who were they going to tell?" She giggled. "Then, senior year of high school, I lured this geeky kid to a secret place in the woods. I made him think I had a crush on him. I told him he couldn't tell anybody he was meeting me, that if he wanted to be with me it had to be a secret. The idiot believed my line of bullshit. I know because nobody ever questioned me after they found his bludgeoned body in the woods." She paused and closed her eyes, apparently reveling in the fond memory. Her eyes snapped open. "What do you think of me now, Jinx?"

Jinx was staring up at her with an expression that was either genuine rapture or prime evidence that the girl was an accomplished actress. "I think I want to be just like you when I grow up."

Sheila smirked. "You'll never be like me. I'm one of a fucking kind. But I bet you'd make an excellent slave. Stand up."

Jinx got to her feet and displayed an anxious, nervous smile. She looked frightened and desperate to please. Sheila knew the bitch would behave in whatever way she sensed would curry favor, and that much of what she said couldn't be trusted. But she also knew life in the freakshow was hard for any human. The ones some freaks kept as personal pets had it a little better than the cage slaves—who were frequently used for various types of sadistic entertainment or were processed as food—but it was still a hellish existence. This girl was smart. She would jump at the chance to be Sheila's slave.

Sheila snapped a hard slap across the girl's face, laughing at the shocked look in her eyes. "Are you mad at me, Jinx? Did you think we were getting to be friends?" She slapped the girl again, harder this time. "Would you like to make me stop if you could?"

Jinx sniffled. "No," she whispered.

Sheila sneered. "You expect me to believe that, bitch? That's sure as shit what I'd be thinking in your place. I'd wanna kill me." She slapped Jinx yet again, even harder, and the imprint of her hand left a red imprint on her face. "Tell me the truth, Jinx—do you want to kill me?"

Jinx was holding a hand to her face and sniffling

now. She was trembling all over. "No . . . please . . . no . . . I'll do whatever you want."

Sheila snorted. "Then tell me what you want. Tell me the truth."

Jinx cleared her throat and drew in a big breath, but she was still shaking. Still, her voice contained clear conviction as she said, "I want to stay here with you."

Sheila nodded. "Of course you do. But I did hurt you. I've hurt you a lot since the moment you stepped through that door. If you want to stay here with me, you're gonna have to prove yourself worthy. Starting now."

Jinx's brow furrowed. "What do you mean?"

Sheila nodded at the man on the floor. "What's that piece of shit's name?"

The young man was sitting up now. He said, "My name is Mike."

*"Shut your fucking hole, maggot!"* Sheila bellowed, her face suddenly a livid, twisted mask. "You don't speak without permission, do you hear me?"

Mike nodded and averted his eyes. "Yes."

Sheila let out a big breath and listened in amazement to the rapid thrumming of her heart. Then she looked at Jinx and smiled. "I want you to think about how you felt while I was tormenting you. I want you to focus the rage you must have felt—don't even bother to deny it—and take it out on that little asshole."

Jinx shot a glance at Mike, then looked uncertaintly at Sheila. "What should I . . . do?"

Sheila shrugged. "That's up to you. Just prove yourself. *Hurt* him."

Jinx smiled then and her eyes appeared to gleam with a genuine wickedness. "Okay."

Sheila went to the command center and settled herself in the leather swivel chair. "Put on a good show, okay? Entertain me."

Jinx approached Mike like a savage jungle cat closing in on cornered, wounded prey, slowly but deliberately, allowing the prey time to anticipate the coming pain, savoring its terror. He was shaking and his face was creased with an expression that must have been confusion. Sheila almost felt sorry for the poor son of a bitch. Here he was, a normal schmoe, caught in a nightmare from which there could be no escape, and now the one person he might have considered an ally in this strange place had turned on him. Well, he was about to learn an important lesson in how tenuous any alliance in this place was. Not that he would ultimately derive much benefit from the lesson, as she intended to kill him within the hour, if not much sooner. She wanted to see him suffer, sure, but at this point she was much more interested in the girl.

Mike began to scoot backward as Jinx neared him, eliciting an angry snarl from Sheila. "Don't you fucking move, boy." Her voice was a hard, merciless thing, and the sound of it made both of her captives flinch. "In fact, you don't do anything unless she says so. Understand?"

Mike stopped moving at once.

Sheila moved to the edge of her seat, making the boy flinch again. "Good." She shot a harsh look at Jinx. "Now get on with it."

Jinx didn't waste another moment. She grabbed a handful of Mike's curly hair and yanked him to a sitting position. She knelt in front of him and punched him hard in the face, making his head snap back and eliciting a startled yelp of pain. A second punch immediately followed the first, a punishing blow that broke his nose and brought forth a gush of blood. Mike cried out again and instinct caused him to slide backward, away from the assault. Jinx lunged at him, driving him hard to the floor. Then she sat astride him and rained down a furious flurry of blows, pummeling his face relentlessly, like a champion boxer hammering away at a punching bag. Sheila settled back in her seat again and slid a hand between her legs as she watched Jinx's fists smashing into the boy's face.

Then Jinx abruptly broke off the assault and stood up, sneering down at Mike's bruised and bloodied face. His nose, lips, and eyes were purple and already swelling. He groaned like a patient coming out of anesthesia, and his head turned in Sheila's direction. He stared at her through eyes bleary with tears. His obvious anguish made Sheila smile.

Jinx drew her foot back and kicked him hard in the side. She kicked him again, even harder than before, and Sheila could stand it no longer. She rose from the leather chair and came at Jinx in a rush. She pulled the girl into her arms and kissed her hungrily. Jinx grabbed handfuls of Sheila's hair, twisted them hard, and leaned into the kiss, driving her tongue deep into her mouth. Electricity seemed to crackle through her body. She'd never felt so aroused. The way Jinx's body was twined so enthusiastically around hers was like something out of a dream, a delight she hadn't experienced since her last time with Kelly, her old secret girlfriend.

So lost was she in the overload of sensual pleasure that she didn't realize Jinx had snatched the shock rod from her hand until she felt the tip of it touch the back of her neck. She went absolutely still when she realized what was about to happen.

Jinx pulled away from Sheila slightly, allowing her to see the smug smile touching her mouth. "This is going to hurt." The smile became a smirk. "Bitch."

Sheila started to say something.

That was when Jinx flicked the switch.

# CHAPTER SIXTEEN

The two-headed woman was waiting for him at the curb as Craig came out of the sandwich shop. She was leaning against the side of the Towncar, her ankles crossed in a relaxed pose as she smoked a thin cigarette through a plastic holder. She cut a sleek, sexy figure beneath the light of the streetlamp in her slinky yet elegant black dress and stiletto heels. This was a woman any guy would fall instantly in lust with—if not for the damnable presence of the ever-leering, hissing hag head.

Both faces smiled as he opened the plastic shopping bag to reveal the decapitated head of the Pakistani shop owner. The middle-aged man's face was a frozen mask of terror, the eyes wide and bulging, the mouth open in a silent scream. In an artistic touch, Craig had shoved the half-eaten remains of a sub sandwich into the dead man's mouth. A limp piece of bloody lettuce was hanging over his chin.

The two-headed woman blew smoke in Craig's face. "Nice work."

Craig coughed and waved smoke away with his free hand. "Thanks." He coughed again. "It's nice to be appreciated."

The comment elicited a smirking half-smile from the pretty head. "It is, indeed. And you've felt underappreciated much of your pathetic life, haven't you?"

"Underappreciated? Sure. Pathetic. No." Craig grinned. "I'm super-cool. Always have been, always will be. I'm the Craigmeister. That's what my fans call me."

The pretty head's smile broadened a bit. She pushed away from the Towncar and linked arms with Craig. "Walk with me a bit. Let's talk."

Craig chuckled. "Right, this is the part where we share our innermost thoughts and dreams. It's a given any time you're dealing with a chick. At some point this sort of thing has to happen. Kind of a drag, but it's the price you gotta pay if you wanna tap that ass. I just thought this case might be an exception to the rule."

The pretty head arched an eyebrow as they walked slowly down the quiet town's empty main street. "Oh? And why is that?'

"Because, well . . . and don't take this personally . . . but you're a monster."

The pretty head laughed softly. The hag head did something disconcerting—it winked. "Yes, I suppose I am a monster, at least by humanity's standards. But many of your kind would use that very word to describe you." She indicated the swinging shopping bag with a slight nod of her head. "By humanity's standards, you have done things tonight that could only be described as 'monstrous.'"

Craig grunted. "Touché."

They walked in silence for a few moments. Craig's gaze alternated between the left and right sides of the street, scanning the dark storefronts for any indication of human presence. They passed a hardware store, a tobacco shop, a video rental store, a pawn shop, a café, a salon, an attorney's office, a used bookstore, and more. No lights were on in any of them. The one other thing the stores had in common was a pervasive sense of desolation. Not just emptiness, but genuine desolation, an impression that not only were the proprietors absent, they were never coming back. Craig wasn't sure why he had this feeling, but it was definitely there, and it wasn't just a product of knowing the town had been overrun by murderous freaks. Suddenly walking down this main street felt like a stroll through the middle of a vast cemetery. Craig shuddered at the thought, spooked despite his own participation in the night's atrocities.

He coughed and loudly cleared his throat to break the gloomy spell. "So . . . what's up? Why the romantic moonlight walk?"

The pretty head smiled. "Is this romantic, then?"

Craig just managed not to roll his eyes. "Uh . . . no offense, but I was just being sarcastic. I'm slowly getting used to you. I've come to grips with the fact that you can reach into my brain and make me do any damned thing you please. I've even stopped being so freaked out by head number two, aka Miss Gruesome, there." He paused. "No, wait. That's a lie. But, in time . . . who knows?"

The pretty head's smile faded a bit. "Are you deliberately trying to provoke me? Do you want me to make you flop around in the middle of this street?"

Craig gave his head an emphatic shake. "No, no, no . . . noooooo." His tone was *this close* to verging on frantic. He forced himself to calm down before continuing. "Look, you can't take half the things I say seriously. I'm a smartass. It's a reflex. Like breathing."

The pretty head's eyes narrowed some. "Mmm, there's an idea. I could make you stop. Breathing, that is."

"Um . . ."

She laughed. "But I won't. In fact, I do understand what you're saying. I like your bluntness." She nodded again at the shopping bag. "And I like your style. We're actually getting to the real point of this little excursion. I have a proposition for you."

Craig frowned. "Uh . . . let me get this straight— you're making me some kind of . . . offer?"

The pretty head nodded. "Oh, yes."

Craig waited a beat. When she didn't elaborate, he said, "Okay. What is it?"

They stopped walking. The two-headed woman pulled him into an embrace. The pretty head kissed him lightly on the mouth while the hag head nipped at his ear. Her sleek, curvy body felt nice pressed against him. The hag head's coarse tongue flicking at his earlobe felt not so nice. In fact, he thought, *Yuck. Fucking yuck*. Yet again he felt simultaneously turned on and grossed out.

Her voice emerged through the pretty head's silken, moist lips as a whisper: "I'm looking for a replacement for Joseph. Someone to be my righthand man and faithful servant. Joseph is good at his job, but he's boring. I like you better."

Craig shrugged. "Okay. I accept. But do I have to wear that fugly chauffeur's uniform?"

The pretty head smiled. "It's not so simple as that. You'll have to kill him to earn the position."

Craig gulped. "Are you fucking kidding?" This time he couldn't keep the frantic edge from his voice. "The guy's a Neanderthal. It's impossible. I'd have better luck against King fucking Kong."

The pretty head's smile didn't waver. "I have faith in you. You will find a way. In fact, I suspect you'll find the task easier by far than you imagine."

Craig cast a glance back down the street. The Towncar was idling at the curb, its rear brake lights gleaming like the red eyes of a demon in the darkness. Joseph was inside the car, waiting patiently behind the wheel for his mistress and her new plaything to return. Craig wondered if the guy had the slightest inkling his employer would even entertain notions of having him killed. The guy was well aware of what the crazy bitch was capable of, and if he possessed even a moderate level of intelligence he'd be half-expecting something like this to happen someday. But maybe not. He struck Craig as the classic hulking goon-type, more brawn than brains. Maybe he was so stupidly secure in his position he'd never see this coming.

*Yeah, right,* Craig thought. *And maybe I'm the sweet, sensitive type.*

He couldn't count on the guy being an idiot. Could be he was a lot smarter than he looked. Don't judge a book by its cover and all that jazz. Craig asked the pretty head, "There a specific time you need this done by?"

She smiled and shrugged. "Now would be nice."

Craig sighed. "I was afraid you'd say that. Excuse me."

He stepped out of the embrace and sauntered back toward the Towncar, his stride projecting a confidence he didn't actually feel. He had only a vague idea how to handle this, but hell, that was better than nothing. He'd just start shit up and see how it developed. It might get him killed, but he wasn't afraid of death. He had a notion an early death was in the cards for him regardless of what happened next.

He tapped on the Towncar's driver's side window. He was just able to make out the outline of Joseph's massive head through the tinted glass. The head rotated slowly to the left and looked up. A moment later Craig heard the electric whir of the power window sliding down.

Joseph's upper lip curled in a slight sneer. "Yes?"

"Hey there, Joey." Craig flashed a faux-friendly grin. "Anyone ever tell you you look like Bruce Banner's meaner half? You ought to consider investing in some green body paint. You'd be a real hit on the celebrity has-been lookalike circuit."

A flicker of confusion passed across the big driver's face. His eyebrows knitted tightly as he considered Craig's words, probably trying to figure out whether they deserved a reply. "What do you want?"

Craig's expression then was one of mock hurt. "Moi? Want?" He heaved an exaggerated sigh. "Look, Joseph, we're going to be working closely together from now on. That's what the thing with two heads was just telling me. She just offered me a job." He smiled brightly. "I'm her new bodyguard. So I figured I ought to make an effort to make friends. So what do you say? We pals now?"

Joseph scowled. "No." But the scowl morphed into a frown. "And *I'm* her bodyguard." He eyed Craig up and down. "You're no pushover, but you're not in my league. Why are you fucking with me?"

Craig chuckled. "I know, I know. It's crazy, right? Like you said, I'm no pushover. I can kick the average dude's ass, easy. But something tells me Miss Thing over there doesn't need protection from Joe Average. All she's gotta do is reach into their brains and make 'em do a funky jitterbug. And then there's the fact that I've only got one eye. What good's a bodyguard with just one eye? My peripheral vision sure ain't what it used to be. Now, I went over all this with her, but she's adamant. I'm the new bodyguard, and from now on you're just the driver."

Joseph's frown deepened as he mulled it over. He glanced in the rearview mirror, studying his boss's distinctly feminine silhouette. She was still standing where Craig had left her down the street. Joseph's head again swiveled toward Craig. "She made me kill the guy who was doing this before me. Ten years ago, that was."

Craig blinked. "Uh . . . yeah? Really? Huh. That's . . . interesting."

*Shit,* he thought. *Didn't see that coming. Should've, though . . .*

Joseph's head inclined slightly, a barely perceptible nod. "I reckon that's what this is all about. You're supposed to kill me." A little smile tweaked the edges of his mouth. "Or try."

Craig shook his head and took a step back from the Towncar, holding his hands up in supplication. "Whoa, hold on there, big fella. You've got it all wrong. She didn't say anything to me about killing you." Craig was certain he'd never know how he managed to keep a straight face while saying those words, but he did. "This is like a departmental reorganization at a big corporation. The only thing that's changed is your job title. No big deal, really."

Joseph smirked. "Right. She knows I'm on to you. She's inside our heads. She hears everything we say, even that far away." He looked briefly toward the rearview mirror again. Then his smirk became a smile. "But it doesn't matter. Nothing will change. I only have to kill you. It'll be one of the easier things I've done."

He opened the door and swung his legs out of the car. Craig's heart beat faster and his breath caught in his throat. He darted a glance at the two-headed woman, hoping desperately to discern some hint of what to do from her expression, but she was too far away and she wasn't looking at them anyway. Her heads were turned skyward, as if she expected to see the mothership descend from the heavens any moment now. Craig turned back to the car in time to see Joseph beginning to lift his substantial bulk off the leather seat.

Craig knew he had to stagger the bigger man immediately or face being beaten to death. And he wasn't so unafraid of death after all. The shopping bag containing the shop owner's severed head slipped from his fingers and fell to the street. His foot shot out and kicked the door against Joseph's knees. Joseph let out a sharp cry of pain and fell back into the car. Craig gripped the door frame, pulled the door open, then swung it hard against the chauffeur's knees again. Then he did it again. And again, repeating the process as Joseph howled and tried to retreat into the car. Then he saw the big man's hand reaching into his jacket. For a gun, probably. Craig threw the door open wide, brushed the man's hand aside, and kicked him twice. First as hard as he could on one of his battered knees, then a scrotum-crushing blast to the crotch. Joseph howled again and tried to roll away, but Craig dove into the car, reached inside the chauffeur's jacket, and jerked a .44 Magnum out of the man's shoulder holster. Joseph let out a gasp and looked up at his attacker with wide-eyed desperation.

Craig shoved the big barrel into one of those dancing eyes and pulled the trigger. The gun kicked and the blast reverberated like a motherfucker in the car's interior. The back of Joseph's head exploded, bathing the upholstery in beautiful gore. Beautiful because it signaled victory, but also because he'd come to appreciate the way a victim's body released its fluids in an almost artistic way. This killing was more brutal and immediate than the others he'd perpetrated tonight, so in some ways the end result was less aesthetically pleasing than the gore outflow from other kills. On the other hand, that didn't matter. He was alive. He'd killed an adversary who theoretically should have presented a far more serious threat than either the kid or the Pakistani shop owner. And now he smiled.

Because the two-headed woman had been right.

It had been easy.

He set the .44 on the Towncar's dash, grabbed handfuls of Joseph's jacket, and hauled the dead man out of the car, depositing him in the street like a bag of garbage. The thought made him chuckle. The plastic shopping bag with the shop owner's head in it was next to the body. The chuckle became a cackle. The sound of high heels clicking on pavement made him look up. The two-headed woman was back.

Craig grinned. "I'm such a litterbug. I hope I don't get fined."

The pretty head smiled and the hag head made a raspy sound that could almost be called laughter. "You did well. I'm proud of you. You'll want to keep that head. Pick it up, please."

Craig knelt to retrieve the plastic bag. "Whatever you say, ma'am. You're the boss."

The two-headed woman opened the Towncar's rear door, then reached inside for something. Craig stared at her ass while she was bent over. It was quite possibly the juiciest, most lust-inducing rear end he'd ever seen. He felt a wild urge to go rub his crotch against it before she could stand up.

But then—too soon—she was out of the car again. In her hands was the burlap sack containing the ragged lump of muscle that had once been the beating heart of a teenage boy. She indicated the shop owner's head with a nod. Craig shrugged. He wasn't sure what the point of collecting these trophies was, but he didn't care. He removed the head from the plastic bag, shook the sticky bag off his hand, and dropped the head in the burlap sack.

The pretty head smiled again. She used the leather drawstring to cinch the bag shut, then tossed it back inside the car. "In a moment, you'll need to return to the sandwich shop for a carving knife. There's a piece of Joseph's anatomy I'll want you to remove." Her smile broadened. "But first . . ."

She turned away from him and lifted her dress over her heads. She draped it over the open door's frame, then bent over at the waist and braced her hands against the Towncar's right rear fender. She shot a sideways smile at him.

"Come get your reward, Craig. You've earned it."

Craig didn't need to be told twice. It didn't even

bother him anymore that she knew his every thought. Truth be told, it was starting to turn him on. Perhaps that was just more of her manipulation, but it didn't really matter at this point, did it? Okay, so the way the hag head looked over her shoulder at him and leered while he was putting it to her was a bit unsettling, but not enough to diminish his ardor much.

When it was over, she put her dress back on and he did as she ordered, returning to the sandwich shop. He came back with a blade honed to a fine edge. He used it to messily remove Joseph's genitals, which he subsequently dropped in the burlap sack.

This time he couldn't help it—he had to ask: "Why the fucked-up keepsakes?"

"You'll know when it's time for you to know." She slid into the Towncar's backseat and looked up at him. "You have a new job. You start now. Drive."

She pulled the door shut, leaving Craig alone in the street.

"Drive? Where?"

But then he knew, the information arriving in his brain like some kind of psychic e-mail. He wiped his bloodstained hands on his already bloody jeans and got behind the Towncar's steering wheel. Spying the .44 on the dash, he took it by the handle and set it on the empty passenger seat. Seemed a safer place for it. He briefly considered liberating Joseph's shoulder holster from his corpse. The big guy wouldn't be needing it anymore, after all.

His head jerked to the right.

Then backward and to the left.

He gripped the steering wheel hard and shuddered, feeling sweat roll from his armpits. "Okay, okay," he muttered. "I'm going. Doing my job. Please don't hurt me again."

He put the car in gear and pulled away from the curb.

Then he did a U-turn and headed away from the town's business center.

Toward the outskirts of town.

# CHAPTER SEVENTEEN

Heather jerked the cord on the big McCulloch chain saw and it roared immediately to life. The big man let go of Josh's throat and jumped to his feet. Heather didn't allow him time to flee, plunging the whirring blade into his back. The man screamed as the blade chewed through his flesh. The chain saw chugged and jumped in Heather's hands, but she fought to keep it under control and pressed it deeper into the big man's body. The spinning blade spit blood and bits of flesh at her, rendering the work more difficult. The man screamed again and somehow managed to pull away from the blade, but he didn't get very far. Tumbling to the rough ground, he howled and rolled onto his side, holding a fluttering hand to the wound in his back.

Heather shut the chain saw off and listened to him whimper. He sounded pitiful, more like a frightened baby than a mad-dog killer. But Heather felt no sympathy for him. She had only to look at the mutilated girl at the edge of the clearing to know he was undeserving of any shred of compassion. She couldn't help staring at him, though. His body had the freakish bulk of a steroid-abusing professional wrestler. He'd used blue body paint to decorate his torso and bald head. The blue stripes looked to have been applied with great precision, rising from his waist to travel in a swirling, crisscross pattern over his belly and chest before winding behind his neck. The thinning stripes culminated in a precise swirl at the crown of his skull. And a closer look showed that he was also wearing mascara.

Josh was sitting up now and staring at the man who'd tried to strangle him. "Son of a bitch." He heaved a big breath and gingerly touched his brutalized throat. "Look at that fucking dude. Ten to one he's got some backwoods house of horrors somewhere out here. Lampshades made of human skin, jars full of preserved human organs, that kind of thing."

Heather shook her head. "Lovely. It isn't enough that we have to be running for our lives from a bunch of goddamned monsters. Now we've stumbled on a real life *Texas Chainsaw* scenario." She sighed. "It's just not fair."

Josh got to his feet with a grunt. Heather saw that he still had the nickel-plated 9mm, having somehow managed to hang onto it while being throttled by the psycho. She was unsurprised when she saw him aim it at the fallen man's head. She thought maybe she should protest. The man was badly wounded and no longer a threat. But she kept her mouth shut and Josh pulled the trigger.

Once, twice, a pause, then a third time.

The man stopped breathing.

His skull was a bullet-riddled mess, the artfully rendered blue swirl at the crown of his skull now obscured by gore. Heather turned away from the sight, but it brought no relief as her gaze settled again on the dead girl. Her stomach churned as she stared in sickened horror at the separated halves of the nude body. Her face—which might have been a pretty one—was a frozen, contorted mask, a study in the limits of human agony. Flies buzzed around the ragged, blade-chewed edges of her waist. A thin column of spine protruded from the torso.

Heather fell to her knees, bent over, and vomited. Her stomach heaved and heaved as her body worked to expel every last bit of her stomach's contents. She was only barely aware of Josh holding her hair away from her face. When at last the convulsions ceased, she broke out in a sweat and her teeth began to chatter.

Josh made soothing noises for a time and squeezed her shoulders. Then he guided her to a sitting position. She hugged herself and continued to shudder as Josh said, "You're gonna be okay, Heather. Sit tight. I'm gonna cut the other girl down."

Heather nodded, but didn't say anything. She watched Josh select a large hunting knife from the dead psycho's collection of torture tools. It hit her again how lucky she was to have him on her side. He was a stoner flake, sure, but he'd proved himself more than capable many times. She thought of the way he'd held her hair back while she was puking and managed a small smile. It was the kind of thing a loving boyfriend might do. The kind of thing Craig Carpenter would never have done.

The girl began to cry as she watched Josh approach her with the knife. Poor thing. Probably thought Josh was about to inflict more pain on her already much-abused body. She bore a striking resemblance to the dead girl, so much so Heather suspected they were sisters. Heather could only imagine what seeing her sister taken apart by the chain saw had done to her mind. The girl whimpered and cringed as Josh stepped behind the tree and went to work on her bonds. When her hands came free, she fell to her knees and began to sob. She looked at Heather through red-rimmed, glassy eyes and tried to speak, but the words were made unintelligible by grief.

Josh flicked his wrist and the knife buried itself in the soft earth. He then stripped off his flannel shirt and offered it to the girl. She flinched at first, but then accepted the shirt and shrugged into it, drawing the front closed over her pale, blood-streaked torso. Josh was over six feet tall and the girl was maybe a shade over five feet, so the shirt hung on her like a dress. Her eyes shone with gratitude as Josh helped her to her feet.

For reasons she couldn't understand, Heather's gaze was drawn helplessly back to the dead girl. She again got a good, long look, but this time her stomach barely fluttered. Her body was through being sick for the time being, so there was that to be grateful for at least. The dead girl didn't look real, somehow—more like a grisly prop from a splatter movie than an actual corpse. Just thinking that made her feel inhuman, but she couldn't help it.

It took her a moment to realize Josh was talking to her.

She blinked and looked up. "What? I'm sorry. I was spacing out there for a minute."

Josh sighed. "I was just saying we have to get out of here."

Heather got to her feet and brushed dirt off her jeans. "Let's go, then."

She was already turning toward Wickman Road when Josh said, "Not that way."

Heather faced him. "Why not?"

The girl was clinging to Josh like a drunk hanging on a buddy. She had one arm around his back and the other looped around his stomach.

"We talked about it before, remember?" Josh sounded tense, like he was weary of repeatedly explaining simple concepts. "The only way out of town is through the woods. You know that."

Heather snorted. "Right." She glanced at the dead psycho. "And run the risk of encountering more charming gentlemen like this Blue Man Group reject?" She shook her head. "I don't think so."

There was an unyielding hardness in Josh's eyes. "My mind's made up, Heather. We're facing serious obstacles either way, but I think we stand a better chance of beating the ones out here. If you want to take your chances with the freaks, that's up to you. I won't stop you."

Heather couldn't believe it. He'd come all this way with her, fighting against impossible odds to stay alive, putting himself at risk again and again, and suddenly he was just going to abandon her. She didn't want to show it, but she was hurt. It was ridiculous. She still didn't really know the guy. But knowing that did little to diminish the hurt.

But the hurt rapidly gave way to anger. She gripped the girl by an elbow and tugged her away from him. The girl let out a little squeak. She tried to move back toward him, but she was still too weak and Heather's grip was still firm.

Josh frowned. "What are you doing, Heather?"

Heather was moving toward the road now, pulling the girl along behind her. "I'm going back to the car."

"I meant what are you doing with *her?*"

Heather glanced over her shoulder at him as she continued to advance toward the edge of the clearing. "Obviously, I'm taking her to the car. How dense are you? She's in no condition to walk miles through the fucking wilderness."

Josh had no retort for that, remaining silent as Heather and the girl stepped out of the clearing and into the small patch of forest that separated the clearing from the road. Heather pulled the girl close and worked hard at holding her upright as they worked their way through the deeper darkness. They nearly took a tumble one time, Heather cursing and the girl letting out a startled yelp as Heather's foot plunged through a shallow hole in the bramble. Somehow they managed to avoid a spill and for the rest of the journey the girl clung as tightly to her as she had to Josh.

As they neared the road, Heather became aware of a sound from somewhere behind them, a crunch of bramble and the snap of a branch. Her heart raced faster for a moment; then she realized it was just Josh following them out of the woods. A petty part of her felt a smug satisfaction at this "victory." She was getting her way and she was happy about it. She realized it was a childish thing to think, but she didn't care. All that mattered at the moment was getting free of the creepy forest.

Heather was stunned when she saw what was waiting for them by the side of the road. Or, rather, the lack thereof.

The Chevelle was gone. As was the body of the

teenager Josh had killed with the last shell from his shotgun. A closer examination of the roadside showed a spray of safety glass and a dark pool of something she knew to be coagulating blood. Evidence that she hadn't imagined the incident. Somehow, though, someone (or some*thing*) had come along and removed both the body and the vehicle without making a sound. Okay, so maybe it'd happened while she was making like Leatherface with the chain saw—the noise generated by the McCulloch certainly would've covered the sound of the Chevelle's engine—but it was still hard to accept.

For one thing, who would've done it? If it'd been the freaks, why hadn't they just come into the woods after them? It made no sense. Regardless of how it had happened, the car was undeniably gone. Along with her mother's body. An aching emptiness threatened to swallow her at that realization. There'd been no opportunity to think of things like funeral preparations or casket selection. And that would have been important. It was the one way in which Alice Campbell had been a staunch traditionalist. Heather and her mother had had many annoyingly morbid debates on the subject of cremation versus burial, the message of which was always very clear—Alice would have wanted her body planted in the ground.

But now there was nothing to bury. Anger and sadness triggered a welling of tears.

Josh came out of the woods and walked out into the road. He stood on the double yellow line and turned in a slow circle before stopping to regard Heather and the girl. He looked as perplexed as she felt, which was a relief. She'd half-expected an annoying "looks-like-we-get-to-do-things-my-way-after-all" attitude, but he seemed as disturbed by the car's disappearance as she was. She understood. It was one thing to heatedly debate which course of action was the best to take. It was another entirely to have one of your options eliminated for you by an outside force.

He took long looks to the left and right again before joining them at the road's shoulder. "Okay, this is seriously fucked up. What the hell happened to the car and the . . . uh . . ."

Josh faltered as he glanced at the girl. He met Heather's gaze and a silent communication passed between them. There was a mutual awareness that the kid with the gun might not have been the villain Josh had feared. In retrospect, it seemed likely he'd been fleeing the madman in the woods. Heather detected a pang of regret in Josh's expression, but he made the look vanish, rendering his face a blank slate for the sake of the girl. Because now it seemed very possibile that she had known the boy.

But the girl was beginning to emerge from the shock of her ordeal and was no longer numb to the rest of the world. The look that passed between Heather and Josh roused her suspicion. "What are you keeping from me?"

Heather cleared her throat and started to speak. "I . . . we . . ." Heather knew what she needed. Good, placating words, the kind that would provide comfort; but she couldn't summon them. She looked desperately at Josh, then gave up, breathing a weary sigh. She'd never been a good liar. She looked at the girl and said, "That guy, the psycho . . . did he have anyone else out there with him? An accomplice, maybe?"

The girl shook her head. "No. Just me and Julie, my sister. And Julie's boyfriend, Steve."

The girl's gaze moved to the pool of blood and lingered there long enough to make the adults distinctly uncomfortable.

A pained look crossed Josh's face. He squeezed his eyes shut and cupped a hand over his mouth for a moment. "Oh, Christ."

The girl turned in his direction. "Something happened to Steve."

A statement, not a question. There was more than just a hint of accusation in those words, as well. The girl's tone made Heather wince. She again found herself flailing for the right words. She failed again. She was sure no right words existed in this case.

Josh opened his eyes and moved his hand from his mouth. He looked the girl in the eye and said, "I shot Steve. He's dead."

The girl stared at him blankly for a long moment. Heather thought maybe she was going into shock again. She was sure that behind that blank look a raw, burning rage was slowly forming. She tensed, expecting that rage to eventually explode.

But before that could happen a rising sound penetrated the tense stillness. The girl blinked, her ears picking up on the sound an instant before the adults. She turned away from Josh and stared at the expanse of road to their right. Josh and Heather followed suit and squinted into the deep darkness.

The sound rose some more and their hearts abruptly accelerated.

Heather gulped. "A car."

"Oh, fuck." Josh grimaced. "We have to get out of here. Back into the woods, before they see us."

Heather nodded and managed a single numb syllable: "Yeah."

But all three remained where they were standing as distant headlights appeared, penetrating the darkness like the sinister, glowing eyes of a movie vampire. The car drew steadily but unhurriedly closer, negotiating the gently curving road at a rate just a hair over the posted speed limit. Under normal circumstances, there would have been more than enough time to flee into the woods.

These were not normal circumstances.

None of them could move.

Something had reached inside their minds. Some powerful presence with the ability to bend their wills with ease. Heather was shaking. Sweat rolled down her back and into her eyes. Despite everything she'd been through that night—including the devastating loss of her mother—nothing she'd faced had induced a fraction of the terror she was feeling at that moment. There was something much more awful about being so helpless, so completely at the mercy of another. She felt like crying. She felt like calling out to her dead mother. And she felt shame at her cowardice.

The younger girl's voice emerged as a shaky whine: "Wh-what's h-happening?"

Heather sniffled and said, "I don't know. I'm sorry."

The car was close enough now to make out its shape. It was an old but very well-maintained Towncar with tinted windows. It had shiny chrome wheels and a buffed exterior. It slowed to a crawl as it neared them, then came to a gentle stop in the middle of the road.

Heather's legs were quaking now. The only thing keeping her from falling to the street was that alien presence in her head. It was holding her upright, like a puppet on a string. She stared at the dark driver's side window and sensed something malevolent lurking behind the glass.

Then the door opened and a living, breathing nightmare stepped out of the car.

Craig grinned. "Hey, Heather, baby. Fancy running into you out here, you goddamned cunt."

Heather whimpered. "Nooo . . ."

Craig laughed. "Sorry, babe, it's true. I've come back for ya." His grin faded some as he took a step toward her. He would've seemed menacing anyway, but the missing eye (or, more accurately, the jelly-stuffed socket once occupied by the missing eye) kicked his already significant creepiness factor into the stratosphere. "I'm gonna put you in your place once and for all."

"How are you doing this?" Heather asked.

Craig smirked. "What, the mind control thing? Afraid I can't take credit for that." The smirk became a grin again. "I see you've made some new friends. Guess what? So have I, baby."

The Towncar's rear door swung slowly open. Heather watched as a slender, shapely female leg emerged. The insinuating tingle in her brain intensified and she knew right away this person was the one controlling them.

Then the woman emerged fully from the car and stood next to Craig.

Josh said, "Ah . . . fuck."

Craig cackled. "I know. It's a trip, right? But, brother, you ain't seen nothin' yet."

Until that instant, Heather would have been willing to bet nothing could eclipse the dismay she felt at the reunion with one-eyed Craig.

The two-headed woman smiled at Heather. "Hello, dear. You are quite lovely."

Heather tried to close her eyes as the freak approached her. But that presence in her head forced them to remain open.

Forced her to watch as the freak's hands reached for her.

# CHAPTER EIGHTEEN

The confident, unhesitating way Jinx moved about the pod's interior and manipulated the command center's controls made Mike nervous. She knew where everything she needed was stored. She knew precisely the function of each button and knob on the control panels. And yet supposedly she'd never before set foot inside the pod. Mike wasn't sure he believed that anymore. On some level he'd probably never believed it, just as he hadn't completely trusted anything said by Jinx since her admission that she'd been using and manipulating him from the beginning.

A hidden speaker somewhere in the pod was playing music broadcast on some strange radio station. A baritone-voiced dj would occasionally come on and say some deeply odd things, things indicating knowledge of the freakshow, and would then play old punk and alternative music. The tune playing now was something apparently called "Bikini Girls With Machine Guns."

The blond girl, Sheila, was hanging several feet off the floor, her body trussed up in a bizarre harness device composed of leather and chains. She was hogtied, her arms and legs secured behind her back. Sheila and the harness were held aloft by a chain descending from an open panel in the pod's ceiling.

Mike had watched in numb disbelief as Jinx roughly maneuvered Sheila into the harness, securing the straps and chains quickly. Again, she went about her work like a person who'd done this very thing countless times before. And again, Mike kept this impression to himself. Like it or not, all he could do now was sit back and watch. He was as powerless as a pawn in a game of chess.

Sheila moaned. She blinked slowly as she lifted her head to look at him. Her face was red and gleamed with a sheen of perspiration. Her body was covered with bruises and cuts that were still weeping blood, wounds she'd suffered in the course of a brutal beating administered by Jinx.

Funny thing, that. He knew exactly how she felt. He gingerly touched his own broken nose and winced.

"What the fuck are you looking at?" Blood dribbled from the corners of Sheila's mouth as she spoke. Her voice was hoarse, and she had to work to push each word through her swollen lips. Mike cringed at the sight of a broken tooth dangling from a thread of tissue. "Stop looking at me . . . mother . . . fucker. . . ."

Mike shuddered and averted his gaze, only too happy to grant her wish. He made eye contact instead with Jinx, who was watching him from the leather swivel chair at the command center. Her expression was cold, so absolutely devoid of emotion it sent another shiver through him. He swallowed hard and said, "So, what happens now?"

Jinx looked at him a moment longer before turning to the column of strange video screens. "Nothing yet," she said at last. "There are still more preparations to be made."

"Preparations for what?"

She tilted her head and squinted at him. "I told you in Jeremiah's trailer. Remember?"

Mike cleared his throat again and nodded. "Sure, I remember. I'm just not sure I believe what you told me. We're going to Freak World. There we'll do something that'll end all this. Which is the part I'm having trouble with."

Jinx stared at him for a long time without speaking. Then she said, "It really isn't important what you believe."

Mike laughed cynically. "I take it that's because I'm no longer needed for whatever you've got in mind. I was a prop, right? A distraction, a way of earning the trust of little miss psycho over here." More of that cynical laughter bubbled out of him, even bleaker than before. "Only, hey, it turns out you're way more psycho. You make blondie seem like an angel."

Jinx's expression turned hard. "Don't you dare judge me, Mike."

He grunted, then shrugged. "Or what? You'll beat me again?" He laughed. "Go ahead. Seriously. Finish the fucking job."

Jinx rose from the chair and came toward him. Mike wanted to run and hide, but he stood his ground. Partly because there was nowhere to run to and no place to hide, but also because part of him desired exactly what he'd requested—an end to this long night of madness. If death was the only escape available, so be it.

Even so, a jolt of panic went through him when she placed a hand around his throat. The burning rage so clearly evident in her eyes made him certain she meant to strangle him, but she applied no pressure. In a moment he realized the hand at his throat was just an intimidation tactic.

"I mean it, Mike. Don't you dare judge me." Her voice was remarkably calm, considering her obvious anger, the words emerging in a low, measured tone. "You've been here one night, Mike. Just one." A slight squeeze of his throat added extra emphasis to this point, just in case he'd been too dense to get it. "I've been here for years. Imagine that, Mike. Imagine going through what you've gone through tonight several hundred more times."

Mike's shoulders sagged and he averted his gaze. "I get it. Okay? Now please let go of me."

"Do you really get it, Mike? Because I want you to seriously consider what I just said. Put yourself in my place. What do you think you'd be capable of after years of this?"

"I don't know."

Jinx let go of his throat. "Like hell you don't. You'd be willing to do anything to end this. Just like I'm willing to do anything." She sighed and there was a flickering spark of sadness in her eyes.. "I'm not a bad person at heart. I'm really not. But this existence has hardened me. I'm sorry."

She stalked back to the control center, dropping into the leather swivel chair with a heavy weariness.

Mike coughed and gently rubbed his throat. She hadn't really hurt him this time, though she'd done a very effective job of letting him know just how badly she *could* hurt him if she wanted. He was still afraid of her. Maybe even more now than before. And yet . . . her words resonated with truth. He could admit that to himself at least, though it pained him. He moved closer to the command center, stepping around the trussed-up girl but stopping short of the swivel chair by several feet.

"So what now?" he asked.

"We wait a bit longer, until the time is just right. Then we enter the Nothing."

"The . . ." He shook his head in confusion. "Excuse me . . . but did I hear you use the word 'nothing' like a proper noun?"

"That's right. Remember that other realm, the place I rescued you from? That's what the freaks call it—the Nothing."

"Huh. Weird. Anyway . . . how am I supposed to help? I know, um, nothing about . . . the Nothing."

The smallest hint of a sad smile touched Jinx's mouth. "There's no way for you to help. You're just along for the ride at this point, I'm afraid."

Mike scowled. "What was my real purpose here, Jinx? Why was it so crucial that I be here?"

"You were a distraction. A wild card." She glanced at Sheila. "I didn't think it was necessary, but Jeremiah insisted. Considering the way things went, I guess he had the right idea after all."

Mike also looked at Sheila. "There some reason she's trussed-up like that? Why didn't you just kill her?"

"At first I thought it might be best to keep her around in case she has information we'll need." She smiled slightly. "But I think we've established the bitch won't give up her secrets even under extreme duress."

Mike's gaze lingered on Sheila's battered face a moment longer. "Extreme duress. Yeah, that's a good word for what happened there."

"She had it coming. Every bit of it."

Mike remembered the jolts from Sheila's shock rod too clearly to argue much with that. Regardless, he couldn't help feeling some sympathy for her. He indicated his broken nose and said, "And did I deserve this?"

"Of course not." She sighed. "And I'm sorry that happened. But I did what I had to do."

"Bullshit."

Jinx chose not to reply to that, a silence Mike considered as damning as an admission of guilt. He chose not to press the point and instead listened more intently as the radio dj's voice came on again: "Ah, yeah. That was the Ramones and their timeless classic 'Beat On the Brat.'" The dj's throaty laughter sounded like the rumbling of a freight train in the pod's interior. "And here's another oldie-but-goodie I'm sure y'all will find appropriate on this glorious evening of Assimilation."

The dj intro'd the track, which was helpful, because Mike wouldn't have recognized the tune. It was "Your Pretty Face Is Going to Hell" by Iggy and the Stooges.

"Hmm." Mike stroked his chin and looked at Sheila again before shifting his attention back to Jinx. "Interesting song selection. Creepy, even. Where the hell is this Radio Ether broadcasting from?"

"From inside the Nothing."

Mike shook his head. "The freaks have a radio station. Huh. What about cable TV? Hey, yeah, I bet they've got a twenty-four hour torture station, right?"

He chuckled. "Or a snuff channel." He assumed the tone of an unctuous TV announcer. "Watch Snuff TV! It's all death, all the time!"

Mike laughed again. He could either laugh or go crazy. For the moment, he was going with the former, though he was resigned to the probable inevitability of the latter. Jinx, though, remained stone-faced. He was about to make a crack about her pronounced lack of a sense of humor when an image on the largest video screen drew a gasp from him instead.

Jinx turned in her chair to face the column of video screens. She didn't so much as flinch at the sight of Jeremiah's bloated, ghastly face, which somehow looked even worse on the video screen than it did in person. The freak was sitting on the bed in his trailer and from the angle of his head looked to be staring at a spot high on the wall, close to the ceiling. Mike had had a good long look at that ceiling during the sex show they'd put on for Jeremiah and he couldn't recall seeing anything even vaguely resembling a camera. Though not seeing one didn't really mean much given the weird, organic technology in use throughout so much of the freakshow. The camera might be as small as a speck of dust.

The edges of the old freak's mouth rippled. A smile, maybe. Then that grating, garbled voice of his emerged through an unseen speaker: "Jinx, darling, pet . . . "—his mouth rippled again as it emitted that breaking-glass laughter of his—"I commend you on a job well done so far."

Jinx's expression remained stoic as she said, "Thank you, sir. I'm honored to have pleased you.

Mike scowled. Honored?

More bullshit.

The bloated head wobbled. A nod? Then the freak spoke again: "You've performed admirably. But your work is far from finished."

Jinx nodded. "I know, sir. And we're almost ready for the next phase."

Jeremiah's head wobbled again. "Good, good. I bid you adieu for now, dear one. I'll see you again on the other side, in this life or the next."

The screen went black.

Mike released a breath he hadn't realized he'd been holding. "Well, that was ominous."

Jinx looked at him and lifted an eyebrow. "Oh?"

"Yeaaaaah. That 'this life or the next' comment betrays a lack of confidence in this scheme you guys have concocted."

Jinx shrugged. "The odds against success are high. We're risking everything."

"And what happens if we fail?"

Jinx tapped the edge of the control panel. "Then we'll be like those movie spies who swallow cyanide capsules rather than be captured by the enemy. I'll enter a self-destruct sequence here. Then . . ." She made a sound mimicking an explosion.

Mike winced. "Lovely. Well, at least with instant incineration there'll be no pain. Maybe a split second of mind-bending agony, but hey, it'll be over fast."

Another period of silence ensued as their conversation lapsed. Jinx busied herself with work at the command center. Mike's attention was drawn back to Sheila when she groaned and mumbled something unintelligible. He moved closer to her and she lifted her head when she sensed his presence, looking at him in a pitiful way through red and swollen eyes. She mouthed something to him. She did it in a very precise and deliberate way, striving to communicate without speaking. Mike glanced past her to see if Jinx was watching them, but her attention was still riveted to the command center.

The Radio Ether dj finished a rather disturbing description of the delightfully tender taste of deep-fried human flesh and the music recommenced. This time it was "Oh, Bondage, Up Yours!" by X-ray Spex.

He didn't know what Sheila was trying to tell him, but he wanted to know. Some instinct compelled him to lean in closer, and he whispered in the trussed-up girl's ear, "I don't think she can hear us over the music. What are you trying to tell me?"

Sheila turned her head toward his and he leaned in even closer. Her mouth was very close to his ear as she said, "Help is coming."

Mike abruptly straightened up and scowled down at her. "What?"

But now she was smiling, an expression made grotesque by her puffy, bleeding lips. And she made a sound he soon recognized as pained laughter.

Jinx at last realized something was happening and tore her gaze away from the video screens. "What's going on over there?"

Mike shook his shead. "Dunno. She said something kinda cryptic. 'Help is coming.'"

Jinx's eyes went wide. "Fuck."

Mike's heart began to race and a rising panic began to grip him as he moved away from the grinning, leering prisoner. "She's just fucking with us, right? There's no way—"

And that was when they heard it.

Jinx leaped out of her chair and Mike spun around in time to see the wheel lock on the hatch begin to turn. Then the hatch popped open.

The pirate leered at them through the opening.

Then he leaped into the pod.

And he wasn't alone.

# CHAPTER NINETEEN

The Chevelle returned sometime during their forced march back through the woods to retrieve the remains of the psycho killer and his dismembered female victim. Heather emerged through the line of trees and saw her car parked alongside the Towncar. She felt nothing upon seeing it. Not surprise, or relief that she again knew the whereabouts of her mother's remains. This was not because she was still numb from the parade of horrors she'd been witness to tonight, but rather because her fractured psyche was reeling from the overwhelming revulsion consuming her.

The dead girl's torso was cradled in her arms. She'd been forced to carry this piece of the ruined body by the two-headed woman, who still controlled her body completely. A length of bloody intestine dangled from the open end of the body, brushing against Heather's leg with every stride. When she'd lifted the torso off the ground, a mass of steaming organs had spilled onto the forest floor. She'd felt instantly sick, but the two-headed puppet master manipulated the part of her mind that controlled such reactions and the feeling abruptly vanished.

So she'd made the return trip through the woods. Josh and the teenage girl followed her back to the road, each carrying their own grisly burden. Josh had been made to dismember the psycho's body with the chain saw, removing the arms, legs, and head. He was carrying as much of the body as he could manage in one trip. The teenager, whose name they'd learned was Stephanie, stumbled out of the woods with the lower half of her sister's body clutched in her thin arms.

And now here they were again, back on Wickman Road. Craig and the two-headed woman appeared oblivious to their return. The woman was sitting on the edge of the Towncar's hood, the black dress hiked up around her waist, her legs splayed with one foot propped on the bumper. Craig was on his knees, his head buried in her crotch. Handfuls of his sandy brown hair were knotted in her fists. The pretty head was silent, but the hag head was making a slurping, panting sound. Heather needed a moment to recognize this as evidence of sexual excitement.

The two-headed woman let go of Craig's hair and pushed him away. He fell onto his back and blinked dumbly up at her for a moment. His eyes had the warm, empty glaze of a heroin addict after a fix. Then he gave his head a hard shake and the dullness seeped out of them. He saw Heather and grinned, leaping to his feet as the two-headed woman moved away from the car and pushed her dress down.

"Whoa." He got up close to Heather and groped the dead girl's breasts. "Holy shit, somebody really did a number on this babe." He grinned. "Friend of yours, Heather? Man, I sure fuckin' hope so."

Heather felt the freak relinquish a bit of control, a deliberate, measured retreat. Just enough to allow Heather to speak. "You sick son of a bitch."

Craig's expression darkened. "What did you say?"

Heather felt an additional relaxing of control. She worked up a mouthful of moisture and delivered a spit dead-center to his face. The wad of saliva ran down the side of his nose and into his mouth. Rage flared in his remaining eye and his features contorted in a silent snarl. Then he raised a fist.

But something odd happened in mid-swing. His arm jerked wildly and the fist went wide of her face. His body followed the momentum of the off-target punch and tumbled to the road. Then he convulsed, his arms and legs flopping about like those of a man being electrocuted. It was a horrifying thing to see, but Heather derived a wicked dose of satisfaction from seeing the evil fuck suffer.

*Do you like that?*

Heather blinked. It took her a moment to realize it was the two-headed woman communicating with her in her mind. She was unsure of the proper way to respond, then just allowed the thought to coalesce in her mind: *I don't know.*

Heather's gaze moved from Craig's twitching form to the two-headed woman. A smug smile touched the pretty head's mouth.

*Nonsense.* The voice resonated in her mind again. *You love it. You want to see him die. It's what he deserves, isn't it?*

Heather regretted the thought the moment it formed. But there was no way she could bring it back, no way she could ever hide her thoughts from this creature. She thought: *You deserve even worse, you evil bitch.*

Craig's body suddenly stopped twitching and he lay panting in the road. The two-headed woman held Heather's gaze a moment longer, delivering a final private communication before retreating: *You had an opportunity, but it is gone. You will suffer for your insolence.*

Craig pushed himself up, first to his hands and knees, then to an unsteady standing position. He cast a wary, frightened glance at the two-headed woman. "You keep doing that, lady, and you'll be in the market for a new driver again real soon. I swear, my heart will flat-out stop the next time you do that."

The two-headed woman's pretty head smiled. "I enjoy playing with you, pet. And your heart will not cease beating even one instant before I will it to do so."

Craig shuddered. "That's . . . comforting. Sort of. But not really."

The pretty head chuckled. "I care not how my treatment of you makes you feel. However, I think you'll be pleased by the next phase of the evening's festivities." Her gaze shifted to Heather. "Especially by what I have in mind for this one."

Craig frowned. "Hmm . . . er . . . say, I was kinda hoping—"

"Shut up."

Craig closed his mouth, whatever protest he'd been about to voice silenced forever by the freak's stern tone. Heather sensed his fear, but it evoked no sympathy in her. Threats aside, it was clear he was reveling in the madness that had gripped this town. The memory of his fascination with serial killers came back to her

with a forceful clarity, and she felt a flush of shame
that she'd known about that and had stayed with him
anyway. Her fear of his temper had only been a minor
part of it, she knew. Mostly she'd attributed his morbid
fixation to a gleeful taste for shock value. Obnoxious,
yes, but ultimately harmless. Jesus, how wrong and
stupid she'd been. All because she'd loved fucking him
so much. She'd been so shallow, so foolish. And the
worst of it was there was no way she'd have a chance
to apply these hard-learned lessons to later relationships. She was going to die tonight, probably right
here on this road. The two-headed woman was watching her again, so intently now it seemed to Heather she
was hearing her thoughts, which was probably the
truth.

The pretty head smirked, erasing all doubt on that
count.

Then the freak turned away and moved to the front
of the car. The pretty head closed its eyes and tilted its
chin skyward. The hag head ceased hissing and
sagged a bit. Its eyes closed, too. Wave after wave of
frustration crashed through Heather as she watched
the freak. Again, it seemed oblivious to them. And yet
again, it retained absolute control over them. She
wished so much she could drop the poor dead girl's
torso and dash into the woods, where she'd gladly
take her chances in the dark maze of trees, rocks, and
bramble. And yet again she felt like a fool as she recalled Josh's insistence that they make their way out of
town through the forest. If she'd just listened to him,
they could be making their way to safety even now. Instead they were frozen like statues on this godforsaken back road. Powerless. Helpless. Victims in
waiting.

The pretty head's mouth was moving, uttering words that were just audible, but unintelligible. As she spoke, a strange thing began to happen to the Town-car. It was vibrating. Not violently, but noticeably, undeniably. The air around the car grew hazy and the car itself shimmered, taking on a malleable, almost organic appearance, like black leather. Or the flesh of a reptile. Then there was a metallic thunk and the hood popped open. The hood rose seemingly of its own accord until it was perfectly vertical. The exposed engine was like a synthesis of a normal car engine and what Heather imagined the inner workings of an extrater-restrial spacecraft would look like. At its center was a gleaming silver disc the size of a large trash can lid. The disc flipped up, revealing a dark, well-like shaft. Occasional flashes of color were visible in that dark-ness and a chilling sound like the commingled voices of millions of damned souls emanated from the open-ing, raising goose bumps all over Heather's body. It was a swirling, howling cascade of agony.

The shaft opening swelled and pushed outward like a fat black lip. The howling increased in volume and intensity and after a moment Heather added a scream of her own to the cacophony of pain, because her body was moving toward the engine and the dark shaft. Again, she exerted every shred of will she possessed in an effort to break free of the two-headed freak's influ-ence, but it was a futile gesture. Soon she was standing at the front of the car and staring into the dark shaft. She felt something drawing her toward that darkness, something perhaps even more powerful than the two-headed woman, and for a moment she hoped that blackness would pull her all the way in and take her away from this world of pain and despair. She felt this even though she sensed something other than damned souls in that space, something big and slavering, a monstrous entity so foul and debased it made the worst human monsters seem like saints by comparison. Maybe this was the opening to hell itself and the thing she sensed lurking in the darkness was Satan, or maybe it was the King of the Freaks, some huge, unspeakably vile, deformed thing, a giant slug or worm with a human face. Whether the place beyond the opening was actually hell or not was almost immaterial. It was clearly a place beyond this world. A very, very *bad* place.

Heather leaned forward over the opening, bending her body slightly at the waist. Her heart raced and terror engulfed her yet again. Her panic-stricken mind sent a desperate plea to the skies (to God, or whoever was really in charge), recanting her earlier wish to fall into that black place. She leaned closer still to the opening and the howling screams now seemed to buffet her face like a hurricane wind. She was sobbing and babbling barely coherent pleas to make this stop.

And then she realized her arms were moving toward the shaft, extending the broken bundle of flesh and bones that had once been one half of a vivacious teenage girl. Tears coursed freely down Heather's cheeks as she pushed the body fragment into the opening. She heard a roar and then sensed something rushing up at her. She loosed another scream as whatever it was grabbed the body part and abruptly sucked it through the opening. Next there was an unmistakeable sound of . . . chewing. A wet, sloppy chewing.

Then another roar. Heather saw a flash in the darkness. A blast of fire. And then she was stepping backward away from the car and watching as Josh went through the same ordeal she'd just endured. She saw the same soul-shredding terror she'd felt etched in his features. She felt a perfect empathy for him. But empathy did nothing to dilute the relief she felt at no longer being the one who had to stare into that awful, hungry darkness. *Anyone but me,* she thought, accepting the selfishness of this and knowing it to be true despite the accompanying burst of shame.

When Josh was done, he staggered away from the car and Stephanie approached the opening. Fresh tears stung Heather's eyes as she watched the weeping, trembling girl stuff the lower half of her sister's body into the darkness. The dead girl's legs protruded from the opening like the legs of a swimmer sticking out of the ocean in mid-dive. Then they were sucked into the shaft and Heather heard that hungry chewing sound again. The two-headed woman seized a handful of Stephanie's long hair and yanked her away from the opening, cackling at the pained sound she made. She gave the teenager a shove, sending her sprawling to the road.

Next up was Craig, who emptied the contents of a burlap sack into the opening. Heather saw a head and what might have been human organs tumble out of the sack. The chorus of agonized voices rose again. Then the silver disc slammed shut, silencing the overwhelming sound so abruptly that the absence of it initially felt like something had sucked all the air out of the world. Heather couldn't breathe for a moment. Then she gasped and sucked in air desperately. As she swallowed hard and tried to regain control of her breathing, the Towncar's hood began to slowly descend, again seeming to move of its own accord, smoothly shutting itself.

The thing wasn't really a car. That much was obvious by now. It was a machine, partly, of some arcane construction, but it was also alive. It was a thing wholly beyond Heather's understanding. And accepting it as something real was something she just couldn't handle. Accepting the freaks as real had been one thing, but this was beyond the fucking pale. It just couldn't be. As far as she was concerned, this meant everything else wasn't real, either. Oh, it all felt real. Tangible. Tactile. But it wasn't. It was just the most vivid nightmare of her life. Either that, or she was a mental patient in an asylum trapped in some kind of permanent delusion. Even the latter possibility, bleak as it was, was better than the ridiculous notion that any of this was real.

The two-headed woman smiled at her. "It's all real, Heather. And you're about to find out just how real."

Heather had no time to ponder the possible significance of these words. The Towncar's four doors popped open at once. Then Heather was again moving against her will, her body being directed toward one of the rear doors. She slid into the backseat, stopping in the middle as Josh and the two-headed woman slid in on either side of her. The rear doors thunked shut. A glass partition separated the front and back seats. The leather seats felt oily, like the flesh of a seal or some other sea creature. The upholstery seemed to adhere to her body. The air in the car felt thick and soupy, like fog minus the visible mist. Her lungs felt congested with it and again she had difficulty breathing.

She looked at the two-headed woman through a new welling of tears. "Please just kill me. If this is really real, I don't want to live anyway."

The pretty head smiled again. "Oh, I'd never dream of letting you off so easily, dear." The hag head hissed loudly and a black length of forked tongue flicked out of its mouth. "This is where the real fun begins."

She snapped her fingers and the glass partition began to shimmer. Then it was gone, as if it had never been there. Heather saw Craig sitting behind the steering wheel, turned sideways in his seat and staring perplexedly at the space once occupied by the partition. Stephanie was in the passenger seat, her back to the door. Her face was a mask of tears, blood, and grime. The poor girl had endured so much. It was wrong that someone so young was trapped in this madness, too. For the first time in a while, anger penetrated Heather's fear and selfish wishes for magical deliverance from this nightmare. But the emotion was as impotent as ever.

The two-headed woman placed a hand on Heather's knee and squeezed. Then she ran a hand up her thigh and squeezed again. The pretty head moved close to her ear and spoke in a whisper, "This'll blow your mind."

Then she laughed and removed her hand. "Watch this."

Heather leaned forward—again impelled by the two-headed woman's will—until she had a clear view of the entire front seat area. As she watched, the molded plastic of the dashboard seemed to thicken and protrude over the radio and air vents. The plastic rippled and seemed to breathe. Then there was a ratcheting sound as the stick shift began to elongate and inflate. The plastic grip took on a fleshy texture, and the entire column began to writhe like something alive. Though it more closely resembled an appendage of some sci-fi movie monster now, it retained some of its stick shift attributes, with the letters P, R, N, D, and L still clearly printed atop the fleshy grip—but now some sticky, oily substance was oozing between the letters and dripping onto the seat. The strange column rose higher still, nearly reaching the car's roof, then flexed toward the backseat, the oily grip hovering over the seat divider, the knobby top part a twitching, questing tendril.

Heather was so entranced by the strange transformation that she didn't immediately feel the grasping hands of the other backseat occupants. Then it hit her. Josh was undoing the buttons of her blouse. The two-headed woman had opened Heather's jeans and was gripping them by the waist. And now Heather was raising herself off the seat so the freak could tug the jeans down past her ass. Except that wasn't exactly right. *Raising herself* implied a choice, and there was no choice here, just the the goddamned freak still manipulating her every move. And now she was sitting on her bare ass, the strangely textured leather adhering almost hungrily to her exposed flesh as she lifted her legs to allow the two-headed woman to pull her jeans the rest of the way off. Then Josh finished getting her blouse and bra off and she was completely stark fucking naked.

The stick shift creature twitched excitedly as Heather shifted position, turning around to brace her knees on the edge of the backseat and lifting her ass up over the seat divider. She knew what was happening now, knew what the thing had become. It was insane. Beyond insane. The terror she felt now was beyond quantifying. It felt like her mind was about to break into a million little pieces. And there was anger again. She imagined twisting the two-headed woman's heads off as easily as a child would decapitate a Barbie doll. Murderous, unadulterated, boiling rage sizzled through her veins. She would do anything—kill anyone, betray anyone, any fucking thing at all—to prevent this most perverse of all possible violations from occurring.

Then she let out a cry as the shaft abruptly penetrated her.

And another as it inflated some more inside her. It reached deep inside her, filling her up, oozing a thick lubricating fluid to allow for smoother movement. Then it began to move in and out. Slowly at first, then building momentum. In a while the artificial lubrication became unnecessary as her own body responded to the thrusting. She cried out again, but this time the sound was elicited by more than just pain, fear, and anger. An intense ecstasy made her whole body quiver. The freak was working in her brain again, manipulating her pleasure centers, forcing her to enjoy this repulsive act. She was angrier than ever now. But, though it was forced, the pleasure was real. She arched her back higher still and thrust herself harder against the shaft. The pleasure began to engulf her, so much so that all the other emotions were temporarily swallowed in its wake. But that was okay for now. The only way to get through this was clearly to lose herself in it. She braced her hands against the backseat and squealed her ecstasy as the thing relentlessly worked at her. The two-headed woman slid beneath her and each head suckled on a breast. Not even the sight of the hag head's forked tongue sliding around her nipple could cause the pleasure to abate as orgasm after orgasm shuddered through her.

The two-headed woman's pretty head moved away from her breast and looked up at her, smiling almost sweetly. "Here it comes."

She slid away from Heather and laughed.

Then the shaft arched inside her, almost lifting her off the seat as it thickly discharged some substance inside her. Heather screamed herself hoarse during the discharge, then fell panting against the seat as the shaft retracted, pulling out of her with a wet plop. Heather kept her face pressed against the upholstery for a long time, waiting for her galloping heart to slow. When she heard crying, she assumed the tears were her own, but her face was dry.

Then she looked to her right and saw that Josh was sobbing. He saw her looking at him and started crying even harder. "Heather . . . I-I'm so . . . sorry. . . ."

Heather sniffled. "It's not your fault. You did nothing wrong."

And it was true. She knew Josh was as much a slave to the two-headed woman's will as she was. And seeing his grief made things a little more bearable. It was human. It was real. Clear evidence of a good soul; good intact even in the face of the most extreme evil she could imagine. She could hear Stephanie softly weeping, as well.

She heard Craig's coarse laughter. "Aw, ain't that sweet? Your new boyfriend's sorry he helped the fucking car rape you." More hearty laughter. "Damn, but that was a kick, baby. You know, I always wanted to do a threesome with you, watch some other dude put it to you while you screamed yourself silly, sort of like a live porno show starring my hot-ass girlfriend, but this is even better."

Heather at last turned around and sat down. She shot Craig the most withering glare she could summon. "Go to hell."

Craig chuckled. "And after all that, you're still feisty." He turned to the two-headed woman. "Hey, that got me all worked up. How's about I have a go at her now?"

The pretty head said, "Perhaps later. But I'm not through with her yet."

Heather looked apprehensively at the still-twitching gearshift, but it was shrinking now, shedding its fleshy appearance as it slowly resumed its guise as an inanimate piece of automotive machinery. Heather noticed that the car was seeming more like a real car with each passing moment. The upholstery was no longer adhering to her flesh. The air was clear and breathable again. The glass partition shimmered back into existence. Whatever weird mojo the freak had worked on the car seemed to be at an end.

The two-headed woman opened the door on her side and stepped out of the car. Josh opened the door on his side, stepped out, and Heather followed. Her hand swiped at her clothing, but failed to grasp it, the impulse overruled by the puppet master. Then she was standing naked on the side of the road, watching as Craig and Stephanie also emerged from the car.

The freak's attention was now focused on Stephanie. "Walk, little girl."

Heather had time enough to see fear flare in the girl's eyes; then she turned away and walked several paces away from the cars. She stopped in the middle of the road and turned to face them. Heather had no idea what was about to happen, but she was suddenly very afraid for the teenager. A dark foreboding stole over her as she pleaded with the freak: "Please, whatever you have in mind, don't do it. You've broken me, okay? I'll do whatever you want, let you do whatever you want to me, just . . . don't."

Craig laughed. "What a fuckin' idiot you are, Heather. Don't you get it yet? She doesn't need your permission for anything."

Heather knew that, but she felt compelled to plead anyway. "Please . . . I mean it . . . anything. I'll do anything . . ."

The pretty head smirked. "Why, yes, that's true. You will."

She moved to the rear of the car, where the trunk was already standing open. The freak reached inside and removed a tire iron. She slammed the trunk shut and moved to where Heather was standing. She pressed the tire iron into Heather's hand, forcing her to wrap her fingers around it. Craig stepped forward and pressed the handle of a large, blood-stained knife into her other hand. She looked at it and knew he'd used it to end the lives of other human beings that night. Just touching it made her feel foul, tainted, and she feared infection by the soul-corruption that had so evidently taken root deep within him.

She strove to keep a quaver out of her voice. "What . . . are . . . you . . . m-making . . . me . . . do?"

The hag head hissed and the pretty head laughed.

Craig grinned. "Pretty obvious, ain't it?"

Then Heather was moving forward toward Stephanie, who was shaking like a small animal cornered by a larger predator in the woods. There was no denying what was about to happen. No way to stop it. Her mind, that bit of it that was still hers, her conscience, rebelled against it. But she kept moving forward, raising the tire iron over her head as she neared the quivering girl.

Heather stopped a few feet away from her. The girl glanced at her once more through red-rimmed eyes, then turned her tear-streaked face to the ground.

Heather sniffed and said, "I'm sorry."

And she brought her arm down with brutal force, cracking the tire iron against the crown of the girl's skull. A sickening sound rang out and the girl toppled to the street. She lay there moaning, barely conscious, her head rolling slowly from one side to the other. Heather straddled her and raised the tire iron again. She reminded herself again it wasn't really her doing this. Her body was being used as a tool, a conduit for evil. Which was true, but knowing this didn't make things one iota better. She wondered if it were possible to divorce herself from what was happening, to allow her consciousness to retreat to some dim recess of her mind while her body was utilized for this grim work. She tried to make it happen even as her arm descended again, working to achieve that distance, to see but not actually see . . . but to no avail. Her awareness was total as metal again met flesh—and again elicited that awful cracking sound. This blow struck the girl's forehead and split it open. Blood gushed from the wound and the frail, brutalized body began to shake. Her eyes opened, a moment of surprising lucidity, awareness that pierced Heather's heart, a condition that vanished as blood from the wound spilled down her face, obscuring those staring eyes.

Heather felt tears flowing down her face. That was one thing the freak couldn't seem to control—human grief. These tears stung like a corrosive rain of the soul, and there was nothing at all cleansing about them. And they continued to flow as she raised the tire iron again and again, pulping the now surely dead girl's skull.

Then she flipped the tire iron aside and went to work with the knife. She plunged the thick, exquisitely sharp blade through a broken space just below the blood-soaked hairline, driving it through tough bone deep into the brainpan. She gripped the knife handle tightly and worked it back and forth with superhuman strength—strength flowing into her from somewhere else—cracking the skull and opening it as easily as she'd crack a walnut. She reached through the mess of bone fragments and tough tissue, pushing her fingers through the viscous slop to find the brain. Her hand closed around the mass of delicate tissue, then ripped out a fistful of gray matter.

She held the grisly prize aloft, brandishing it like a trophy. Then she brought it to her mouth and took a bite out of it, ripping into the tissue like a Rottweiler tearing apart a chunk of raw meat. The brain matter was warm and slimy in her mouth and as it slid down her gullet she realized she would have to kill herself if the unlikely happened and she survived this relentlessly appalling ordeal. There was simply no way she could go through the rest of her life carrying these memories.

And it wasn't over after she swallowed the last of the brain matter. Of course not. The freak's utter depravity seemed to have no limits. So she was unsurprised when she was made to use the knife to extract the dead girl's eyeballs from her collapsed eye sockets. And was less than shocked when the freak's damnable, undeniable will compelled her to eat them.

Even that wasn't the end. She plunged the knife into the girl's head, neck, and torso several dozen times, ripping at the dead but still warm flesh like a frenzied wild animal. At last, after what seemed like a million years in hell, it was over. She dropped the knife and rose to stand on shaky legs. She cast her gaze downward and examined her own body with a mixture of disbelief and disgust. She was covered in gore. She looked like Carrie after the high school prom. Like a brain-fried maniac in a splatter movie. She'd never felt so dirty, so much like a wallowing pig. She wanted to take an endless shower, just step under a scalding blast of purifying water for hours and hours.

She turned to face the others, who were still standing next to the Towncar. The freak's pretty head was grinning broadly, but she was the only one who'd enjoyed the show. Josh's eyes shone with empathy and pain. Even Craig seemed a little pale.

Heather met the pretty head's gaze and said, "Goddamn you."

The pretty head chuckled. "Such venom. I suspect on some level you're hoping I'll kill you now. But I'm far from done with you." She licked her lips. "You look so lovely covered in blood. I think I'll keep you around indefinitely. You'll be my pet, just like this silly boy." The hag head hissed at Craig. "And you'll learn to love it just as much as he does."

Heather said nothing as the freak laughed again. The threat of a very prolonged period spent in this monster's thrall made her want to scream again. Instead she walked back to the Towncar and slid into the rear seat again. The two-headed woman and Josh took their previous places to either side of her and pulled the doors shut. She heard another door thunk shut and knew Craig was behind the wheel again. The car shifted slightly as Craig reached across the front seat to pull the door shut that Stephanie had left standing open.

No one said anything as Craig started the engine and pulled the big black car forward. There was a slight bounce as the wheels rolled over something in the road. *Stephanie,* Heather thought, feeling a fresh stab of pain and remorse. Then the car turned around and drove over the ruined body again, heading back toward Pleasant Hills. As they drove past Heather's Chevelle, she caught a glimpse of something big situated behind the wheel, a silhouette hinting at deformity. A freak. Heather didn't need to look back to know the thing driving her car would follow them. She thought of her mother's body nestled in the tight confines of that trunk and derived a smidgen of comfort that it would remain nearby. She was suddenly possessed by a desperate need to talk to her mother, to hear that tenacious old broad's cigarettes-and-whiskey voice again. Though she'd disagreed with her mom on many things, she'd loved her very much. Whenever she'd been feeling especially low through the years, a talk with Alice Campbell had always been able to turn her around, make her stop feeling sorry for herself and see that things weren't so bad after all. In retrospect, she'd been an amazing source of strength and an object lesson in self-reliance.

But she was never going to hear that voice again.

Heather began to weep. A trickle of tears that turned into a torrent. She was so lost in her grief that she barely noticed the freak had started licking sticky, coagulating blood from her body. She turned to the left, looking past Josh at the window, watching as the Towncar zipped down Wickman Road. The trees were an indistinguishable blur, a dead mass, the sky above like a twinkling funeral shroud. She felt the hag head push between her legs and shifted slightly on the seat to allow its forked tongue easier access. What happened then should have repulsed her, but it hardly mattered anymore. Her debasement was complete. Regardless of what the freak said, there was nothing else that could be done to wound her spirit more deeply—and irrevocably—than it already had been. She didn't just feel numb, she felt dead inside.

The Towncar turned onto the main road, heading left back toward town. Heather's gaze remained glued to the stand of trees, the wooded expanse thinning, then disappearing as it gave way to the outer circle of residential areas. Individual houses and whole neighborhoods. An apartment complex and a grocery store. And seemingly just an eyeblink later they were rolling through the heart of Pleasant Hills, the small city's pretty but modest downtown.

Josh was looking out the window now, too, suddenly much more attentive than he'd been since prior to Stephanie's murder. And now he glanced at Heather, his eyes bulging and gleaming with fear. "We're going to the park."

In a moment Heather saw that he was right. They turned down a narrow road and the park came into view. The first thing she saw was the dark silhouette of a ferris wheel standing against the sky. Then, as they drew closer, a grouping of vehicles and tents. She could see what looked like a darkened midway nearby.

The two-headed woman sat up, the pretty head licking blood from its lips before it smiled and said, "Oh, goodie. We're home."

# CHAPTER TWENTY

Everything happened so fast in those moments after the pod hatch popped open. Everything was a speeded-up blur, like videotaped images on fast forward. The pirate came through the door and drew a sword. Three of those bloated clown-things followed him inside. The only weapons wielded by the latter were elongated, glistening fingernails. Fingernails like knives, clicking against each other like the pincers of giant crabs. Mike stumbled backward as the invaders approached, bumping against Sheila and setting her to swinging in the dangling harness. He grabbed onto her to keep from falling and she snarled at him like a trapped animal.

Then there was a loud bang followed by a large red bloom across the front of one of the clown-things. The clown-thing exploded and its body shot toward the vaulted ceiling like a popped balloon. Then two more

bangs in rapid succession and two more clown remnants went zipping across the pod's interior, each trailing a stream of blood, some of which spattered across
Sheila's back and the top of Mike's head.

Then Jinx was rushing forward, aiming the barrel of
some kind of submachine gun at the pirate's face. Mike
tensed, expecting her to squeeze the trigger and blow
his head apart with a few dozen rounds. He couldn't
imagine where she'd gotten the weapon. He hadn't
even seen her retrieving it from wherever it'd been
hidden, but he couldn't say he was surprised, given her
apparently intimate knowedge of every nook and
cranny of the pod's interior. For his part, Mike continued to cling to Sheila for dear life, relegated to a role
as sideline observer. He felt like a reporter cowering in
a trench on the front lines of a war, right on the edge of
the action but incapable of making a difference
through actual combat participation. Which didn't
seem to matter, as Jinx appeared to have the situation
well in hand already.

The pirate never moved, didn't so much as flinch
when Jinx pressed the gun's thin barrel below his one
good eye.

"Who gave us away, motherfucker?" Jinx's voice
was low and tense, each syllable vibrant with raw fury.
"Tell me now or you're dead."

The pirate smiled. "Ah, Jinx. Sweet girl. Why do you
assume we were sent against you? Maybe we're here to
help."

Jinx shook her head and pressed the barrel harder
against his face, pushing his head back. "Yeah, right.
And that's why you drew the sword. How stupid do
you think I am? I know everything that's supposed to
happen and you ain't part of it. So maybe you should

come up with a better story before my fucking trigger finger slips."

The pirate's smile didn't waver, but Mike was sure he saw a flicker of nervousness cross his features. It was there and then gone and Mike wondered if Jinx had seen it, too. His good eye flicked to the floor before lifting to stare calmly at Jinx again. "Dearheart, there's no need for threats. The truth is, I heard whispers of something happening and came to see for myself. I wasn't *sent* here by anyone." His smile broadened and the skin around his eye patch puckered. "So let's be smart about this. I've been a part of this madness far longer than you and you can bet your missing knickers I want out. Let's join forces and double your chances of pulling off whatever it is you have in mind."

The pirate's commentary elicited a humorless laugh from Jinx. "Nice try, Wallace. But I don't buy a word of it. You're like a Nazi collaborator in World War Two, in too deep to ever risk going against the powers that be."

The pirate's eye flicked to the floor again, up, and then back in less than the space of a heartbeat. "Well, that's where you're wrong, lovely Jinx, because . . ."

Mike didn't hear the rest of what Wallace had to say because he'd followed the man's gaze and saw the deflated, shredded remnants of a clown-thing dragging itself slowly across the pod's floor. Its elongated fingernails dug into the dirty carpet and pulled the thing forward a few feet at a time. It was drawing steadily closer to Jinx and Mike had no doubt it was still deadly in its diminished condition. And Jinx seemed completely oblivious to its approach. Mike saw through Wallace's delaying tactic at once—the one-eyed son of a bitch had hoped to distract her long enough to allow the clown-thing to get close enough to rake her legs with its finger-knives.

What happened next was pure instinct, a bit of bravery Mike would later scarcely believe. He let go of Sheila and dashed forward, scooping up the clown-thing by its orange hair and flinging it through the open pod hatch before it could even react.

Jinx's mouth froze in midsentence at the sight of the flapping creature passing through the door into the darkness beyond. Keeping the barrel pressed to Wallace's cheek, she glanced backward at Mike, her eyes wide with astonishment. She started to say something, but Mike saw Wallace raise his sword. Mike's heart almost seized in his chest as he realized there would be no time to shout a warning, but Jinx must have read something in his face because her finger squeezed the trigger. The submachine gun loosed a series of stuttering blasts that blew apart Wallace's face and sent his body backward, the legs doing a momentary wild dance before the big man flopped heavily to the floor and lay still.

Mike heaved a breath of relief, but it proved premature as another of the clown-things descended from the ceiling, where it'd been hanging since being blown apart by Jinx's gun. It landed atop her with a wet plop, dousing her with its blood even as its finger-knives slashed at her belly, opening shallow red grooves that seeped blood. Jinx dropped the gun and flailed blindly against the creature. The finger-knives and its elongating, flexible teeth sought her belly again, looking to disembowel her. She was managing to hold it off, but she couldn't get a good grip on its slippery body and

Mike knew it'd only be a matter of moments before it successfully managed to spill her guts on the pod floor. He knew he had to act soon to prevent that, but the spurt of adrenalized bravery that had helped him before was gone. He stood frozen to the spot, helpless, ineffectual—until he heard a sound that galvanized him.

Sheila was laughing. "You're finished." Her swollen lips twisted in a grotesque grin. "You're both dead, you fuckers."

Mike punched her in the face and set her to swinging again. Then he hurried to Jinx's side and grabbed the clown-thing by its wrists, yanking it off Jinx's head before it could deliver a fatal wound. Her face was covered in its blood and she stumbled blindly for a moment as she swiped gore from her eyes. The clown-thing flailed against Mike, but he wrestled it to the floor, pinning it by its wrists. His eyes went wide as he saw the flexible teeth elongate again, stretching toward his flesh.

But then Jinx was back with the gun. She jammed the barrel against the top of the thing's head and told Mike to let go. He didn't need to be told twice, relinquishing his hold on the creature's wrists and jumping backward an instant before Jinx pulled the trigger, pumping rounds into its alien brain. It stopped fighting immediately, its gnarled, reaching hands suddenly flopping to the floor. Jinx picked up the dead thing and hurled it through the open hatch.

Mike looked up at Jinx. She was wild-eyed, her face streaked with freak blood. Her gaze seemed to be trying to go everywhere at once, her head jerking this way and that, aiming the gun here, there, everywhere—

even, more than once, over his own head. He cringed as the barrel swept in his direction yet again and tried not to think of what he'd seen the gun do to the dead pirate's face. Sheila was raging at them the whole time, more fully awake than she'd been at any point since the savage beating she'd taken from Jinx. The sounds that came through her throat were animalistic growls (puncuated with the occasional intelligible bit of profanity), and a red mist of saliva and blood accompanied each outburst. Mike suspected she'd been partly feigning insensibility earlier, just biding her time for the rescue she knew was coming. But how had she known that?

That was a question for another time, though, as Jinx looked to be on the verge of a nervous breakdown. She was moving about the pod's interior now, pushing the gun's barrel into every hole, corner, and recess.

"What's going on? What are you looking for?"

She glanced Mike's way for a millisecond before again resuming her frantic visual search of the pod. "There was another one. It's hiding somewhere. We can't do shit until we flush the fucker out and get rid of it."

Mike frowned. "What are you—" Then awareness dawned and he felt his heart speed up. "There were three of them, those clown monsters. . . ."

Jinx nodded. "Yeah."

Mike got to his feet. "Let me help you look for—"

She cut him off with an intense glare. "Just stay where you are." Her hard expression softened by a small degree. "Hey, I appreciate what you've done. You saved my ass. But you're safer right there for the moment. Hell, who knows, maybe you'll have a chance to rescue me again."

Mike's protest died on the end of his tongue as it occurred to him this was the first time since the beginning of the night's ordeal that she'd expressed any concern for his well-being. His broken nose still hurt like hell, but the notion that she gave even a little bit of a damn what happened to him made him feel a little more warmly toward her. So he stayed where he was, obeying her, watching as she prowled the pod in search of the last surviving clown-thing. Remembering the way the second thing had attacked, he turned his gaze to the ceiling. Seeing that there was nothing there—and no apparent place for such a creature to hide—he shifted his gaze back to Jinx. He wished she'd hurry up and locate the abominable thing. Just thinking about it lurking somewhere in the pod, waiting to pounce on either of them at any moment, set his nerves on edge. It didn't help that the music on Radio Ether at the moment was some creepy, insinuating, sinister thing, with some singer repeatedly moaning the word "undead."

So when the freak finally revealed itself the moment came as both a shock and a relief. As Jinx walked by the open hatch, the creature squealed and launched itself from its hiding place. It'd been clinging to the other side of the hatch, waiting for the right moment. Mike saw it come scampering over the top of the hatch in plenty of time to shout a warning. Jinx, who'd been facing the opposite way, did a spin a ballerina would've been proud of, drew an accurate (and perhaps lucky) bead on the thing in the same instant, and blew it away. She then stood over it to pump a coup de grâce through the top of its orange-haired skull.

Mike let out another big breath. "Holy fuck. I mean, seriously, holy fucking shit. Is that all of them now? Are we sure?"

Jinx nodded. "Yeah. We're sure."

She kicked the thing's remains through the open hatch, then grabbed the wheel lock and pulled the hatch shut. She turned the wheel lock until it thunked shut.

Mike shook his head. "How'd they manage to open that thing from the outside? I thought this thing was an impenetrable fucking fortress."

Jinx kicked Wallace's bullet-riddled corpse. "Nothing's impenetrable, as the motherfucking freaks are about to find out when we invade the Nothing. But a few keys to the pod exist. I'm guessing this fat fuck had one. I'd search him for it, but it's not worth the effort. It's just about showtime."

Mike sighed. "You keep talking about the Nothing. But this is a pretty badass machine we've commandeered. Couldn't we just kill all the freaks with it, then bludgeon our way out of here and not worry about the fucking Nothing?"

Jinx's face hardened. "No."

Mike's brow furrowed. "But why? Seems to me taking the battle into their own territory considerably lessens the odds of our own survival."

Some of the earlier coldness stole into Jinx's eyes now. "I'm committed to a course of action. I will not abandon it. Nor will I continue to debate it with you."

Mike's spirit wilted at that last statement—its air of finality was too total. He sighed again. "Okay."

Jinx shifted her attention to Sheila. She aimed the gun's barrel at the top of the bound girl's head and said, "You knew they were coming. How?"

Sheila lifted her head and leveled a defiant glare at Jinx. "Because I'm the chosen one, bitch. Braddock's successor." She grinned and licked her swollen lips. "You think you've got everything under control, but you're wrong. If you think what just happened was the end of it, you're a fool."

Jinx's lips pursed as she considered what Sheila had said. Then she did something Mike considered strange as all get-out under the circumstances—she smiled. She poked the gun barrel against Sheila's temple and said, "They've put something in your head, haven't they?"

"I don't know what you're talking about."

But Mike was suddenly sure Jinx was onto something. He didn't know for sure what she was talking about (a surgically implanted microchip, perhaps?), but the look of astonished recognition that flashed across Sheila's face was unmistakable. She tried to cover it up, but it was too late—Jinx had seen it, too.

She pushed the gun barrel harder against the side of Sheila's head. "Oh, I think you know exactly what I'm talking about. They implanted a seeing orb in your brain, didn't they?"

Sheila flashed another grotesque grin. "So you figured it out. Big deal. You're already fucked, bitch. Soon you'll be kissing my feet again and begging for your worthless life."

Mike was shaking his head. "Whoa, whoa, whoa . . . hold up. What's a seeing orb?"

Jinx spoke without moving her gaze from Sheila's bloodied countenance. "More freak technology. An organic device they put in her brain that allows someone, probably the ringmaster, to see through her eyes."

Mike flinched at the mention of the tall man. "Oh, shit. Not him. You mean he's seen everything we're doing?" He started shaking, terrified almost beyond measure at the notion of being observed by the top hat-wearing freak. "Won't he be coming after us himself? Oh, Christ, we are so fucked."

But Jinx was shaking her head again. "No. Not if we act quickly enough."

The submachine gun erupted and blew apart Sheila's head.

Mike's whole body was shaking. His teeth chattered as he struggled to get himself under control. "J-Jesus f-fucking Christ! Won't the ringmaster be after us now? She had that goddamned seeing orb whatsit in her head! Now that she's gone . . ."

But Jinx was shaking her head. "Chill out, okay? Think of seeing orbs as being like channels on a TV set. Maybe the ringmaster was watching what just happened, and maybe he wasn't. We'll hope for the former."

Jinx turned away from him and strode back to the command center. Mike followed her, but kept a careful distance as she settled herself in the swivel chair and set the gun on the floor. She glanced his way briefly, then leaned over the control panel and started fiddling with the controls. "We're gonna do this thing, Mike. *Now.* Those fuckers." She smiled bitterly. "They thought they were playing a big game, just toying with the stupid humans, but they never counted on Jeremiah turning traitor."

Mike sighed. "I haven't been here long enough to know what you're talking about. And I don't get this game stuff. Who're the players?"

Jinx paused in her work to look at him. "The ringmaster and Jeremiah sent opposing factions to the pod. They're the players. It was a game, a variation on a kind they've played endlessly through the years. Pit us against each other and see what happens. A bit of casual amusement for bored freaks. In this case a mutual understanding was reached regarding Braddock, the former pod commander. He was old and wouldn't last much longer. The game would determine who would assume the position. That would be me now, but we've changed the rules of the game. Oh, and there's another player out there. Miss Monique, the most dangerous of all. She's out on the town, mixing it up with the human stragglers. It's what she always does. We have to get to the Nothing before she returns."

Jinx again shifted her attention to the control panel, manipulating buttons and knobs as she continued to elaborate. "Jeremiah betrayed them, as you know. My knowledge of this . . . thing . . ."—she indicated the pod with a quick wave of her hand—"comes from him. The others assumed he taught me just enough about the pod's operation to make things interesting. Instead he taught me everything."

"I still don't get what's in it for him."

Jinx's voice took on a somber tone as she said, "He's dying." She glanced at him. "With the exception of Miss Monique, the freaks are as vulnerable to disease and the effects of aging as we are. Jeremiah's time is near. He wants to atone."

Mike grunted. "That's nice. Sounds like a great guy. Except for the bit about making us fuck in front of him. But hey, nobody's perfect, right?"

Jinx sighed. "No. Nobody's perfect, Mike."

Mike detected a pronounced sense of mixed feelings

on the subject of Jeremiah in Jinx's tone. On the one hand, the fucker got his jollies from the sexual debasement of his human protégé. Jinx had been with the freak for some time, so tonight's performance likely had been nothing new for her. To some degree, she probably repressed her true feelings on being used that way. It was either that or go crazy. On the other hand, life as Jeremiah's pet was about the best a human imprisoned by the freakshow could hope for. Which was why he chose to forego giving Jinx any further grief on the subject.

The large video screen shifted from an image of the empty midway to a shot of the rippling big top tent. The pod began to move in that direction. Jinx shot an intense look Mike's way and said, "They'll be onto us by now. It's time. You'll want to grab on to something."

Mike wanted to ask Jinx what she meant, but the opportunity to do so passed as she gripped a big toggle in the middle of the control panel and gave it a savage twist.

The pod lurched and Mike flew backward.

Then there was a metallic screech and everything went black.

# CHAPTER TWENTY-ONE

A hastily thrown-up chain-link fence surrounded the freakshow grounds. The Towncar drove slowly alongside the fence until arriving at an admissions gate, where it drew to a stop. A moment later Heather heard the engine cut off, followed by the sound of a front door opening, then slamming shut. Then the door to her left came open and she could see Craig standing on the other side, holding the door handle like a real chauffeur. The concept of Craig as a chauffeur struck her as funny on a very basic level and she was unable to hold back a burst of laughter. The sound of unrestrained mirth seemed obscenely inappropriate given the circumstances, so she was only mildly bothered when the two-headed woman reached into her mind again and made her stop.

Then she was following Josh out of the car. They walked to a spot near the padlocked admissions gate and stopped. Heather hugged herself and shivered in the cooling late night air. The slight breeze that was kicking up made the chill worse and she wished again she'd been allowed to put her clothes back on. The two-headed woman slid out of the car and headed their way. She had a walk like a runway model, an exaggerated sashay that made her look like a bizarro world version of Marilyn Monroe.

The pretty head smiled. "Oh, Heather. You look cold. Would you like something to cover up with?"

Heather nodded, perhaps a tad too eagerly. "Yes, please."

The pretty head laughed. "Too bad. I like you this way."

Craig had joined them now, and he was eyeing Heather up and down again in his typically slimy way. "Yeah, I do, too."

Heather's angry retort went unsaid as the sound of a chain rattling distracted her. She turned toward the fence (the freak seemed to be allowing them some limited range of motion now) and saw the padlock pop open. Then there was a creak of rusty hinges as the chain-link gate swung open. A lone figure, a freak with a face like a dog, stood on the other side of the fence, waiting for them. His elongated jaw and mouth strongly resembled a muzzle. His face was covered with a thick down that looked like white fur. He even had whiskers and a large wet nose.

They passed quickly through the opening and the freak Heather immediately thought of as Dog Boy closed the gate and snapped the padlock back into place. Dog Boy glanced at Josh and Heather in a clearly disdainful way before focusing his attention on the two-headed woman. He bowed before her and licked her hand. Then she patted his head and he made a sound very similar to a doggy pant before standing fully erect again.

His black lips peeled back, revealing rows of sharp teeth protruding from pink gums. "Everything's in place, Miss Monique. We're ready when you are."

Hearing Dog Boy speak was disconcerting, even considering the virtually nonstop parade of oddities and atrocities this long night had encompassed. Having a name for the two-headed bitch was disconcerting on another, only slightly less surreal level. Miss Monique sounded like it should be the name of a teen pop diva, some bottle-blond music industry hype machine creation. This thing masquerading as a woman was the queen bitch of pain and humiliation, an evil monster capable of levels of cruelty that were beyond human comprehension. Cruella De Cunt—that would be a good name for her.

Miss Monique glanced her way then and Heather flinched, expecting a punishment similar to what Craig had endured. But the freak just smiled and after a long moment Heather released a shuddery breath. Miss Monique made a *tsk-tsk* sound and waggled an admonishing forefinger at her. "Now, Heather, you know better. You should mind your manners when you're a guest in someone else's home. Your mother taught you better than that." Her smile brightened and the hag head made a chuffing sound Heather supposed was some form of freak laughter. "Didn't she?"

Heather's eyes narrowed as fresh anger coursed through her, overriding her better judgement. "Burn in hell, bitch."

Dog Boy glared at her and growled, hunkering down for a moment like a wolf about to pounce, but Miss Monique must have exerted some kind of influence over him because he immediately backed down and moved to stand behind his mistress. The two-headed freak smiled again, an expression invested with a surprising degree of genuine cheerfulness. A taunting quality remained, but the overwhelming malice the creature normally exuded was absent. Heather had no doubt this was a temporary change. The freak was clearly happy to be back home. But her sadistic tendencies would manifest again soon enough, Heather was sure.

Miss Monique swept a hand toward a row of turnstiles, beyond which stood the shadow-cloaked midway. "This way, please."

Heather felt the freak reassert a basic level of control over her body and in a moment she was marching toward the turnstiles, with Josh and Craig following along behind her. Three female freaks stood on the opposite side of the turnstile stanchions. Attired in white short-shorts and skimpy halter tops, their bodies were slim and physically attractive. But one, a curvy blonde with a pierced belly button, had a third eye in the middle of her forehead. The eye protruded in a . . . well, in a freakish way and throbbed like something infected. The freak to her left was almost as curvy and had fiery red hair that fell to her waist, but each of her hands had several more fingers than the standard amount and her eyes were like lumps of coal, black and flinty. The third freak girl was slimmer and not quite as curvy as the other two, but she exuded a slinky sensuality Heather was sure most men would find irresistible—if not for the yellow beak. The beak opened and emitted a shrill squawk as this one took note of Heather's scrutiny.

Heather stepped up to the turnstile manned by the girl with the throbbing third eye. There was a liquidy sound as the eye bulged outward, the pupil dilating as the orb throbbed harder. The third-eye scrutiny made her squirm inwardly. There was something so consummately vile and slimy about it. She'd rather be made to parade naked before a thousand dirty old perverts than endure one more second of this unnatural appraisal.

The blonde smiled and said, "Special admission rate of one finger tonight, ma'am."

Heather frowned. "What?"

The blonde kept smiling as she seized Heather's wrist and brought her hand to her mouth. She sucked Heather's pinky finger between her pink lips and chomped down. Heather screamed and knew a second of mind-bending pain. Her stomach turned at the sound of bone crunching. Then the little finger separated from her hand and blood jetted against the blond freak's face. The blonde maintained an iron grip on Heather's wrist as she chewed on her finger. Then she knelt and calmly lifted a small acetylene torch. Heather screamed again as the torch flared to life and moved toward the wound on her hand. Another searing wave of pain swept over her as she felt the flame touch her flesh, but she felt Miss Monique enter her mind again and in a moment the pain was gone. Most of her left hand felt numb. She was crying again. And though she hated herself for it, a wave of gratitude flowed from the most primal part of her to Miss Monique.

The scent of her own charred flesh made her woozy, and she would've tumbled to the ground if not for the freak's continued control of her body. The blond ticket-taker paced as she continued to chew on the severed body part. She was clearly savoring the morsel, working at it slowly as the corners of her blood-spattered mouth curved upward in a ghoulish grin. Heather moved past her toward the midway, and heard the freak swallow what remained of her finger. The freak groped her as she went by and giggled like a schoolgirl.

Heather heard more screams behind her as she continued toward the midway. She tried to cast a glance backward, but Miss Monique kept her gaze focused on the array of amusement and game booths and sideshow tents that comprised the midway. Something about the timbre of the first scream made her think it came from Josh, even though it was a shockingly girlish sound. Heather cringed inwardly, recalling too clearly how immense the pain had been. Then there was the familiar whoosh of the acetylene torch igniting, followed by yet another, even more shrill scream. She wondered for a moment why their wounds had been cauterized with the torches rather than numbed with the anesthetizing jelly. But the answer was clear—it was just pure sadism.

A moment later another scream reverberated in the nighttime stillness. This scream was also shrill and girlish, but she knew at once it came from Craig. Which was an interesting development. He'd been a willing participant in the evening's atrocities, and he'd apparently been led to believe he was now in the two-headed freak's employ. He'd likely reveled in the agony suffered by Heather and Josh as they paid the gruesome price of admission to the freakshow, never suspecting he would have to pay the same price. She wondered what he was thinking now, whether he was feeling betrayed and scared. She hoped so. He deserved to know unadulterated terror.

As she reached the midway a series of loud pops sounded as previously hidden klieg lights snapped on, spiriting away the darkness and replacing it with a brand of artificial daylight that was initially so bright she had to squint. The game booths were manned by freaks and people who looked human, each of them attired in colorful carnie outfits. Had the freakshow staff been called to duty solely for their benefit? The notion seemed absurd and surreal. Then again, that only made it in keeping with the major themes of the night.

Josh and Craig were standing to either side of her now. Miss Monique moved past them, spun around, and struck a showgirl-type pose, spreading her arms wide as she grinned like a lunatic. "Lady and gentlemen, welcome to the freakshow!"

There was a pause, a moment of near utter silence, then the music started. Loud, jaunty calliope music. The ferris wheel beyond the midway began to turn. The flaps of the big top tent at the opposite end of the midway suddenly opened and a stream of people—human beings, or so they appeared—emerged from the opening and began to hurry into the midway. There were boys and girls, men and women of all ages, and upon each face was a beatific smile. They filled the midway and approached the booths. Some disappeared into sideshow tents. Heather saw a father hoist a small child for a better view of a ring toss competition.

Heather heard Josh draw in a sharp breath. "I wouldn't have thought it possible, but this is a whole new level of fucked-up."

Heather nodded.

The laughing, apparently joyous people filling the midway were all nude. And not one of them seemed aware of that fact.

Miss Monique's pretty head winked at Heather. Her hands swept toward the midway as she said, "Come, dear. Join the fun."

Miss Monique turned away from her and started down the midway.

And though she didn't want to, Heather followed.

# CHAPTER TWENTY-TWO

For a time Mike was sure he was dead. His conscious mind—his soul?—was awake and aware, but floating in black nothingness. There was no awareness of his body and the physical world. In these moments he felt a tentative relief. He was dead, but apparently there was some kind of continued existence after the extinguishing of life. He had passed through the veil separating the mortal world and the afterlife, and, yes, it was a relief to no longer bear the burdens of a mortal existence. He supposed this floating in blackness business could get old after a while, but maybe it was just temporary, this nothing realm perhaps a way station of the afterlife, a place where he must wait while the ultimate disposition of his soul was decided by . . . well, God, or whoever was in charge. But he wasn't really worried about that. He'd been a good person. Not perfect, certainly, but a thoroughly decent human being nonetheless. The more he thought about it, the happier he became—he couldn't wait to get to heaven!

The moment he thought this, of course, was when everything began to go to hell.

Mike let out a gasp as bright light displaced the nothing blackness and he experienced the return of the physical world like a hard shot to the gut from a champion fighter. He was flat on his back in the pod, lying directly beneath the suspended body of their former tormentor. Blood was still leaking from her blown-apart head. A drop of it hit his forehead. He laid there for a moment, temporarily paralyzed by a wave of melancholy. There was no relief at the revelation that he was still alive. A large part of him longed for a return to that empty place, that black realm devoid of hurt and fear. A place where there was a marked absence of bullet-riddled heads.

Then the moment was gone and he was primarily aware of a sound he'd heard before—*bambambambam*—a grinding, banging sound that was loud, but not as loud as he remembered. And he realized why that was—because now they were inside the machine creating that noise, whereas before they'd been pursued by it. The pod was on the move. He remembered the deadly metallic tentacles and wondered if Jinx knew how to operate them. He sure fucking hoped so. The fearsome things would come in handy now that they were in the enemy's home territory. And he suspected they would need every weapon at their disposal to do whatever it was they'd come here to do without being killed first.

He rolled away from Sheila's suspended corpse a moment before another drop of her blood would have struck him. He sat up and saw Jinx seated at the command center. She was leaning over the control panel, one hand fastened around a toggle while the other worked different controls. Her gaze was fixed on the largest video screen, which was displaying an image of the world beyond the pod. The Nothing. From Mike's vantage point, it looked like a place only a lunatic could love. He could discern shapes here and there, things that might have been buildings or strange monuments, but everything was swamped in low-lying mist. This had the effect of making the place look like an alien city floating on a cloud.

Mike got to his feet and approached the command center for a closer look. Jinx glanced at him as he came up beside her. The set of her face was grim, but her eyes flashed with what he was sure was excitement. It was the look of a fighter plane pilot descending from the clouds to strike at enemy territory.

"Sorry I can't offer you a seat, Mike. You might want to go grab onto the dead bitch again in a minute. Things will be getting rough again soon."

Mike sighed. "I was afraid of that. So what happened a minute ago, when everything went black?"

Her gaze went back to the large video screen as she addressed Mike's question. "That was this thing, the pod, forcing a temporary rift between dimensions, allowing us to pass into the Nothing."

"I thought I was dead."

Jinx nodded. "Temporal displacement. It's what happens when you force a rift to open rather than passing through one of the naturally accessible gaps."

Mike grunted. "I was happy. I thought this was over. I thought I was on my way to heaven."

She glanced at him again and her expression was

softer this time. "I'm sorry, Mike. But this will be over soon."

Mike watched the big video screen. The sky in the Nothing was a bright arterial red. As he stared in amazement at the alien landscape, he began to perceive another sound filtering through the grind of the pod's progress. The sound sent a chill through him and made his heart flutter. It was like a chorus of screams. He wanted to think it was just a strong whistling wind, but that was impossible to believe after only a few moments of focusing on it.

Screams. Those were definitely screams.

He shuddered. "What the hell is that screaming sound?" He leaned forward a bit, squinting his eyes and craning his neck up at the big screen. "I don't see any people out there. No freaks, either. Where is that coming from?"

Jinx looked at him. "Those are wailing souls. Human souls. They're trapped in the Nothing, where their physical bodies died. They can't escape to the afterlife, because that realm is only accessible from our world."

The notion disturbed Mike to the core. "They sound like they're in pain."

Jinx nodded. "They are, inasmuch as disembodied souls can experience pain."

Mike frowned, feeling sudden empathy. "It's a spiritual pain. It must be horrible. They might as well be in hell. Isn't there anything we—"

Jinx shook her head. "There's not a damn thing we can do for them. We'll be hard-pressed just to do what we came here to do."

Mike heaved an exasperated sigh. "Which is what, exactly? Cut the mystery bullshit and just tell me."

Jinx opened her mouth to respond, but the words remained unspoken, as something on the big screen seized her attention. Mike's gaze went to the screen again. He saw something, a hint of darkness at the edge of the crimson horizon, but at first it was unclear what they were seeing. Whatever it was was drawing rapidly closer and Mike felt his mouth go dry as terror stole over him again. Jinx tapped a series of buttons and zoomed in on the approaching darkness.

Mike felt dizzy and he grabbed the back of Jinx's chair to keep from falling over. "Oh shit. This is impossible, Jinx. Open a rift again, please. Let's get back to our world and make a run for it."

Jinx drew in a deep breath. Mike had expected another instant denial, but he sensed she was giving his suggestion serious thought. In a way that scared him more than the looming threat. He hadn't been really cognizant of it before, but he realized now he'd drawn some degree of comfort from her confidence and surety of purpose.

She sighed and spoke in the resigned tone of one who knows her fate: "Shit. Even if I wanted to do that, it's too late."

Mike nodded, but didn't say anything. Her reply was what he'd expected.

The image filling the screen was that of a wave of flying creatures. They looked like demonic pterodactyls with huge, flapping black wings, elongated jaws gleaming with rows of sharp teeth, and enormous forelimbs equipped with talons that looked large enough to decapitate a regiment of marching soldiers with one swipe.

Jinx at last recovered the ability to speak. "Grab onto the dead bitch, Mike. *Now.*"

She had some steel in her voice again and Mike

obeyed her at once. "We're so fucked, Jinx. What're we gonna do?"

Jinx didn't hesitate. "We're gonna fight."

Blackness filled the video screen.

Something thumped the pod, making it sway on its segmented, metallic legs. There was a roar from outside the pod and Mike closed his eyes, expecting true death to arrive at any moment.

# CHAPTER TWENTY-THREE

The people strolling up and down the midway were oblivious to more than their nudity. They were smiling, laughing, and talking amongst one another. Heather focused briefly on many random bits of mundane conversation as she followed Miss Monique down the midway. One man was telling another man about his lawn care problems. The other man was chuckling and shaking his head in sympathy. A young mother was admonishing a loud child who wanted money for buying souvenirs. A teenager at one of the gaming booths was loudly proclaiming the game rigged. On more than one occasion she bumped into a nude freakshow patron, who would stumble a bit but not seem to notice that anything had happened.

Heather caught Josh's gaze at one point and whispered, "This is just creepy. It's like they can't even see us."

Josh nodded, his mouth a grim, tight line. "I'm sure they can't."

As they neared the end of the midway, Heather had become sure of another slowly dawning suspicion—the midway people weren't real human beings. Oh, they appeared to be upon first glance. And even at second glance. It took a prolonged appraisal of their bodies to discern the anomalies. It boiled down to them all being too physically perfect. Even the fat ones and older ones. Not one of them had a single blemish or mole. None of the teenagers had a spot of acne. The supposedly older ones had grey hair and seamed faces, but their skin was otherwise perfect, unmarred by age spots, surgery scars, or any other indicator of a long life. Heather believed this was because they were all precisely the same age, and were all freshly "born" (or, perhaps more accurately, created) via some inexplicable freak magic or technology.

Josh just came out and said it: "They're clones."

Heather let out a shuddery, nervous breath. "Yes. They're replicas of all the people who came out to see the freakshow tonight. And I bet when the freakshow rolls out of Pleasant Hills these imitation people will be left behind to assume the lives of the real people the freaks killed."

They had reached the end of the midway by now and were crossing an open patch of ground between the midway and the looming big top. Miss Monique addressed Heather's suspicions without breaking stride or turning to face her. "Such a perceptive girl. You are correct on all counts. This is our annual period of Assimilation. Next year we'll replace the inhabitants of another town with our creations. And another the next year and so on."

Heather didn't relish the idea of conversing with the sadistic freak, but her curiosity level was too high. "What's the ultimate point of this? To take over the world?"

Miss Monique's pretty head laughed. "Why, of course."

Heather frowned. "But it would take forever that way. One town at a time. All of them little towns like this one, I'd imagine. It would take centuries."

They arrived at the big top and came to a stop outside the huge red and white tent. Miss Monique turned to face Heather, a bemused smile playing at the corners of her bright red lips. "We've been at it for centuries already, dear. We are a patient race. In the fullness of time your world will be ours. And when that glorious day comes, we will step out of the shadows and assume control of everything." She breathed a wistful sigh. "Your kind's illusion of normality will be shattered, and those who are different, freaks, will no longer be objects of derision or ostracization. You're all so afraid of anything that threatens your fragile sense of the way things should be." She smirked. "Your kind will wilt and fall before us, and eventually be extinguished from the face of this earth."

Heather's heart fluttered. "Genocide. That's what you're talking about."

Miss Monique smiled again. "Use whatever word you wish. When a human's home is infested with pests, she calls an exterminator to get rid of the pests. Well, that's what we're doing. Getting rid of the pests, except on a global scale." Her smile broadened at the sight of Heather's astonished expression. But enought chitchat about business. It's time for some entertainment!"

Miss Monique entered the big top and Heather helplessly followed her inside. Josh and Craig shuffled along to either side of her. Josh's expression remained grim but otherwise unreadable, whereas Craig's evinced quite a bit more fear and uncertainty with every passing moment.

Her former boyfriend saw Heather looking his way and flinched. "Stop looking at me like that."

Heather's expression remained blank, but she felt a smug satisfaction at seeing his discomfort. "She made you think you'd been taken into her inner circle. Or something like that, right? And now you know you're just another pest."

Craig nostrils flared as he ground his teeth. "Shut . . . up . . . bitch."

Heather didn't bother taunting him any further. It was enough to know big bad Craig was as afraid as she was now.

They followed Miss Monique through a mini-concourse lined with empty souvenir and refreshment stands, then between sections of silver metal bleachers until they arrived at the edge of a makeshift circus arena. The ranks of metal bleachers formed a silver oval around a large open area. The open area contained an array of acrobatic equipment, including a high wire that stretched nearly from one end of the arena to the other. There were no safety nets beneath the high wire or below any of the other acrobatic equipment. Heather felt a lump form in her throat as she saw a freak prodding a nude human woman up the rope ladder to the high wire. This woman was no replica; the pink stretch marks on her flabby tummy marked her as the real thing. The woman was sobbing as she climbed up the rungs, glancing backward frequently to plead with the green-skinned freak. But every pause earned her a zap from a thin metal rod. One prolonged zap made her sag against the rope ladder and nearly lose her grip. Heather's breath caught in her throat as she waited for the woman to fall. She was nearly halfway up the tall ladder, and even at that height a fall would probably be fatal.

But the freak slid the prod between the woman's legs and she abruptly recovered in time to pull herself to the next rung. Her progress remained halting and unsure the whole way, but she eventually reached the platform at the top of the ladder. The freak prodded her to the edge of the platform. He was saying something to her, words Heather couldn't make out at this distance, but the woman eventually nodded and picked up the balancing rod at the edge of the platform.

Miss Monique laughed and applauded.

Heather glowered at her. "You evil fucking cunt. She's going to fall. You know that."

Miss Monique grinned and the hag head emitted some more of that unsettling, chuffing laughter. "Of course she'll fall. She has no training. I said there'd be entertainment, didn't I? Now then, let's take a seat and enjoy the show. Don't worry, this is just the warm-up act."

They followed the two-headed freak to a bleacher section at the midpoint of the arena, then ascended five rows and sat down. Heather was sat next to Miss Monique, so close that their knees touched. She hadn't had a choice in the matter, of course. Craig was seated several feet to the right of Miss Monique, and he regarded the two of them with an expression that was equal parts jealousy and relief. Josh sat to Heather's left, closer but not within touching distance. She wondered briefly why the bitch was focusing so much of her attention on her, but the train of thought made her uncomfortable and she forced her mind in other directions.

Her gaze went back to the woman on the high wire platform. She was standing at the edge of the platform, shaking like a woman forced to stand outside in sub-freezing temperatures. Her face gleamed with tears that spilled like a rushing river, a perpetual flow Heather knew would only cease when the woman was dead, which was probably going to be any moment. She half-suspected the woman would tumble off the platform before taking a single step on the high wire. But the green-skinned freak mounted the platform and gave her another good jolt from the prod. The woman screamed and wobbled dangerously. Heather sucked in her breath and tried to close her eyes, but Miss Monique, ever the sadist, wouldn't let her, forcing her to keep her unblinking gaze riveted to the platform drama.

By some miracle, the woman managed to right herself and shuffled closer to the very edge of the platform. Though it made her feel like a monster to think it, Heather's coolly pragmatic side wished she'd fallen off the platform. It would have been merciful, that sudden end to this ugly ordeal. Sudden, rushing death had to be a better option than the terror of the impossible trial she was facing.

The woman seemed to compose herself. Heather saw her take a deep breath, then place the bare sole of one foot very tentatively on the high wire. The way the wire vibrated at her touch made Heather cringe. Then the woman extended her arms in front of her, attempting to find some measure of equilibrium with the balancing rod. She was obviously acting on instinct—and probably on dim memories of circus acts seen as a child—but it didn't take a genius to know instinct wouldn't be nearly enough to carry her from one end of the high wire to the other.

Heather said, "What do you get out of this? What's the point of this staged cruelty?"

Miss Monique patted her knee. "Pleasure, dear. Pure, sadistic pleasure. There is no deeper reason. I love to make humans suffer."

"You hate us."

Miss Monique laughed. "Yes."

"Why?"

Miss Monique seized Heather's mutilated hand and held it aloft, forcing Heather to look at the expanse of cauterized flesh. Miss Monique grinned and Heather felt a subtle shift in the atmosphere. Then the numbness was gone and the pain came blazing back in. She cried out and tried to pull her hand away, but the freak exerted no apparent effort in holding it in place. Then there was another subtle shift and the pain was gone. But Heather was shaking, the memory of the pain still fresh.

Miss Monique leered at her. "Any other questions, dear?"

Heather gave her head an emphatic shake. She opened her mouth to produce one weak, quavery syllable: ". . . No . . ."

Miss Monique chuckled. "Good. Remember, curiosity killed the dumb human bitch."

By the time Heather recovered enough of her senses to be fully cognizant of everything happening around her again, the woman on the high wire had traversed a quarter of the wire's distance. Pure astonishment swept away the last vestiges of the prior shock. A helpless grin spread across her face as she watched the woman move her right leg forward with great deliberation, taking time to fit the sole of her foot on the wire in a way that gave her balance and grip, the wire smoothly fitted against the expanse of flesh between the ball of her foot and the heel. Amazingly, she wasn't crying anymore. She seemed to have found a zone within herself, a place where there was no room for terror, just perfect concentration on the act at hand. Heather's grin broadened as the woman took another careful, perfect step forward. Then another and another. She couldn't believe what she was seeing. It seemed to defy all reason. But there was no denying the evidence of her eyes. The woman still had a long ways to go—she was closing in on a third of the way across now—but Heather was beginning to feel a cautious optimism. As crazy as it seemed, she really thought the woman had a shot at accomplishing this amazing, seemingly impossible feat.

At which point Miss Monique flatly intoned, "This is boring."

Heather felt another of those subtle shifts, which was really more mental than atmospheric, though it did produce a sensation of warmth and caused the hairs on the back of her neck to stand up. The woman on the high wire immediately wobbled. Heather's heart lurched and she heard startled gasps to either side of her. Craig and Josh. Human monster though he was, Craig was apparently still capable of some degree of baseline empathy.

Somehow the woman managed to remain upright. It took a monumental effort, but she did it, every muscle in her arms and legs standing out in stark relief beneath the bright klieg lights. Heather bit her lip as the woman tried to take another step forward, not willing to give up after having come so far, her goal so tantalizingly close. Then the hairs on the back of Heather's neck stood up again and what happened next didn't surprise her, though was no less heartbreaking for the knowing.

The woman's right foot slid off the wire. She wobbled again and for one last nanosecond it looked like she would pull off another miracle, be able to raise the foot again and slide the wire into that perfect flesh groove. But she missed the wire and fell to her left, the balancing rod spinning out of her grip as she plunged to the ground. The fall was shockingly fast. The woman's head hit the hard ground first and exploded like a dropped watermelon. Heather screamed and tried to look away, but Miss Monique forbade even that little mercy.

Someone was crying. She felt tears on her own face, but the vocal sobbing was coming from Josh. Even Craig's eyes gleamed with faint moisture. The sound of Miss Monique's enthusiastic applause added a taunting counterpoint to their grief. And then the bitch let out a squeal of delight when a lion and its bare-chested tamer emerged from between bleacher sections on the opposite side of the arena. The lion tamer closely resembled a normal human man, but with one glaring exception—the ramlike spiral horns curling away from either side of his head. He had the massive build of a Mr. Universe contestant, and his black leather pants adhered to his flesh like a gleaming second skin. He led the lion to a spot near the center of the arena, where he guided it through a series of flaming hoops. Standard circus animal acrobatics. But what happened next was anything but standard.

Heather let out a helpless moan as the lion tamer led his growling charge to the pile of bloody flesh that until moments before had been a living human being. A very brave woman who deserved so much more respect than this. The lion loosed a loud growl and pounced on the warm mound of flesh, digging into it with a ruthless abandon that was at once sickening and gruesomely awesome in its unthinking savagery. By the time it was finished with the woman's remains its regal face and coat were heavily flecked with her blood.

Miss Monique leaned over to whisper in Heather's ear. "Isn't the animal magnificent? Such power. Such savage grace." She made a low sound of pleasure and nipped at Heather's earlobe. "And so arousing. Didn't that turn you on, dear?"

Heather was shaking. "N-no. It was . . . awful."

The freak stroked Heather's thigh, her cool fingers raising goose bumps on Heather's flesh. She chuckled. "Oh, pooh. I'll have you purring with desire soon enough. The show's just begun. Wait till you see what's next."

Heather drew in a calming breath. "I'd rather not."

Miss Monique laughed some more. "Nonetheless, the show must go on."

The barrel-chested lion tamer spoke some command and the sated animal came to his side at once. The tamer bowed in a very stiff and formal manner, a gesture Miss Monique acknowledged with a curt nod. Then he stood erect, crisply clicked the heels of his boots, and quickly strode out of the arena, the lion trotting along at his heel. Almost immediately more people emerged through the same gap between bleachers and entered the arena. Some were freaks, but most of the new arrivals were haggard, bleary-eyed human beings. The freaks forced the humans to march in a single file to the center of the arena, where they formed a neat row facing the bleacher where Miss Monique and her captive companions were seated. One of the freaks barked a command and the humans (all nude, of course) dropped immediately to their knees and bowed their heads. This had the look of something rehearsed.

Heather's brow creased. "What's going on? This . . . isn't . . ."

Miss Monique smiled. "You're wondering where the circus angle is?"

Heather nodded.

The pretty head arched an eyebrow. "There isn't one, dear. This is merely a mass execution of slaves."

Dread rose from the pit of Heather's stomach like a flush of poison. She suddenly knew she was about to see something very bad. Her jaw quivered as she said, "Please don't make me watch this. Please just kill me now. Get it over with. Please."

Miss Monique drew close again and her voice dropped to a whisper. "I'll tell you a secret." Her breath was very hot on Heather's ear. "You're the only one I'm not going to kill."

Heather whimpered. "No . . ."

Miss Monique's fingertips tickled the small of her back. The pretty head's lips brushed her ear and the hag head grinned at her, its forked tongue flicking at the air inches from her face. "I've selected you to fulfill a special purpose. You should feel honored."

Heather swallowed hard and said, "That's funny, because I just feel sick."

Miss Monique giggled and started to reply, but that was when the freak Heather thought of as Dog Boy reappeared and came pounding up the metal steps. He moved rapidly up the row ahead of theirs and stood panting before his mistress. Panic was etched in the folds of his fur-lined features.

"Madam," he said, struggling to speak between heaving breaths. "A word. Please." His gaze swept over the humans seated around Miss Monique. "In private. Please."

Miss Monique heaved a sigh, a sound that indicated annoyance. But Heather saw the glittering anxiety in Dog Boy's eyes as clearly as a sniper sees the head of an enemy lined up in the crosshairs of his rifle. She was amazed to realize the two-headed freak hadn't immediately sensed her underling's urgency. The bitch was too immersed in her sadistic pleasures to register what should have been blindingly apparent. Heather experienced a flicker of hope. It was probably a stupid thing to feel, especially since at any moment Miss Monique could look into her mind and see this thought. But the feeling was there and refused to go away.

Cruella De Cunt could be distracted.

And if she could be distracted long enough . . . and in the right way . . . maybe . . . just maybe . . .

"Madam!"

Miss Monique at last focused the whole of her attention on Dog Boy. And he must have seen something in her cool gaze that frightened him because he flinched. Probably she didn't like to be yelled at by her servants.

But any punishment the act of insolence might normally have incurred wasn't forthcoming, because she'd finally recognized that something might be seriously amiss.

Heather prayed.

*Here's hoping the cavalry has arrived. . . .*

Miss Monique rose from her seat, stepped over the bleacher row in front of her, and walked with Dog Boy to the end of the aisle. Dog Boy leaned close to her and spoke in urgent but hushed tones.

Then the pretty head snapped back, eyes wide with disbelief. A single exclamatory syllable rang out: *"What?"*

Dog Boy glanced nervously at Heather before again inclining his head toward Miss Monique. He still spoke in an agitated whisper. Though the words weren't quite intelligible, the desperate panic the creature felt came through loud and clear.

Miss Monique was fuming. She silenced Dog Boy with a hard slap across his furry face that rang out like a shot. *"No fucking excuses!"* she screamed. *"Find it! Find it right fucking now!"*

Dog Boy bowed his head and nodded in a frantic way as he backed away from her. Then he turned and dashed back down the steps to the arena floor, where he quickly ducked between bleacher sections and disappeared. Miss Monique remained where she was for several tense moments, her bosom heaving as she breathed hard. Then her gaze snapped back toward Heather.

Heather's facial muscles slowly unclenched.

She realized in horror that she'd been smiling.

Miss Monique held her gaze for a long moment. Heather felt her insides curdle. Then Miss Monique sneered and turned toward the arena. She snapped out a single command: "Off with their heads!"

Heather's gaze went back to the kneeling row of humans. A freak stood behind each of them now.

In the hands of each freak was a gleaming machete.

Heather bit the inside of her lower lip hard enough to draw blood. Its salty tang filled her mouth as the machetes rose high into the air. . . .

# CHAPTER TWENTY-FOUR

The flying creatures swooped out of the crimson sky one after another with a chilling grace, like a formation of fighter planes peeling away to take strafing runs at a target. They battered the pod, making it sway precariously. Radio Ether gave way to a whooping internal alarm, and strobe lights bolted to the wall suddenly came on, bathing the pod's interior in flashing red light.

The strobe lights made Mike feel like he was trapped in Satan's private discotheque, and the piercing alarm tone felt like a drill penetrating to the center of his brain. When a particularly dramatic series of thumps caused the pod to tilt hard to the left, he closed his eyes and screamed, expecting the machine to topple at any moment. But the pod rocked back to the right and seemed to again find a shaky equilibrium.

The assault on the pod continued. Thump after

thump rattled its interior. Mike felt an instinctive relief that the machine was still upright, but he suspected they'd only temporarily averted the inevitable.
He hung on to Sheila's suspended corpse as desperately as a shipwreck survivor clinging to a life raft. He
heard another thump, then a loud, horrendous screech
of pain.

Jinx let out an ecstatic war whoop and Mike's eyes
snapped open. "What was that?"

She didn't acknowledge his question and didn't
seem able to hear him over the whooping alarm. Mike
wanted to go to her, but he was reluctant to let go of
Sheila, knowing another dramatic jolt to the pod could
send him flying against one of its curved walls. He
imagined himself with a broken neck on the floor, dying, useless to anybody—not that Jinx needed his assis-
tance at this point anyway.

He watched her manipulate a double toggle thing
that resembled early video game joysticks. It had
popped out of a previously hidden recess in the control
panel. Mike wondered for a moment what she was doing, but a glance at the big video screen provided the
answer. He saw the metallic tentacles snaking across
the blazing red sky, their pincers snapping at the air-
borne freaks. The creatures came at the pod in waves
now, apparently hoping to overwhelm the pod's external defenses with sheer numbers. It seemed to be a
solid strategy, because for every creature brought
down by the snapping pincers, two or three more got
through to crash against the pod kamikaze-style. And
there were so many of them, enough that Mike
couldn't share Jinx's apparent new surge of confidence.
On the screen a pincer sheered off the wing of an approaching creature. It let out a loud, pained screech

and went spinning down into the mist. Yet another series of bone-rattling thumps ensued.

It was then that Mike noticed something Jinx seemed oblivious to, a pulsing red button embedded in the center of the control panel, just above the double-toggle device she was using to operate the tentacles. Either she didn't think the flashing button was important, or the whole of her attention was on the battle playing out on the big screen. Mike had no idea what the button was, why it was flashing like that, or what might happen if it was pressed, but he was suddenly seized by the notion that pressing the button was critically important to their survival. Maybe he was wrong. Maybe it was a self-destruct button instead. But he didn't think so. He didn't have anything more than gut instinct to go on, but he didn't care. Jinx was putting up a valiant fight, granted, but it was an effort doomed to failure.

He took a deep breath and made his decision.

He got his feet firmly planted beneath him, then let go of Sheila and dashed toward the command center. The pod lurched beneath a fresh barrage of crashing bodies. Mike teetered sideways and only managed to remain upright by falling forward and seizing the back of the swivel chair. Jinx let out a cry at the sudden jolt and twisted around in the seat to scowl at Mike.

"What the fuck are you doing?"

"Got . . . to . . ."—Mike struggled to speak between heaving breaths—". . . push . . . the button. . . ."

Jinx frowned as she saw Mike reaching past her. She faced the control panel again and finally noticed the flashing red button. Mike's fingers were inches from it when she let out a scream and swatted his hand away. But Mike was determined. He leaped at the control

panel and again reached for the button. This time Jinx
drove a fist into the side of his head, a blow that sent
him to the floor. Jinx surged out of her seat, the battle
forgotten for the moment. Unimpeded now by the
darting tentacles, the flying creatures intensified their
assault on the pod. The pod rocked and rolled and
now there was a sound of squealing metal. Mike feared
the creatures would eventually manage to tear the pod
open and snatch them out.

But Jinx was so consumed with rage at Mike's inter-
ference that she no longer seemed to care. Her eyes
were wide and her nostrils flared as she seethed. Her
hands clenched and unclenched. She looked like she
wanted to tear Mike apart. "Are you out of your fucking mind!?" she shouted above the blaring alarm.
"You don't know what that goddamned button is, you
fucking idiot! Hell, I don't know what it is, either."

Mike tried to sit up.

Jinx kicked him in the stomach and he folded up on
the floor, moaning in pain. "Stay down. Get up again
and I'll break your fucking neck! I won't let you get me
killed before I finish this, do you fucking hear me?"

The pod lurched hard to the left again and Jinx fell
on top of him. She immediately tried to rise, but Mike
grabbed hold of her and pulled her close. He spoke
with an intense urgency, hoping to get through to her
before it was too late. "Listen to me. That button may
be our only chance. Maybe it'll blow this goddamn
thing to bits. But maybe it's something else, something
that'll help."

Jinx's expression remained a study in unadulterated
anger. She looked ready to fulfill the neck-breaking
threat any second. But something within her must

have responded to Mike's suggestion, because she hesitated. She shook her head and said, "Goddammit, Mike."

Another metallic squeal from above caused her to break out of Mike's embrace. She held his gaze for another moment as the pod swayed like a thin tree in a hurricane gale. Then she scrambled toward the command center on her hands and knees, pulled herself into the swivel chair and leaned over the control panel. Mike's heart pounded as he watched her stare at the blinking red button for a long moment. He wanted to scream at her. She was taking too long. There was no time to think about this; couldn't she see that?

Then he saw her grit her teeth and stab the button with an index finger.

Mike heard a dim electronic pulse, a sound emanating from the pod's exterior. It didn't sound like anything too fearsome to him, but the effect it had on the flying creatures proved otherwise. Their screeches blotted out any other perceivable sound for several moments. The pod stopped swaying. Mike's gaze went to the big screen and he watched in astonishment as the creatures spun about in pained confusion. They screamed and flew into each other. All of them eventually plummeted into the mist below.

There was a strange moment of absolute stillness. The creatures were gone. Their anguished cries no longer filled the air. The pod was still standing. The blaring alarm had ceased and the strobe lights had given way to the pod's normal interior lighting. Jinx sat hunched over the control panel, blinking up at the screen in disbelief.

Then Mike let out a big breath and said, "Holy shit."

Radio Ether came back on as he got to his feet, for once playing a song Mike recognized, "Psycho Killer" by the Talking Heads. He cringed as a flash of pain rippled through his abdomen. Then he staggered over to the command center and stood next to Jinx. He stared up at the screen and shook his head. "I'll be damned. It really worked."

Jinx sighed. "I'm sorry."

Mike waved his hand in a dismissing gesture. "Don't worry about it. So what do you think that was? Some EMP-type thing?"

Jinx shrugged. "Must be. Only way more hardcore and lethal." She shook her head. "Jeremiah never mentioned anything like that. Jesus. Okay, let's get back to business."

She leaned over the control panel again and pressed a button that caused the double-toggle device to flip over and slide back into its recess. Then she again gripped what Mike now thought of as the steering toggle. The pod gave a metallic groan and again began to move deeper into the Nothing.

Mike sucked moisture from the corners of his mouth. "That doesn't sound good. This thing couldn't have taken much more of that."

Jinx shot him a grin. "At least we'll know to use your magic button right away if they send more of those fuckers against us."

Mike frowned. "Yeah . . . hmm, I wonder if it'd work on anything other than those flying things."

Jinx shrugged again. "I sure hope so."

Mike went back to watching the big screen. They moved through an open space. The screen showed only red sky and that swirling mist. Then the pod tilted forward slightly and they seemed to be moving downhill. The mist receded somewhat a few minutes later as they reached level ground again, and soon they came upon another cluster of buildings and tall dark towers.

Mike stroked his chin as he stared at the screen and thought about what he was seeing. There had obviously been some sort of established freak civilization in this place Jinx called the Nothing. The buildings alone were evidence of that. But there was no indication of a thriving society inhabiting this strange city. And little wonder—everything about this queer realm marked it as a blighted, dying place.

"I think I get it now."

Jinx glanced at him. "Yeah? Get what?"

Mike cleared his throat. "This place, the Nothing, it's . . . diseased somehow. It's been dying for a long time. For centuries. And that's why the freaks are slowly and subtly worming their way into our world. They want to leave this tainted place behind and claim our world as their own."

Jinx smiled. "That's a very interesting theory."

Mike shifted his gaze from the screen to Jinx. "Am I right?"

"Yeah, pretty much."

"So what are we gonna do about it?"

Jinx's almost langorous smile faded, gave way to a pinched expression that hinted at a deep anxiety. "We're going to put a stop to it."

Mike made a sound of disbelief and shook his head. "How? With just this thing . . ."—he indicated the pod with an expansive flap of his arms—"against a whole freak army? I appreciate your confidence, Jinx, but forgive me, because I don't share it."

Jinx regarded him somberly. "Make no mistake, Mike, it won't be easy. But it *can* be done. The freaks seem very powerful, and they are. But they're not so powerful that you should overestimate them, either. I don't know this for certain, but I suspect we've already weathered the worst of what they can throw at us here. They're strong, yes, but their resources are stretched very thin. They can't keep us from going where we need to go, or from doing what we need to do when we get there."

Mike arched an eyebrow. "Which is? Seriously, the time has come to share this fucking information with me."

Jinx held his gaze for a long moment, seeming to take the measure of him. She must have finally found him worthy of genuine trust, because she chose that moment to at last share the truth with him.

"We're going to annihilate the thing that keeps them going, Mike, the thing that gives them their power." Her eyes gleamed with feverish intensity. "We're going to kill their god."

# CHAPTER TWENTY-FIVE

The machetes came down.

Heather let out a helpless wail of horror and anguish as she watched the blades chop through several dozen exposed necks. The heads fell away from the bodies as cleanly as those of anyone ever executed by a guillotine. Blood spurted from shorn neck stumps as the bodies fell over and twitched. Heather continued to wail as Miss Monique threw her arms into the air in exultation. The two-headed freak stomped down the stairs to the bottom row of bleacher seats and shouted to the heavens, "Yes-yes-*yes!*"

She sounded like a woman having an orgasm. Maybe she was. Heather was too numb, her emotions too ravaged by the horror of what she'd just witnessed, to register disgust at the notion. She still couldn't believe that it had happened. All along she'd thought some miracle would prevent it. But there had been no last moment of salvation for those poor people, no deliverance from this place of evil by some divine hand. She now knew there could be no God. Or if there was a God, then surely He had deserted this hopeless world, allowing it to become hell on earth. She'd never devoted much thought to whether she believed in a higher power that was overseeing everything, but on some level there must have been some degree of primal acceptance of God. How else to explain this bereft feeling now consuming her? She felt abandoned, alone in a cold universe, a person consigned to an ugly fate with no promise of a reward in heaven. The tears she cried now were bitter ones.

She heard Josh gasp beside her and thought he must be crying again, too. She glanced at him and saw that he was shaking. He was trying to hide it and he was doing a fair job of it, because the shaking was barely perceptible. But Heather saw it, mostly in the way his clasped hands were trembling. And he was sweating, a slight sheen at his hairline. Then it struck her—he was feeling the pain of his wound. She glanced at her own wound, which was still perfectly numb. Had Miss Monique turned those pain receptors on again for Josh? This seemed the most likely explanation at first blush, but then why was he trying so hard to hide it?

Heather looked him in the eye and whispered, "What's going on, Josh?"

Josh flashed her a tight grin. His eyes darted to Miss Monique, who was still standing at the bottom row. She was now engaged in animated conversation with Dog Boy and two other freaks. She again seemed agitated, even worried. Heather desperately wanted to know what could possibly alarm such a creature, but she had to let that go for now.

Heather leaned slightly closer to Josh. "If you need to say something, now's the time."

His thin lips issued a soft, nervous laugh. Then another. To Heather's astonishment, he softly sang the chorus of the Rolling Stones song "Time Is On My Side."

Heather frowned. "Josh . . . what the hell is wrong with you?"

Josh uttered another of those low laughs, then finally sobered. Something in the tight set of his face told Heather this was only temporary. Though it seemed ghoulish and completely inexplicable, her new friend and frequent savior seemed on the verge of sliding into uncontrollable hilarity. Only an extraordinary focus of will—and perhaps the pain—was keeping this from happening.

He exhaled a slow breath and grinned tightly again. "Have you ever heard of Marinol?"

Heather's frown deepened and she shook her head. "No. But it sounds like—"

Josh cut her off: "It's medical grade synthetic marijuana. Used primarily for either terminally ill patients or patients having a particularly rough time with chemo. Now, I'm not proud of this, understand, but I recently bought some off my neighbor. Her mother just died and had some left over."

Heather gaped at him. "Jesus, Josh."

Josh nodded. "Yep. I'm a scumbag. A regular reprobate and rapscallion. Feel free to call the DEA on me if we get out of this." He giggled. The sound alarmed Heather and made her glance again at Miss Monique, but the freak was still immersed in conversation with her underlings. Josh spoke again as her gaze shifted back to him. "Thing is, I had one left over. In my pocket. Well, it *was* in my pocket." Another of those alarming giggles, only slightly louder this time. "I took it about twenty minutes ago on the midway. I reckon I'm about five minutes or so from bein' high as the proverbial fuckin' kite."

Heather shook her head again. "But . . . why? Our lives are on the line and all you can think of to do is get high?"

Josh winced and closed his eyes a moment. Heather saw him grip his wounded hand more tightly for a moment. Then the pain surge seemed to recede as he blew out a breath and opened his eyes. A bemused smile touched the corners of his mouth. "You have a short memory, Heather. Remember what I told you about getting high and watching the freakshow set up earlier today? I thought getting baked helped me resist whatever called damn near everyone else in Pleasant Hills here. I figured maybe the THC turned off a necessary receptor or something."

His gaze went briefly to Miss Monique. The two-headed bitch glanced up at them and frowned a moment before speaking again to Dog Boy and company. When his gaze came back to Heather he spoke with a renewed intensity. "And you know what? I think I was right. The pain in my hand started creeping in about ten minutes after I took the pill. It's getting worse by the moment. But I can handle it. This gives us a chance. Do you understand? She doesn't control me anymore."

Heather's heart began to race. If what Josh was saying was true, then maybe he could overpower Miss Monique, perhaps even kill her. Just thinking that this might be possible made her tremble with excitement, but Josh gripped her by the hand and squeezed it tight. "I'm probably saying too much, but this drug is beginning to make me loopy, cloud my judgment. Here's the main thing to keep in mind. She's still got control over you. She's distracted right now, but you know it's true. Try not to think about what I've just told you. I'm gonna wait and see if an opening to make a move comes up. Until then don't even look at me or think about what I've just said."

And with that he wrenched his gaze away from her and stared down in feigned (well, maybe only partly feigned) shock at the bloody killing floor. Heather's mind was spinning. She wanted to do as Josh said, force the revelation out of her mind, but doing so was going to be difficult, if not impossible. His words had acted on her like magic, lifting her from the depths of bleakest despair to a place where it was possible to hope for salvation again. She wished Josh had kept the information to himself. Better to be out of the loop altogether than be assigned this impossible task. For a moment she was mad at him, but she quickly reined in that emotion. He'd said it himself—his judgment had been clouded. The situation was what it was and there was nothing to be done about it now. She couldn't extract the information from her memory. Doing this thing would be hard as hell, but worth it. Any attempt to escape or overpower the two-headed freak was still likely to fail, but at least now there was a chance— albeit slight—that they could get away.

Except that they wouldn't even have an opportunity to give it a shot if she couldn't stop thinking about it. She started trying to fill her mind with other things, but the attempt was derailed when she happened to glance in Craig's direction. He was still several feet to her right and was staring straight ahead, his eyes wide and radiating shock. Sudden panic made her heart skip a beat. What if he'd overheard their conversation? If he had, they were doomed. The asshole would blab to Miss Monique at the first opportunity, perhaps recognizing it as his last shot at getting in her good graces again. Heather forced herself to take a calming breath. This was another case of the genie being out of the bottle. Either Craig had overheard or he hadn't, and there was nothing she could do about it either way.

So she at last turned her attention to the task at hand. It was true that she couldn't extract the information from her memory, but perhaps she could push it far enough beneath the surface to keep it away from Miss Monique. And that might just be good enough, given how agitated and distracted she was at the moment.

Heather thought of random things. Her first real boyfriend in junior high. Jimmy O'Bannon, whose older brother had gone on to become a cop in Dandridge before that town was wiped out in a terrorist attack. Many continued to insist that had been a cover story for something even more sinister, something the U.S. government was behind, but Heather chalked this up as the usual conspiracy theory babble. She wondered what the authorities would say had happened to Pleasant Hills if the impossible happened and they were able to thwart the freakshow's dark design for the town.

*Aw, shit.*

Not random enough. Or too random, maybe. Potentially anything she could think of might lead her conscious mind back to the last place it needed to be. Heather sighed in frustration. She needed something deeply compelling to focus on, something so big and overwhelming it would smother the unwanted thoughts.

Then she had it—and her heart sank.

Her eyes watered.

*Mom.*

Alice Campbell was the only reason Heather was in Pleasant Hills at all. She didn't hate the town, but she felt no particular nostalgia for it. Alice hadn't loved the place either, going so far as to call it a "blight on the map" when she got riled up about some irritating bit of local politics. But Alice had been stubborn and set in her ways. She was too old to start over somewhere else, she'd said. Heather's eyes moistened again as she recalled her long-held desire to kick Craig out and badger her mother into moving in with her. Now she'd never have that chance. Her mother was gone and she'd never see her again. Never talk to her again. That was bad, but even worse was the knowledge that she'd died in agony. This after an evening spent in terror of what was happening around her. There'd been no final moment of peace or grace, and she'd deserved that. She might have died even if they'd managed to slip out of town, but at least there might have been an opportunity to go gently in some hospital room as morphine swirled through her system and took the pain away. Instead she was a lump of dead, badly damaged meat in the trunk of Heather's Chevelle.

Tears spilled down Heather's face and her lower lip trembled uncontrollably. She barely noticed Miss Monique return, despite the rage the freak was in as she rapidly ascended the steps. Heather let out a startled gasp as Miss Monique gripped her by the arm and jerked her to her feet.

The freak forced Heather to meet her gaze. The pretty head's eyes narrowed as she appeared to do a quick scan of Heather's thoughts. Then she sneered. "Aww . . . do you miss your mommy? Excellent. I've got a situation to deal with here, but maybe later we can get Mommy Dearest out of the trunk and do something creative with her mangled remains."

A sob burst from Heather's throat.

Miss Monique squeezed her arm more tightly and laughed. "Beautiful. I'd lick the tears off your face, but there simply isn't time to savor your exquisite grief. Let's go."

She started to drag Heather toward the end of the row. Craig and Josh rose and followed her down the bleacher steps to the arena floor. From there they exited the big top and began to move at a brisk pace down the now deserted midway. Now this was a strange sight. The midway was dark again and there was no sign at all of the bustle of activity they'd witnessed so recently. You could almost believe it had all been a dream, but Heather remembered the strange nude replicas of Pleasant Hills's doomed citizens too clearly to buy that. She also remembered the sense that it had all been a show put on for their benefit to convey to them the scope of the freakshow's capabilities in one extraordinary display, and she reckoned this was the final proof of that.

They continued at a hurried pace as they neared the turnstiles beyond the midway. The three skimpily attired freak girls were still at their posts, leaning against the turnstile stanchions. Heather cringed as the girl with the throbbing third eye caught her gaze. The girl grinned and inserted one of her own fingers in her mouth and mimed chewing. The other girls giggled.

"Mmmmm." The girl slipped the now wet and glistening finger from her mouth. "I love the taste of human. I'm hungry all over again."

The girl took a step in Heather's direction, but went abruptly still when Miss Monique shot a glare at her. "Back off." Her voice was low and guttural, almost a growl. "Unless you want to die."

The girl lowered her eyes and stepped back after a slight bow in Miss Monique's direction. "Yes, ma'am. I'm sorry."

But then they were moving again and Heather couldn't help casting a last glance backward as they passed through the turnstiles. Third-Eye Girl was looking right at her again. She was smirking and licking her lips. Miss Monique gave her arm a hard yank and she was at last able to shift her gaze elsewhere. Ahead of them was the main gate. It was standing open. The gleaming black Towncar and Heather's dumpy old Chevelle were visible on the other side of the chain-link fence.

As they passed through the gate, Craig blurted out the question Heather had been afraid to voice: "Where are we going?" A hint of his former psychotic swagger tinged his voice. "And what the fuck's got you all in a tizzy?"

Miss Monique whirled on him once they were standing outside the freakshow grounds. The hag head snarled and hissed at him, its eyes narrow slits of fury. Heather experienced a sudden revelation—the hag head's brain was the two-headed freak's real source of power. She had no direct or anecdotal evidence upon which to base this notion, but she felt the undeniable truth of it in her gut. The hag was the power, the source of the freak's ability to control minds and bod-

ies, and the pretty head was only a conduit, a puppet
the creature used to verbalize its thoughts.

The hag head's forked tongue darted out of its
mouth and twitched wildly in the cool evening air. The
pretty head said, "We aren't going anywhere. This is
where you get off, you annoying whelp."

Craig cried out and dropped to his knees. He put his
hands to his ears and released a bloodcurdling scream.
Then his hands came away from his ears and Heather
saw blood leaking from the ear canals. He was shaking
and crying. The freak had done something to his brain.
The whites of his eyes filled with red. But he was still
alive. Whatever she'd done to him, she was holding
back a bit, stemming the flow of blood from the rup-
tured artery long enough for him to experience the
horror of what was happening to him; to be fully
aware of what was happening and know there was not
a thing he could do to stop it. For maybe the millionth
time that night, tears blurred Heather's vision. Craig
had revealed himself to be many vile things, but until a
few hours ago the man had been her boyfriend. She'd
laughed with him. Had sex with him. They had even
robbed a liquor store together. That had been early in
their relationship, back when she'd still been so turned
on by his bad-boy allure. Drugs, of course, had been a
factor, too. Later she'd dealt with almost crippling
feelings of guilt and shame, and they never did anything like that again. But there was no denying the
wild exhilaration she'd felt in the immediate aftermath
of her one and only foray into the world of crime.
Later that evening Craig had scattered the cash from
the liquor store's register and safe over their bed and
they had a long, wild lovemaking session that remained easily the best sex she'd ever had.

And now the guy she'd had that experience with was likely within moments of his death. Despite everything, she couldn't help the twinge of pity she felt for him. But then he managed to speak and the feeling evaporated: "No, wait! There's something you need to know. I'll tell you if you keep me alive." His jittering, red-filled eyes darted to Heather, then to Josh, and back to Miss Monique. "They're tricking you, they—"

"*Shut up!*" Miss Monique's stentorian voice rang out like an explosion in the night. Craig stopped talking at once. He whimpered and his red eyes glimmered with tears as the freak sneered at him. "Fool. You think I don't know about their pitiful little scheme? You should know better than to underestimate me."

The hag head swiveled in Heather's direction as the pretty head kept talking: "You all should know better."

Heather felt like she'd been punched in the stomach. She'd tried so hard to suppress what Josh had told her, foolishly believing they might actually be able to escape. But now it didn't matter. The freak knew of their plans. Heather felt the extinguishing of the tiny spark of hope Josh's words had ignited like a little death.

The pretty head made a *tsk-tsk* sound. "I've wasted enough time with you."

Craig's face went suddenly slack and his body toppled over.

He was dead. A helpless cry of reflexive grief escaped Heather's lips. But any lingering sympathy she felt for Craig was forgotten as Miss Monique turned toward her. The pretty head was smiling in a creepily knowing way that made Heather's knees shake. "You didn't really think you could hide your thoughts from me, did you?" She made that *tsk-tsk* sound again. "I hadn't suspected you were that stupid, dear."

Josh let out a roar and came at the two-headed freak in a rush. It looked like he meant to tackle the bitch around the midsection and drive her to the ground. Another surge of adrenaline made Heather's heart race. He was so much bigger than Miss Monique. So powerfully built. Maybe there was still a chance after all! In her mind she saw a flashing image—Josh tackling her, pinning her to the ground as he used his big fists to beat her to death.

What actually happened was quite different and instantly deflated Heather's suddenly surging spirit. The freak never flinched. She sidestepped him and delivered a hard punch to the side of the head. Then she picked him up and threw him high into the air. Heather gasped as she watched his flailing body go up and come back down. And she screamed when he landed with a sickening crash atop the Towncar's roof.

Miss Monique smiled at Heather. "Now, then. Where was I? Oh, yes. We were discussing your stupidity. Well, luckily it's not your mind I care about. You see, you were right about the real source of my power." The hag head made that chuffing pseudo-laughter sound again. Her hands roamed over the front of her body in a way that was at once obscene and oddly compelling. "This body is actually a human body. A host body. I took possession of it during an earlier Assimilation many years ago. It has served me well since then, but host bodies eventually begin to decay from the inside out and I'm afraid this one is very near the end of its usefulness. I require a new host."

Heather was shaking her head. "N-no . . ."

The pretty head chuckled. "Oh, yes. I'm afraid so, dear. *Your* body will be my new host. I'm as much a slave to vanity as any human female, so I'm very particular about the bodies I choose. I'd thought I might put this off until next year's Assimilation, just keep you around as a slave, an object of amusement and humiliation, but things are happening that are forcing my hand. When I assume control of your body, I'll be even stronger than I am now. A thousand times stronger. One of the many benefits of a fresh host. I'll need every bit of that strength before this night is finished. Your consciousness won't die when I enter your body. Your essence will reside in your brain for as many years or decades as I choose to use your body. And you will always be conscious, always aware. You'll watch me use your body to kill and torture countless human beings and there'll never be anything you can do about it. I tell you all this because I want you to know ahead of time what's about to happen to you, so we can both savor the anticipation."

Heather swallowed a lump in her throat. She wanted to run, but Miss Monique had reasserted firm control of her motor functions. She stood utterly still as the freak pulled the slinky black dress off over her heads. The freak's host body was gorgeous, the legs very long and shapely. She had a flat stomach and her breasts were large and firm. Standing there in nothing but high heels and black stockings, with her long blond hair flowing behind her, she looked like a vision out of some X-rated horror comic, simultaneously hideous and irresistibly alluring. Take away the hag head and she'd have looked as perfect as any Victoria's Secret model. It was a body that certainly evinced no external indications of decay.

Heather said, "What about my hand?"

The pretty head smiled. "Your wounded hand, you mean?"

"Yes."

Miss Monique shrugged. "Clever girl, attempting to appeal to my admitted vanity. But you've seen some of the amazing things we can do. A new finger will be grafted to your hand later. It will be perfect, I assure you."

Heather didn't doubt it.

*Clip-clop.*

*Clip-clop.*

*Clip-clop.*

Heather frowned. "What is that?"

Miss Monique glanced beyond where Heather was standing and smiled. "That's one of my associates, dear. My old and very good friend, Roland Stark-weather, the ringmaster of the Freakshow. I'd won-dered where he was and had frankly become concerned for his well-being."

*Clip-clop.*

*CLIP-CLOP.*

Miss Monique's associate was very close now. Heather had a moment to wonder what manner of gruesome deformity this Roland guy would have; then she got her first glimpse of the ringmaster as he clomped by her on what had to be the highest pair of stilts in existence. Heather's eyes lifted as she took in the sight of the towering figure. He looked strangely elegant in his velvet waistcoat and top hat. He had long black hair and a meticulously trimmed goatee. His eyes were hidden behind lenses that were a swirling kaleidoscope of colors.

Heather stared at the two of them. What a bizarre spectacle. The two-headed supermodel psycho vixen and Ringmaster Kong. She doubted anyone who had ever used LSD or shrooms had ever seen anything even remotely as trippy as what she was now seeing.

Miss Monique smiled again. "Roland tells me a small army has been dispatched to retrieve something of mine that was stolen." She saw Heather's look of confusion and laughed. "Roland and I have no need of verbal communication, dear. And I must tell you the news he's brought is very welcome. I have quite a sense of relief. Roland wasn't as vigilant as he might have been and I was afraid I might have to kill my dear friend. Happily, this will not be necessary." Then her expression darkened. "But this changes nothing for you. The extraction process has already begun. In a moment I will depart this body and enter yours. During this time my power over you will falter. Roland, however, can ensure everything goes smoothly."

Heather's eyes went again to the creepy ringmaster. He was grinning. She couldn't bear the feel of that creepy gaze upon her and looked again at Miss Monique.

Fear stabbed her heart.

She sniffled. "Oh . . . no . . ."

Miss Monique's host body began to shudder. Heather heard a cracking, grinding sound. Her gaze was riveted now to the hag head, which was working furiously to pull itself free of the host body. Literally *pull*. Two tiny, clawlike hands pushed through the flesh surrounding the hag head and grasped handfuls of flesh. The hag head's leathery flesh stretched taut over the withered skull, evidence of the tremendous strain it was under. A low whine issued through its open mouth. Its eyes were wide and gleaming. Evidently extraction was a painful process. The cracking, grinding sound grew louder for a moment; then the freak abruptly popped out of the host body and plopped to the ground, where it lay writhing in the green, dew-laden park grass.

She heard someone say, "Thank God."

Heather looked at the woman Miss Monique had used as a host and saw relief fill eyes that were suddenly very tired. The poor woman. After who knew how long, she was herself again. Human again.

Then she fell over dead.

Heather's gaze went back to Miss Monique and she shivered again at the sight of the freak's true physical appearance. The hag head and tiny clawlike hands were the only parts of the thing's body that were even remotely humanoid. The body below the thing's neck looked like a grey two-foot slug. The thing sensed her horrified scrutiny. It looked up at her and grinned. And it hissed.

Then it began to slither toward her across the green grass. Terror consumed Heather's entire consciousness, obliterating awareness of everything except the extraordinarily vile and atrocious thing that was about to happen to her. But she didn't actually start screaming until she felt Miss Monique's claws grip one of her legs.

And she screamed some more as it began to climb. . . .

# CHAPTER TWENTY-SIX

The pod passed a tall, conical building with the words *Radio Ether* emblazoned in wavy red letters on a side of the black structure. The words looked like they'd been put there by a highway graffiti artist armed with a can of red spray paint. Underneath the letters was the anarchy symbol, also in red spray paint.

Mike shook his head at the image on the video screen. "So what's the deal with the radio station? Except for those bat-people, I haven't seen a single living thing here. But there's obviously someone holed up in the Radio Ether building, right? The dj's between-song commentary sounds live to me."

Jinx nodded. "There's someone in there, but we don't need to worry about him."

"Why not? He's a freak, right?"

"No, Mike." Jinx glanced at him, her expression serious. "He's human. And he hasn't left the radio tower since he was installed there twenty years ago. It's a similar situation to Braddock, the former military guy who used to pilot the pod."

"The one you said Sheila killed, right?"

"Right."

"He can't leave Radio Ether or something in his head goes kablooey?"

Jinx grunted. "Yep."

Mike rubbed at his eyes and yawned. It seemed wrong to feel so tired in the face of what was likely to be mortal danger—he should be so wired on adrenaline and fear that sleep wasn't even a remote consideration. But he nonetheless craved rest. He knew he would sleep for days if he were to ever have an opportunity to lie down somewhere and close his eyes. Thinking about it made him yawn once more.

Jinx looked at him again, her expression softening. "This is almost over, Mike. I know this has been hard on you. I know *I've* been hard on you. And you haven't deserved any of this. I just want you to know how deeply sorry I am that things had to be this way."

Mike dismissed the belated apology with a wave of his hand. He wasn't bothered by the unspoken implication behind her words, that she wanted this said before they went to meet their doom. He knew what was coming and he didn't fear it anymore. Surviving this ordeal would be nothing to celebrate, anyway. His town was gone. Everyone he'd known was dead. "It's okay. Let's just make this worth it, okay?"

A tired smile dimpled the corners of Jinx's mouth. "Okay."

The gratitude conveyed in the single word tugged at Mike's heart. For the first time in a while he was able to appreciate her on a very basic, human level. She was so pretty, her face a study in delicate, sexy beauty.

Her big eyes were so compelling, and her plump lips perpetually invited a kiss. In another life, maybe some alternate reality, he would have quickly fallen in love with this girl. For a long, breath-stealing moment, they shared a look that communicated these things. Then, with clear regret flashing in her eyes, Jinx wrenched her eyes away from him and returned her attention to the command center and the big video screen.

They were now moving downhill. Mike had felt it earlier in the pod's subtle forward tilt, but now the downward angle became much steeper. Mike staggered forward and again gripped the back of the swivel chair. The low-lying mist had given way to a swirling fog that seemed to encompass everything, but Mike saw enough to deduce that they were moving through a rocky valley. The fog would occasionally part in places to reveal ridges and rocky outcroppings. The pod's flexible metallic legs handled the rough terrain so well it became clear its designers had constructed it with this capability in mind. Jinx guided the machine deeper and deeper into the valley, making corrections every time a green light pulsed on one of the control panel's meters, a thing Mike supposed was the ancient freak equivalent of a GPS.

Some fifteen minutes later they'd apparently reached the valley floor, because they seemed to be on level ground again. The video screen showed glimpses of a barren riverbed. "I think I know why they call this place the Nothing. It's because there's fucking next to nothing in it."

Jinx laughed softly. "Yeah. And you were right earlier about this being a dying place. I don't know much about it, but Jeremiah told me there was a war here a long time ago between the different freak races. A big one, like one of our world wars. It's why their world is almost dead. They used what we would call weapons of mass destruction."

Mike let out a low whistle. "This machine . . . it's a relic of that war, isn't it?"

Jinx nodded. "Supposedly there are skeletons of similar war machines scattered all over this valley. This is where one of the final battles was fought, something like seven hundred years ago."

"Damn. And the survivors have been working at this Assimilation thing ever since?"

Jinx shook her head. "Not quite. Jeremiah says it took the survivors a few generations to realize they could never revitalize their own world. That was when they came up with the Assimilation scheme and used what was left of the fallen world's technology to cross over to our world."

"How many earth communities have been Assimilated?"

Jinx shrugged. "Hundreds. Maybe thousands. *Probably* thousands."

Despair fell over Mike like a blanket, causing him to fall to his knees next to the swivel chair. He glanced up at the big video screen and saw telltale evidence of the story told by Jinx—occasional bits of twisted, scorched metal, piles of bones that might have been the remains of centuries-dead soldiers, and a long, phallic-looking metallic device buried in the sand. Mike immediately guessed the latter was an unexploded missile, a thought that made him hold his breath until they were well past it. They continued on for miles, and the barren riverbed twisted and turned like a highway winding through a mountain. At last they left the riverbed and began to move downhill again, the pod smashing its way through the rotten remains of a dead forest. On the other side of the expanse of barren trees was another sloping valley, and at the bottom of this one was the dark mouth of what appeared to be a large cave.

A feeling of dreadful precognition set Mike's teeth to chattering the instant he spied the cave opening. "Don't tell me—that's where we're going."

Jinx sighed. "Yeah."

Mike glanced up at her. "How did you know the way?"

Jinx's smile this time was the most unguarded and genuine she'd ever shown him. "Oh, guess." She nodded at the trunk of video screens. "Watch."

A smaller video screen to the left of the big screen flickered, turned black, then white, then filled with the image of Jeremiah. Of course. The freak's glassy features rippled in an apparent smile. "Jinx, I see you have arrived at your destination."

Mike frowned. "How the fuck could he know that?"

Jinx's gaze remained on the image of Jeremiah as she said, "Seeing Orb in my brain, like the kind the ringmaster had implanted in Sheila. It's linked to a similar device in his own brain."

Mike grunted. "Huh. Yeah. Figures."

The freak spoke again: "The end is near. Roland fell for the ruse. And why not? We'd played similar games so many times. . . ."

Jinx smiled. "You were brilliant, sir. As usual."

The freak's face rippled in that unsettling way again. "Yes. As were you. You know what awaits you in the Dark One's lair. I wish I could spare you this final sacrifice. I wish I were there in your place."

"So why aren't you?" Mike snapped.

The freak's expression and tone didn't change as he

responded, "Because I am old and far weaker than I seem. And because if I'd attempted to commandeer that device myself, Roland and Miss Monique would've known something was amiss. They've long known I've harbored some misgivings about our methods, though I've been careful not to be very vocal about them. They would've stopped me before I could get anywhere, and I would've been killed."

Jinx's nod was grim. "And the process of Assimilation would've continued unchecked."

And now Jeremiah nodded. "Yes. And now the time for talk is at an end. Go forth and kill the Dark One."

The screen again went black.

The pod began to move toward the cave opening.

Mike pulled himself to his feet again. "Just tell me one more thing. Who the fuck is this 'Dark One'? I assume he's the 'god' you referred to before."

Jinx's attention was now fully on the pod's operation. "Mmm-hmm . . ."

Mike frowned. "Do you mean 'god' in the literal sense—a divine, all-powerful being? Omnipotent, omniscient, all that shit? Because if you do, I don't see how we're gonna kill the damn thing. Divine beings are supposed to be immortal."

Jinx glanced at him. The pod was now a hundred feet from the cave opening. "The Dark One is not literally a god, not in the way you understand the word, anyway. It's a freak. The mother of all freaks, or so Jeremiah says. It isn't immortal, but it is ancient— thousands, if not millions of years old. In its original form, it birthed the first freaks, so it is the progenitor of the species."

Mike's laugh then was without humor. "You're

telling me something millions of years old, a capital C Creator of sorts, according to you, isn't immortal?"

Jinx nodded. "It can be killed."

Mike laughed again. "Forgive my skepticism, but how can anyone know that?"

Jinx sighed. "Jeremiah says the Dark One can be killed, and I choose to believe him. He also says when the Dark One dies, all freaks will die. At this point, Mike, we can only act on faith. There is no other choice now."

Mike thought of several retorts, all of them argumentative and angry, but he eventually sighed and let it go. She was right, after all. It was too late to turn back, too late for any course of action but the one that had been chosen for him.

But he was still curious about some things. "There are so many different varieties of freak, it seems. Did they all evolve from the creatures this thing gave birth to?"

Jinx shook her head. "The ones you saw in the operating theater, the—"

"The Pumpkin Heads."

Jinx ignored the interruption and continued: "They are the descendents of the original race. The first freaks, you could say. Most of the others you've seen are a result of centuries of genetic engineering, an effort to perpetuate the species through science that continues to this day. The original intent was to make freaks look more like humans to better facilitate Assimilation. Now the descendents of the original scientists basically do it just for the pure hell of it, to see what new strains of fucked-up humanoid freaks they can produce. Others creatures, the clown-things and human replicas, are just constructs, what you might think of as a cyborg—a synthesis of living flesh and freak technology."

The pod entered the cave and the large video screen went dark. But the pod's external lighting system came on an instant later and provided partial, flickering illumination. The image on the screen made Mike think of a tiny submersible exploring the depths of a sea. The pod's tentacles skittered over the floor of the cave as they moved deeper through the tunnel, revealing an alternate use as a sensory device. The tunnel was narrow at the beginning and continued to contract as they plunged deeper below this dying world's surface. At one point Mike feared the tunnel would become too narrow to allow the pod passage, but then it abruptly widened again and soon gave way to a massive underground cavern. A winding trail led to the bottom of the cavern, where a giant, pulsing yellow blob sat in a vast lake of churning blood. Other than its immensity, the nearly amorphous blob was virtually featureless. It was just an organic mass, an enormous . . . thing.

Mike's stomach did a sudden flop. "Oh . . . shit . . . is that the super-freak?"

Jinx released a shuddering breath. "Yes."

"And we're gonna kill that . . . thing . . . that . . . giant fucking brain of doom?"

For one awful moment Jinx's confidence deserted her and she seemed diminished. She looked like exactly what she was—a slightly built human girl of no special powers. Then the moment passed and Mike's heart started beating again. Jinx sat up straighter in her chair and pushed the steering toggle forward.

The pod descended the winding trail so quickly Mike had little time to think about the apparent impossibility of the task assigned them. The descent was aided by the cavern's natural illumination, which was in the form of glowing organic orbs embedded in the cavern walls. They reached the bottom of the cavern in just a few minutes, and as they drew closer to the throbbing thing and the lake of blood it wallowed in, Mike was able to see huge piles of bones scattered around it, like rocks or shells on a dirty beach. He also saw what looked to be very fresh human body parts.

Mike pointed at the screen. "The body parts . . . where did they come from?"

"Miss Monique. She possesses another of the old one's machines, one that can act as a conduit to the Nothing. She uses it to feed the Dark One. Which is why the wailing souls are louder here."

Mike grimaced. "Fuck! You mean she could show up here any time?"

Jinx shook her head. "Only dead things can pass through that conduit. That's its whole purpose. A kind of interdimensional feeding tube."

"It feeds on people? Jesus."

Something struck the pod from behind as they neared the edge of the blood lake, causing the machine to wobble wildly for a moment. Mike fell against the swivel chair and managed to grab hold of it just before the pod was hit again. Then there was a sound of grinding metal and the pod's whooping alarm started to blare again. This time Jinx silenced it with a flick of a single button.

Mike was breathing heavily. "What the fuck is going on?"

"We're under attack again."

"No shit."

Jinx tapped some buttons and the view on the big

video screen changed to a shot from the rear of the pod. What looked like an army of freaks was charging down the winding path to the bottom of the cavern. They looked crazed, their features twisted with anger and fear. The charge down the path quickly became more like a stampede, with many of the freaks leaping and crawling over their comrades in the frenzied rush to reach the pod before Jinx could do whatever it was she'd come to do. Many fell beneath the feet of the on-rushing horde and were crushed. The leading edge of the stampede had already reached the pod. Freaks were throwing themselves at the metallic legs. Others were throwing grappling hooks at the pod itself. Most of the grappling hooks flew awry, but a few snagged on various bolts and brackets. Freaks scampered up the dangling wires, several on each one. The combined weight of them was slowing the machine a bit, dragging it down. This was the cause of the metallic grinding. The sense of tired resignation deserted Mike then, burned away by a fresh jolt of adrenaline.

He was wild-eyed as he shifted his eyes from the video screen to Jinx. "Goddammit, look at all those crazy fuckers! Where the hell did they come from? And how did they get here so fucking fast!?"

Jinx seemed almost ethereally calm in the face of this latest threat. It was an odd contrast to the way she'd briefly faltered upon entering the cavern. Her tone was very even as she said, "They're here because either the ringmaster or Miss Monique figured out what was going on and sent them. They got here as fast as they did because one of them tapped the very limits of their power reserves to force open a path between dimensions."

"I thought that kind of thing was a piece of cake for the likes of those bastards."

Jinx chewed her lower lip a moment. "Yeah. Under normal circumstances. If the path is from a corresponding geographical space between worlds. But this is different. We're many miles from the section of the Nothing that corresponds with where the freakshow is parked. Sending these freaks from there to here would require immense power, immense effort, even for creatures as powerful as Miss Monique and the ringmaster. Perhaps even enough to kill them."

Mike frowned. "Why would they risk that?"

"Because they don't have any choice." She flashed Mike a bright smile he thought incongruous given the circumstances. "They'll all die anyway if we kill the Dark One."

The pod swayed some more as many more freaks scaled the metal legs and grappling wires. The metal tentacles snapped at them, the pincers shearing off body parts of dozens of the attackers. But there were just too many of them. Soon enough the swarm of freaks would overwhelm the pod and drive it to the ground. Two freaks were clinging to the hatch's external wheel crank. One had his feet braced against the edge of the metal plate upon which the pod sat and was desperately attempting to turn the crank. Mike's eyes darted from the video screen to the hatch. The wheel lock rattled, but it remained firmly locked in place. Though he wouldn't bet on that remaining the case for long.

He ran his hands through his hair. "Shit! We are so fucked, Jinx. Maybe you should hit that EMP button again."

"Already tried that, actually. Didn't work again." Amazingly, Jinx was still smiling. "Everything's fine, Mike. In fact . . . in some ways it's better so many of them were sent against us."

Mike gaped at her. "How in the name of sweet living fuck can you say that!? That's fucking insane!" He gestured wildly at the scene on the big screen. "In what way is there anything good about that!?"

"Because we're gonna be taking them with us."

Mike opened his mouth to say something, but fell into a contemplative silence as he absorbed the meaning of her words. Then he sighed and said, "Oh."

Jinx pressed a button and the image on the big screen shifted from the marauding freaks to the so-called Dark One, who, Mike thought with an inner smirk, was on a very superficial level, the opposite of "dark."

*The Yellow One.*

Mike chortled. "Nah, doesn't have the same ring. Lacks panache."

Jinx raised an eyebrow. "Talking to yourself now?"

Mike shrugged. "Hell, why not?" He nodded at the screen. "Last thing a guy should worry about in a situation like this is his sanity, because clearly it's already gone."

The pod had reached the lake of blood and was now wading in. Many of the clinging freaks screamed as they fell below the swirling surface and were swept away. The pod wobbled more violently than ever, but still managed to remain upright as it went below the lake's surface and continued toward the freak god. The big video screen went dark and Mike knew that this time it was for good.

Mike cleared his throat. "*A-hem.* I think it's high time you tell me how this is gonna happen. If this is the source of freak power, what passes for their god, doesn't it have any way of fighting back?"

"Of course. But it won't matter."

Mike grunted. "*Ooo*kay . . ."

"Have faith, remember?"

Mike sighed and, with great reluctance, said, "Yeah. Okay."

They fell silent as the pod plodded on through the dark sea of blood. The pod's progress seemed lethargic and halting. It was wearing down. The blood was flooding its organic circuitry. The old machine was enduring more abuse than it had seen at any time since that war of the freaks. Mike began to fear it would sputter and die before it could reach its destination. Then the pod rocked as it encountered resistance and came to an abrupt stop.

Jinx assumed a relaxed posture in the swivel seat and closed her eyes. Mike thought he'd never seen anyone more simultaneously relieved and worn-out. Their journey was at an end. But the job wasn't finished. And she was allowing herself a last moment's peace before doing the thing she'd come to do.

Mike reached down and squeezed her shoulder. "We're gonna detonate this thing, aren't we?"

Jinx's eyes fluttered open. She covered his hand with hers and smiled. "Yes."

Mike nodded and sighed. "So this is really it, then. More than once tonight I've thought I'd rather die than continue facing this madness. But now that we're down to it, that old survival instinct's trying to kick in. I don't really want to die."

Jinx's expression turned sad. "Neither do I."

Now it was Mike's turn to smile. "So let's not prolong our misery."

Jinx released his hand and leaned over the control panel one more time, where she tapped a series of glowing buttons, what Mike figured was the self-destruct sequence. When she was finished, she stood and again took Mike by the hand. She pulled him close and kissed him on the mouth. Then she wrapped her arms around him and said, "I'm so sorry."

Mike made a shushing sound and kissed the side of her face. "Don't be."

Jinx pressed her face against his neck. He felt her tears on his skin. "I'm so afraid."

Mike stroked her back. "It's okay. It'll be over in the blink of an eye. It won't hurt or—"

The pod lurched. Someone screamed. Then Jinx was falling away from him as something lifted the pod out of the lake of blood. Mike grabbed onto Sheila one last time as the pod was turned upside down. He heard a sickening sound, a crunch he realized was Jinx's body smashing into the pod's ceiling. Mike wrapped his body around Sheila and clung to her with all his might as he twisted his head to look at the big video screen one more time. The Dark One was no longer just an amorphous blob. The mass had shifted, as something like an enormous black mouth formed in the midst of the rippling yellow matter. Limbs had formed from the yellow mass as well, and these gripped the sides of the pod. Mike closed his eyes and said a prayer. The limbs released the pod and the old machine hurtled toward that yawning blackness. . . .

The detonation was mammoth. It vaporized everything inside the cavern and blew off the top of the small mountain. Debris rained across the lifeless valley like a delayed echo of the war waged there once upon a time.

Somewhere in the distance, Radio Ether went quiet. The Nothing itself was as silent as a tomb.

# CHAPTER TWENTY-SEVEN

Miss Monique's claws pierced Heather's flesh as the creature continued to climb. Blood spilled from the shallow wounds and etched a wet trail down her thigh and over her calf. The creature ceased its ascent as it reached her crotch. Heather didn't want to look, but the freak reached into her mind yet again and made her turn her gaze downward. The freak grinned broadly and hissed, then its psychic tendrils flexed in Heather's mind another time. Heather had been standing rigidly upright, her legs together, but now she shifted her stance, swinging one leg to the left as the freak's slimy head began to prod at the opening to her vagina.

Heather had thought herself incapable of experiencing any deeper sense of horror than what she'd already endured that night. She had been wrong. Because now a fresh sense of horror swept through her with the force of a tsunami, buffeting her already shattered psyche with wave after wave of mind-twisting terror and revulsion. She screamed inwardly as the crown of the creature's skull began to enter her.

She knew she was in the last moments of her existence as a normal human being. Her body would undergo changes from which it could not recover. She'd seen the evidence of that mere moments ago, as the creature's former host expired seconds after Miss Monique exited her body. She'd rather die than face imprisonment in her own body, forced to watch as her flesh was manipulated by an alien consciousness, and used to bring pain and suffering to countless innocents in the coming years. But she was powerless to do a goddamned thing about it.

The vile thing continued to push inward, slipping in another inch, then another. Soon it would be all the way inside her. Then, through some method Heather couldn't fathom, it would worm its way through her body, shifting aside vital organs without puncturing or destroying them, and then it would claw or chew a hole through her flesh, the withered head popping through to take up residence next to her own head.

Another fraction of an inch farther in it reached into her mind again, this time to trigger a physical reaction in Heather to allow smoother entry. Heather spread her legs farther apart and squatted, allowing the thing to move more smoothly and easily into her freshly lubricated vagina.

Heather despaired. As much as the process repulsed her, she now wanted nothing more than to have it over with.

Then something happened. Something that felt like

a miracle, that divine deliverance from the hand of God she'd so hoped for when those poor people were executed under the big top. The creature went suddenly rigid inside her and let out a single muffled cry of pain. One moment Miss Monique had full control over her mind and motor function, and the next she was completely gone from her mind.

Heather's body and soul were her own again.

She remained in that squatting position a moment longer, frozen in shock. She heard a noise nearby and turned her head to see the ringmaster falter on his stilts before toppling over. He crashed against the chain-link fence and went still. Heather watched him for a moment, half-expecting him to rise again.

But he stayed down. He was dead. Somehow. And she had a sudden insight. They were all dead. All the fucking freaks. She didn't know how she knew this, but she felt it deep inside, and with a loud cry of rage and revulsion she gripped the end of Miss Monique's sluglike tail and yanked the foul thing out of her body. She held it aloft and stared at its dead face, waiting for its slack features to become animate again.

It didn't happen. And it wasn't going to happen.

This time the cry Heather loosed was a cry of triumph. She ran to a nearby lamppost, braced her feet, and gripped the dead creature's slimy tail with both hands; then she smashed its head against the lamppost, swinging the thing again and again as its ugly features disintegrated into a pulpy, unrecognizable mess. She screamed at it the whole time, damning it for all the death and pain it had caused, cursing it especially for the death of her mother. Tears spilled down her face in a hot flood as her arms grew tired, but she continued to smash the creature against the lamppost until what little remained of it slipped out of her hands and dropped to the ground with a wet plop. She gave it a final kick, then stood there panting.

As the whirlwind of rage, heartbreak, and confusion began to subside a bit in her head, she turned to look at the freakshow. She saw the crumpled bodies of the three dead freak girls and knew what she'd surmised earlier was true. They were all dead. How this had occurred hardly mattered. It was enough that it had happened. With great reluctance, she shifted her gaze to the Towncar. Josh was still unmoving, still sprawled across the roof, hands and legs hanging limply over the sides.

With fresh tears in her eyes, she turned away and began to wander deeper into the park, away from the freakshow. In a while she would return to drive the Chevelle and her dead mother away from this hell on earth. She was grateful for that one little thing, at least—that she would be afforded the opportunity to grant her mother a proper and decent burial. But now she was too numb. Too tired. She needed time to rest.

She kept going until she reached the outskirts of the park, where she settled down on the grass near a park bench. She folded her legs beneath her, crossed her arms over her breasts, and rocked like an old lady in a rocking chair. Or like a straitjacketed mental patient in a padded asylum room. She thought the latter scenario was a more likely glimpse of her future. Given everything that had happened—the deaths, the unspeakable physical violations, and the things she'd been forced to do—how could she not go crazy?

She sat and rocked like that for a long, long time. Her scarred hand throbbed as she rocked, a painful pulse that served as the clearest, most undeniable reminder that she had survived, that this wasn't some fever dream conjured by her tortured psyche after surrendering her body to Miss Monique.

The dark nighttime sky gave way to predawn gray. Daylight was beginning to creep in at the horizon's edge as she heard the footsteps approach.

She sucked in a breath and tensed.

Then Josh let out a loud groan and sat down next to her. He kissed the side of her head and she began to sob as he drew her into his arms.

A while later she asked him a question: "What do you think happened? What killed them?"

Josh breathed a sigh of immense fatigue. "I don't know. But I think . . ."—he hesitated a moment before going on—"I think somebody did something. Somebody we'll never know did something amazing. They were the real heroes tonight, whoever they were. And we'll never fucking know them."

Heather sniffled. "That's so goddamned sad."

Josh sighed again. "I know."

Heather looked at him. "So what now?"

He frowned. "What do you mean?"

Heather turned again to the horizon, where a strip of violet light was encroaching on Pleasant Hills like a radioactive cloud. She shivered and snuggled more firmly into Josh's embrace. Then she sighed and said, "I mean, I can't just slip back into the life I was leading before the freakshow. I can't just go home and pretend everything is normal again. I can't pretend this never happened."

Josh studied his own scarred hand. "I know."

"I want to bury my mother. I want to grieve for her." She pushed out of Josh's embrace and regarded him somberly. "Then I want to go far away from this place. Thousands of miles from here."

He took her unwounded hand in his and squeezed it. "How would you like a traveling companion?"

Her eyes misted again as a fragile smile trembled at the corners of her mouth. "I'd like that. But you should know something. I haven't always been a good person. I've done bad things. One really bad thing."

Josh shrugged. "It doesn't matter. You're good at heart. I know you are."

Heather let out a cry at that; then he pulled her into another embrace and they stayed that way, locked in each other's arms, until full daylight held sway over Pleasant Hills.

Then they rose and made the journey back to Heather's car. Josh had to haul the bodies of two dead freaks out of it. Then he got behind the wheel and started the Chevelle as Heather slipped into the shotgun seat.

A few minutes later Pleasant Hills and the freakshow were behind them.


The sun shone brightly over Pleasant Hills all that day, exposing the tawdry and gruesome truth of the freakshow. A lone traveler, a college student who had just been passing through, filled his digital camera with the bizarre and grisly images. These were later posted all over the Internet. As it had in the aftermath of the demise of another Tennessee town, the federal government hatched a coverup. And almost everyone accepted the government's story of yet another unlikely terrorist assault on a small community in the heartland.

Proof of the truth was out there. It was everywhere, most prominently in the form of the thousands of still functioning clones populating the assimilated towns. But it was ignored and dismissed as a hoax.

But the people in power knew the truth.

And they learned some things.

Some secret laboratories began experimenting with these things.

New and exciting weapons systems were developed.

Just in time for the winds of war to begin blowing again. . . .

# BRYAN SMITH

Beautiful. Sexy. Inhuman. Jake McAllister knows that his brother Trey's new girlfriend is a bad influence, but he doesn't know what Myra's really after—Trey's soul. Trey is just one of her new playthings, a pawn in her centuries-long game. One by one, Myra has seduced and enslaved the young men of the town. The women have joined her cult as eager priestesses, lured by promises of sex and power. But Myra's unholy plan is almost complete. Can one man hope to battle such seductive evil? Will he be able to resist the...

# SOULTAKER

ISBN 13: 978-0-8439-6193-5

# BRYAN SMITH

It was known as the House of Blood. It sat at the entrance to a netherworld of unimaginable torture and terror. Very few who entered its front door lived to ever again see the outside world. But a few did survive. They thought they had found a way to destroy the house of horrors…but they were wrong. A new house has arisen. A new mistress now wields its unholy power—and she wants revenge. She will not rest until those who dared to challenge her and her former master are made to pay with their very souls.

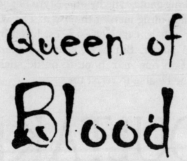

ISBN 13: 978-0-8439-6061-7

To order a book or to request a catalog call:
**1-800-481-9191**

This book is also available at your local bookstore, or you can check out our Web site **www.dorchesterpub.com** where you can look up your favorite authors, read excerpts, or glance at our discussion forum to see what people have to say about your favorite books.

# ☐ YES!

Sign me up for the Leisure Horror Book Club and send my FREE BOOKS! If I choose to stay in the club, I will pay only $8.50* each month, a savings of $7.48!

NAME: _____

ADDRESS: _____

TELEPHONE: _____

EMAIL: _____

☐ I want to pay by credit card.

☐ **VISA**    ☐ **MasterCard**    ☐ **DISCOVER**

ACCOUNT #: _____

EXPIRATION DATE: _____

SIGNATURE: _____

Mail this page along with $2.00 shipping and handling to:
**Leisure Horror Book Club**
**PO Box 6640**
**Wayne, PA 19087**
Or fax (must include credit card information) to:
**610-995-9274**

You can also sign up online at **www.dorchesterpub.com**.

*Plus $2.00 for shipping. Offer open to residents of the U.S. and Canada only.
Canadian residents please call 1-800-481-9191 for pricing information.

If under 18, a parent or guardian must sign. Terms, prices and conditions subject to change. Subscription subject to acceptance. Dorchester Publishing reserves the right to reject any order or cancel any subscription.

# GET FREE BOOKS!

You can have the best fiction delivered to your door for less than what you'd pay in a bookstore or online. Sign up for one of our book clubs today, and we'll send you *FREE\* BOOKS* just for trying it out... **with no obligation to buy, ever!**

As a member of the Leisure Horror Book Club, you'll receive books by authors such as **RICHARD LAYMON, JACK KETCHUM, JOHN SKIPP, BRIAN KEENE** and many more.

As a book club member you also receive the following special benefits:
- **30% off all orders!**
- **Exclusive access to special discounts!**
- **Convenient home delivery and 10 days to return any books you don't want to keep.**

## Visit www.dorchesterpub.com or call 1-800-481-9191

There is no minimum number of books to buy, and you may cancel membership at any time.
\*Please include $2.00 for shipping and handling.